Soulstorm Keep

Many centuries after the passing of mankind, the blight known as the Craven still lingered, lurking within the shadows; a dark hunger awaiting its chance to consume what little was left of their fragile world.

Only one among the Elves knew the true face of their enemy, with the knowledge to awaken the Undying and save the Faerylands before the living veil of the Evermore was forever lost.

Ivy Elvenborn was presented with an impossible quest - one that would take her on a distant journey to the Tower of Madness to seek the guidance of an ancient relic guarded within; but it would lead her to trespass beyond the gates of a forgotten castle; a ghostly fortress of despair where no living Faerie had ever tread. If she failed in her task, the entire race of Fey would be the last of their kind.

www.Faerylands.com

JAN   2011

Titles by Michel Savage

Faerylands
The Grey Forest
Soulstorm Keep

Outlaws of Europa
Rebels of Alpha Prime

Hellbot • Battle Planet

Islands in the Sky

Forgotten Future

Shadoworld
Veil of Shadows
Shadows Gate

Faerylands

II

MICHEL SAVAGE

This is a work of fiction. All the characters and events portrayed in this book are fictitious, and any resemblance to real people or events is purely coincidental.

FAERYLANDS – Soulstorm Keep

Copyright © 1992 by Michel Savage

The Grey Forest
P.O. Box 71494
Eugene, OR 97401

www.GreyForest.com • www.Faerylands.com

Cover art by Michel Savage

ISBN: 978-09719168-7-6

First Edition: Dec 2010

Printed in the United States of America

0 9 8 7 6 5 4 3 2 1

Faerylands

Soulstorm Keep

Enter the Grey Forest

www.GreyForest.com

Sequel from Book 1

The Grey Forest

After the Age of Men

Among the races of magical creatures, humankind was known as the clan of huskmen, savage mortals who had driven the Faerie into hiding long ago. After countless ages in the underworld, mankind was forgotten, their memory having faded to nothing more than a childhood myth among the many tribes of fey.

The Elven lords had kept this secret from the Faerie even as the spirits of the land began to wane, abandoning their dying race until the passing of men from the face of the earth. However, in their wake rose an ancient darkness, one that destroyed all that it touched; an evil they called the Craven. Now the protective aura of the Evermore was vanishing, and those that dwelled within the Faerylands had nowhere left to turn. If the Elvenborn could not save their world, this dreadful blight would consume them all.

Awakening

"Ivy ...it's time to wake up," a soft voice drifted within her dreams as flitting images from her past melted like a melody into her mind. A colorful memory of the long journey from her modest home in the Undergrove into a maze of gloomy tunnels and ruined cities; through forests of glass that glittered with shards of light, past wastelands of sand and fire. Images of a giant golem, of floating isles and jungles of deep green danced through her head. A painted mermaid singing some strange forgotten song echoed through her thoughts; as she recalled a glistening face in a waterfall and the empty void of darkness that followed, visions of a place she couldn't quite grasp.

She had sailed the waters beneath the seas to the land above, in her long and arduous journey to reach the world tree; birthplace of the Faerie. The Elven Lords, however, were now but few, and sadly could do little to aid her. A prism of light ferried her to a place that was once the world of humankind; with nothing but a single leaf from the tree of life to protect her in their now dead and poisoned realm. As a wood sprite, she had taken root under the stars deep within the heart of the grey forest. The race of men were reduced to nothing more than dust that covered the land as far as the eye could see, discoloring the world in a blanket of ash. All that was left of their once great civilization was crumbled stones buried beneath the deadfall.

As an Elvenborn, it was Ivy's legacy to heal the shameful wounds the world had suffered, and had planted herself as a tree to cleanse the lingering taint from mother earth. For over a hundred years she had slumbered to the gentle sway of her branches and the wind through her leaves, but now a whisper intruded into her solace; awakening her from her deep sleep.

"Ivy, you must wake up." The demanding voice was familiar, with a tinge of wisdom and strength; a musical voice as soft as a summer breeze, "We need you," Dawn pleaded. She remembered now, it was the elven maiden who had shown her the secret truth of their world hidden from the other faeries. As she stirred, branches twisted and withdrew, as did her embrace from the soft earth beneath her, and Ivy was once again herself. With a flutter of her long green wings and a wave of her raven black hair, she gave a sigh of ecstasy and exhilaration.

They stood in a pocket of green, the forests purified by her presence over the years. Scores of other faeries had also wandered back into the lands above to purge the bitter poison mankind had left behind, that tarnished every plant and stream and stone. So many of the faeries had sacrificed their essence, their very lives, to rid the world of its pain and to nurture the spark of life back into the surface realm at the edge of the Evermore. Slowly, color began to return to this once dying world. Dawn was there standing beside her, appearing unchanged; but the look in her eyes heavy and worn by time.

"Welcome back to us, child, it has been nearly eight score winters you have slept." Dawn apprised her in a gentle tone as she brushed a lock of Ivy's hair from her long pointed ears. The faerie girl squinted as she opened her emerald green eyes for the first time in over a century. The area around her was transformed from the dying woodlands she had remembered; thick beds of moss now mottled the forest floor, as grass and flowers struggled towards the ray of sunlight shining through the canopy. Though the distant clouds still had an air of gloom, the sky above had begun to assume its natural shade of blue.

"I had such strange dreams, of giants and deserts and jungles and trolls," Ivy reminisced, "and I remember someone calling, a voice saying that they needed me..."

"They weren't dreams little one, all that did happen in another place and time, for dreams are but a shadow of something real," Dawn replied, "but you are needed here and now ...the Elvenborn are in danger."

Ivy looked down at her hands to find the glowing leaf, a gift from the tree of life, still resting in her palm. Looking again, she faltered as she tried to lift it with her fingers, as it had absorbed into her skin, now forever a part of her.

"But, why me?" she asked innocently.

"You are special, Ivy, and much has happened since we last

spoke. Follow me and I will enlighten you along the way." Dawn advised as she motioned with her slender arm towards a faint trail through the forest that appeared to open up before them, only to grow closed upon their passing. Around them a mist of threads began to form, and the passing of the trees beyond seemed to blur.

"What is happening?" the young fairy asked as the tall elf took her hand.

"These are wind spiders," Dawn explained to Ivy with a shy smile and a wave to the tiny silver specks floating about them, "they help us traverse great distances. They weave a silk that allows us to move as the breeze. Certainly you have seen the strings of their webs throughout the forest before, a lingering marking of our passage?" the elfin maiden questioned the curious girl.

Ivy was mesmerized by the coils of shining strings twisting about them, and the mountains and lakes they drifted over at speeds far beyond what she alone could fly. She recalled seeing insects so small that they would let loose their fine thread to be carried away in the breeze; never knowing their true magic. They whisked through darkened woods and valleys like a storm cloud, to finally come to rest at a lone grove surrounded by worn ancient stones.

The cocoon of threads gently released them into a circle of rock decorated with mystic glyphs. Ivy recognized it as one of the doorways to the Faerylands below. Beneath the hills and valleys, vast networks of tunnels were home to the Faerie folk who were banished from the world above long ago. At the center of the henge of stones sat a pyre of blue flames, burning slowly as if out of sync with the world around them. Within the cone of its strange flickering light stood two tall lords dressed in green velvet and laced with patterns of gold. Their long white hair flowed over their shoulders like a shower of summer rain, each with a grim stare in their almond shaped eyes. These were high elves, fathers of the Elvenborn.

Ivy nervously fluttered her wings nervously, while brushing her hair out of her eyes as a cool breeze caressed her naked form. Since she had departed the Undergrove those many years ago, she had matured in mind and spirit and had grown to know that as an Elvenborn, she had a legacy to fulfill. Though bare and unclothed, she stood before them unashamed, as this was her natural form.

"I have brought you here, Ivy, to this audience to ask you for your aid," Dawn spoke in humbled tones, "Before you stand two of our honored elves, seers of prophecy and past; guardians of the fey."

"You ...you need *my* help?" Ivy stumbled on her words.

"Yes child, you have been chosen." One of the lords answered, though his lips did not move. At knee level behind him a small head poked out into the blue light, a young girl with short unkempt hair, green as forest moss. Her eyes were wide with curiosity as she stepped out into the open at the urging hand of her elders. A shy and innocent smile crept upon her face, as she tiptoed out. Though her wings were as white as snow, her arms and feet were speckled with moss. She had a wild and sassy look about her; more so than most faeries do.

"This is Jinx," Dawn introduced the coy fey to Ivy, as the slender girl toyed with a small pebble at her feet while giving a cute pout, "she will be accompanying you on your journey."

"And where are we to go?" Ivy asked with a frown, boggled by the hasty request. Turning to Dawn, the lady tilted her head down to the girl, with a hand to her shoulder in gentle assurance.

"Both of you will be sent to a distant land to retrieve something we cannot do alone." Dawn replied, "Since you have slept, Ivy, many a fairy has perished to help us cleanse this realm as you have done by your example; however, countless others have been consumed by the Craven which now pools in dark recesses throughout the Faerylands." A look of pity fell from her doleful eyes, "The Evermore is dying, strangled by the growing presence of the Craven which lurks in every shadow. You must find a way to reawaken the Undying, the spirits of our land; only then can we release the stranglehold it has on our world," Dawn conveyed with a soft touch to Ivy's cheek.

Ivy had seen this darkness before: a turbulent fog of gloom and despair, and she was powerless before it. It could take almost any form from what the legends had told; an ancient and foul sickness that twisted and destroyed all that it touched. Ivy's eyes turned up towards the elf, feeling helpless in this monumental task placed so suddenly upon her.

"How am I to do this? What you ask is beyond me," Ivy pleaded.

"We have watched the pools of time and the churning of the stars; and with you, Ivy, there is a way..." the tall seer spoke into her mind.

"As I said before, you are special Ivy," Dawn assured, "Listen carefully young fey, for it is all I can tell you at this time; you must travel to the Cliffs of Chaos and seek the heart of flames," she ordered firmly. "Take care of Jinx, for she will aid you on your quest." The elven maiden withdrew her soothing touch as she and the other lords stepped back into the shadows beyond the edge of the firelight; her last words haunting Ivy as they faded away, "Our faith is in you, child; for if you fail, we fear we will be the last of our kind."

Ivy was puzzled and confused. The elven lords had left her burdened with a an impossible quest. She had heard tales from her old mentor Grubroot about the cliffs of chaos, but had no clue as to where they might be. The map she once possessed of the Faerylands was no more, taken by Dawn more than a century ago ...which she now remembered the elf had transformed into a twig which sprouted the glowing leaf from the tree of life. Ivy opened her palm to see the soft glow of the tiny leaf that was now a part of her, and pondered at its purpose with a heavy scowl. She had absolutely no idea how this magic worked. She sat down before the weirding fire, entirely perplexed. Jinx strolled over to stand beside her.

"Just like elves to talk in riddles." she exclaimed, her cheeky tone surprised Ivy more than a little, "Can you believe they just left us here without even bothering to point us in the right direction? pssh..." Jinx folded her arms and snorted with an air of contempt.

"Where are you from, Jinx, and why exactly were you recruited for this quest?" Ivy had to ask.

"I used to live in a small grove next to a magic well deep

within the celestial valley. One day the elves showed up and
snatched me away to this place. I don't know why ...just my
bad luck I guess." she scowled. Ivy was bewildered that the
elves had not bothered to explain their plan to her either.

"So you have no idea where the cliffs of chaos are?"

"Not a clue..." Jinx returned with a sassy smirk and a shrug of
her shoulders. Ivy had to agree the small fey had a point;
sometimes the high elves could be a bit aggravating. Leaving
her to figure this out on her own seemed almost rude of them,
let alone having to baby-sit this impudent child. She looked
again at the impression of the leaf in her hand; a golden glow
pulsated through it with a life of its own. Her hand didn't feel
any different, and though it was pretty to behold, she couldn't
understand why it had joined with her.

Ivy tried to remember the tales her old friend and scholar Grub
had told her about the Cliffs she sought; it was the place where
he had acquired an elemental gem from the living soil beyond
the Dwarven Mountains. At least that was a clue. Ivy turned to
her small companion who still stood within circle of stones,
warming herself by the slowly drifting fire.

"Might you know where the dwarves dwell, Jinx?"

"Well, certainly, but it will take a long time to get there from
here," she advised, "and we can't travel within the veil to get
there." Jinx mentioned, referring to the shroud of the Evermore
beneath the surface. "Perhaps you could use the wind spiders
like the elves do, and take us there?" the girl suggested, but Ivy
was unable to do so. Ivy was a wood sprite, able to transform
into a tree ...but not much else; her magic was limited. Ivy
must have had a puzzled look on her face, because her new
companion gave her an accusing glare of impatience.

"I don't know how." Ivy finally admitted, feeling like she was
looking a smidge stupid in front of this presumptuous girl for
whom she was responsible. "If I knew the direction we could
fly there." But Jinx just gave her an aggravated groan at that
comment.

"Actually, I'm not so great at flight," she responded, as the
small girl ruffled her wings once, more moth-like than sturdy
and slender as were Ivy's, and not made for covering long

distances. They were stuck in a pretty predicament; Elves were expecting every other fey to be up to speed on what needed to be done, they were talking in riddles and rhymes most of the time which usually left everyone around them in a state of confusion. Maybe they got some morbid pleasure out of making others feel inadequate and stupid. Ivy thought they could at least be a tad more helpful if they were going to be so insistent.

Woken up from a century of sleep and dragged into the middle of nowhere only to be abandoned with a saucy little whelp was causing Ivy more than a shred of anxiety. But deep down, Ivy realized the Elves must have had their reasons not to inform her of the fine specifics of their mission; prophecies tended to work that way. Ivy looked at her hand once again, wondering what form of magic lay within the leaf imprinted into her palm. Her left hand was stained where she had once touched a powerful water spirit, leaving her with the ability to enter the realms of water; but it was nothing she had control over. The leaf was something new, something potent; from the very branch of the world tree itself ...if only she knew how to use it.

"Well then, we will have to travel by foot," Ivy said with an air of confidence, and started to exit the ring of stones, expecting Jinx to follow. The girl, however, grabbed her by the arm, and yanked her back before she passed the threshold of the ancient stone henge.

"Are you daft?" Jinx accused, with a scrunch of her eyebrows, "Why they put you in charge is beyond me? ...The blue flame protects us here, keeping us out of phase with the world beyond." She explained.

"But we can't stay here forever." Ivy shot back at the girl, whose bratty attitude was starting to get on her nerves. The small girl ruffled her wings and placed her other hand on her on hip with a spark of conceit.

"Look here, *maybe* you got some gift or whatever, and that's why the Elves chose you; but don't get the idea you can boss me around." Jinx shot back at Ivy, who was bewildered by her tone; Ivy didn't think she was being bossy.

"I, I didn't mean," Ivy responded, but was interrupted by the small sassy girl, whose attitude suddenly and surprisingly turned apologetic as she withdrew her hand from where she had grabbed Ivy's arm.

"Oh damn, I did it again." She whispered out loud as she backed away from the tall wood sprite. Ivy figured the girl was remorseful for showing her disrespect and turned to console her that no harm was done. But as she took her first step, roots sprung out of her feet in every direction, and Ivy stumbled and fell to the ground with a yelp. Ivy laid there with her face in the dirt, feeling very undignified; mystified as to what exactly had just happened. Errant roots and branches that had lashed out of her body slowly began to withdraw, and Ivy sat up with a mixed feeling of embarrassment and worry. She had thought she had mastered control over her transformation. Jinx, however, stood there giggling to herself as Ivy brushed the dirt from her face. Ivy gave her an incredulous glare, not knowing what to think.

"I'm sorry ...I jinxed you." she continued to giggle, though the apology seemed sincere. "It would be better if you didn't touch me." she advised. Ivy had heard of luck fairies who influence positive circumstance, but why would the high elves in all their wisdom partner her up with a fey who brings misfortune?

* * *

Bloodmoon

"So what do you propose we do?" Ivy asked after brushing herself off, now wary of how close the little fey got to her. Jinx herself seemed to be in deep thought for a moment as she peered out at the countryside beyond.

"We must wait for the moon to rise." she declared, though not seeming quite sure of herself. "Yes, I believe we can leave when the moon shines."

Ivy looked out over the hilly plains and darkened forests beyond the ring of stone. Thick clouds had drifted over the horizon since she and Dawn had arrived at this small sanctuary. Now stars speckled the heavens above as the sounds of night echoed through the wooded hills. Not far beyond, a shallow lake glittered as the trees at its banks gently swayed in the evening breeze.

"So ...what exactly are we waiting for?" Ivy inquired, watching the little girl who stared out at distant hillside.

"Oh, you'll see." she answered back curtly, clearly being intentionally obnoxious towards the wood sprite. With a snort, Ivy bided her time inspecting the intricate carvings within the stones surrounding them, filled with gaunt faces coiled within twisting spirals and cryptic runes. This was one of the few doorways to the Faerylands below, but this portal was now closed. In many parts of the underworld the protective veil of the Evermore had lapsed; leaving those below within the grasp of the Craven which it had once kept at bay. It was said all the surface world was once the land of the Faerie, but that was a time long past, which now seemed like an eternity ago.

"Jinx, how do you know about the Dwarves?" Ivy asked, deciding to break the aching boredom they now suffered.

"The valley where I am from is on the opposite side of the Dwarven Mountains. They would visit from time to time trying to pawn off diamonds and gems and nuggets of gold and other useless junk." Jinx relayed, "We were protected by the wishing well located there, but many of the fey had begun to disappear recently. Our elders warned us not to leave the grove when the shadows in the forests began to move." she finished with a dire tone. Even as short a moment as it was that still lingered in her eyes, Ivy could tell the look on her face was one of serious fear.

Over the distant mountains, a glimmer of silvery light washed across them. A dark cloud parted to reveal the glowing moon as it rose into the midnight sky. Jinx stood there with her eyes squinted shut and her fingers crossed as the moonlight reached the hillside she had been watching with such intent. Ivy looked on in amazement as the hillside began to slowly shake. She had heard stories of giants that slept in the earth, but this seemed to be something different. The whole side of the mound rose up and tore itself from the soil around it and wobbled there as wide enormous feet protruded out from underneath.

"Come Ivy, we must hurry." Jinx said with excitement. Leading the way, they breached the barrier of the azure fairy flame out into the cold night. Jinx bounded up and took flight with her tiny wings, fluttering her way towards the heaving mound. Ivy jumped into the air to follow as they soared to the top of the moving hill. As Ivy got closer, a giant head of a turtle lunged forth from the shadows beneath the mound. Jinx landed and grabbed a bush still anchored atop the grassy shell as Ivy came to rest beside her.

"What kind of creature is this?" Ivy dared to ask. It appeared similar to a sea turtle she had once ridden in the emerald oceans with the mermaids long ago, though this one was distinctly different.

"This is a Chukwa, a moving mountain, though, this one is just a baby." Jinx exclaimed as the turtle lurched forward from the ground towards the lake.

"But how did you know it was here?"

"The fairy flame silly, you can see what things truly are when you're within the glow of its light. Didn't anybody tell you that?" Jinx responded with a shrug. Ivy only gave a pout, her mother had in fact kept many things from her while she was growing up. Then again, it was Ivy's fault for never making time with all her running about.

As the great turtle neared the lake's edge, Ivy started to become worried as she was anticipating what was about to happen. The turtle was certainly enormous and covered a great deal of ground, but even a tiny fairy could easily fly faster than its achingly slow pace.

"This thing isn't exactly fast, you know." she finally had to mention. "Is it going into that lake?"

"Just be patient, Ivy," Jinx chimed back, "wait until it gets to the water." But Ivy was a little troubled by this turn of events, especially since it didn't seem like they were really getting anywhere at the moment. Because of her brush with a water spirit, Ivy was able to exist in the realms of water; but she presumed Jinx could not.

"Won't we sink when it goes into the lake?" Ivy had to inquire, not knowing what to expect.

"Wow, you *really* don't know the meaning of patience do you?" the tiny fey shot back with a condescending tone, though a playful one at that. Ivy just gave a disgruntled sigh, realizing this was going to be a very, very long journey considering her present company. What irked Ivy the most, was realizing she once used to treat others the same way Jinx spoke to her, and was guilty herself of acting like an ill-behaved brat. So, with that reflection, she took the insults with a touch of salt.

The huge turtle lugged forward, pitching its bulk upon the shore. Jinx seemed calm and unworried as the entire hill slowly drifted into the middle of the lake. Like a tiny island, they floated there, as the lapping of the cool water washed upon the edge of the earth covered shell. So that is how islands got into the middle of lakes. Ivy had always wondered about that.

"So um ...now what?"

"Now we wait," Jinx answered, "see there?" she pointed out towards the night sky, as a large cloud approached the shining moon. Ivy was confused; it was just a cloud, so what? But as the cloud passed over it, blocking out the moonlight, and everything around them changed. The air felt heavy and the landscape turned dark, rippling like the surface of a pond. As the moonlight shone once more when the cloud parted, Ivy could see that the scenery around them had changed. They were no longer where they once were, but somewhere else entirely.

"Ah, well, let's see where we are." Jinx uttered as she looked about the horizon. Sharp rocky hills gave way to majestic mountains that loomed high above. The wide lake that once surrounded them was now no more than a deep pond with a bare sandy shore spotted with ferns and cattails. The glowing eyes of tiny creatures skittered away from the two fey who had magically appeared in front of them. The air here was wet with the mists of distant rain. Where had they been transported?

"What just happened?" Ivy frowned, and began to worry how they were going to get back. Jinx on the other hand, seemed certain they were on the right track, despite Ivy's personal lack of confidence.

Beside them a shallow river of bare stones coursed down through a narrow canyon. The dark rocky cliffs stretching high above, left only a slender crack of clouds viewable through their sharply leaning walls. Light mists of rain floated down upon them, leaving the two naked fey glittering with dew.

"That's how those creatures move from place to place, and sometimes you can hitch along for the ride." Jinx answered gleefully, accompanied by what Ivy took as an impish grin,

Far above, Ivy noticed bridges of stone linked between the cliff sides, layered with fortifications. Half covered in the ethereal mists, it was difficult to make out any details. As they walked, Jinx scanned the cliffs with a measure of curiosity, but failed to enlighten Ivy on her observations. Several hours later, they encroached upon a wide set of steps that led up to a massive stone door, imbedded into the side of the cliff face. Four giant statues of strange beasts carved from the same black stone decorated the entry. Links of chain carved from the living rock lined the door; more decorative than of practical use from what Ivy could tell. Jinx tiptoed up to the top step and plopped down on the wet stair; her hair now matted from the light rain.

"Well, this appears to be a doorway to the dwarven lairs, but it's not the right time. Looks like we're in for a little wait." Jinx stated with a pout.

"What do you mean?" Ivy wondered, as she dared to inspect the strange statues, "How long of a wait are we talking about?"

"Oh, I dunno, maybe a few days or so; can't really tell just yet." she said with an air of indifference. Ivy only blinked her eyes in astonishment, truly confounded by her companions immeasurable quantity of patience. That was something Ivy's own personality lacked by nature, and had a great deal of trouble understanding.

"We can't stay here that long," Ivy contended, while looking around the area of barren stones. Certainly she could handle a day or two without food, but there wasn't even soil here for mushrooms to grow; let alone that it was mighty unpleasant being exposed to this constant drizzle of rain. "What are we waiting out here for, why not just knock on the door?" Ivy spouted as she made her way over to the large double doors and placed her ears against them; but it was silent as stone beyond.

"You're funny," the small girl laughed back, "you really don't know anything about dwarves do you?" she chastised Ivy with a roll of her eyes. "Dwarves do not come to the surface except to collect dream stones from the river during the nights of the full moon; when it is the only time they can be seen," Jinx advised, "Knock all you want, nobody is going to answer."

"What are these dream stones you're talking about?" Ivy asked, as she peered out toward the flowing river.

"Oh, they're just a type of light blue gem which are hoarded by the dwarves as symbols of fertility, but the elves use them for their magical ability to influence visions and dreams. But they can only be seen under the direct moonlight, otherwise the stones are nearly impossible to find." she noted.

"So, why aren't they called moonstones instead?" Ivy inquired.

"Don't be silly," Jinx giggled, "they don't come from the moon." Getting up from her seat, Jinx wandered over to inspect the statues with light curiosity. They had long sharp claws and appeared to be an unpleasant mix of something between a wolf and a large cat. The stonework around the doorway appeared to be unremarkable and plain; only the entry itself seemed to share any amount of detail. The constant shower of fine mist from the clouds above that funneled down to the canyon floor wasn't all that bad, except for the fact that there was nowhere to escape from it. The slight overhang from the gigantic doorway did little to shield them from the blanketing haze.

"Jinx, why is it that dwarves built everything on such a large scale when they are actually quite short themselves?" Ivy wondered, pondering over the use of such a massive door to those of a much smaller stature.

"Some stories say that when the Dwarves came to the surface to battle the orcs and goblins and other nasties a long time ago; they brought with them giant constructs they called machines plated with steel and belching steam." the girl enlightened her, "But I think they just make everything larger, like those doors, to scare intruders away." she finished with a casual sigh.

Well, that made sense, Ivy thought to herself. She was taught that dwarves had distanced themselves from the Elves untold centuries ago, and their kind held a grudge against them ever since. What their dispute was over was still a point of rumor among the Elvenborn. It had brewed back when the tribes of centaurs roamed the lands, but their people had been extinguished by the huskmen, the race otherwise known as mankind. It was told dwarves didn't have much tolerance for fairies either, which would make their quest that much more difficult.

"Maybe we should try looking farther downriver," Ivy suggested to the girl. Had the weather been dry here, they could have flown up to investigate the dark bridges overhead; but their wings were soaked, making such a flight impossible.

"I don't think so, we were lucky to find this doorway actually," Jinx responded with a catty glance towards her companion. Ivy truly didn't understand why Jinx acted so insolent at moments, and her condescending attitude had a habit of rubbing her the wrong way.

"What does luck have to do with it?"

"Um ...everything!" Jinx shot back with a huff, raising her hands in exaggeration. What Ivy didn't realize is that Jinx was in fact a luck fairy, though, there are many different types of luck. Though Jinx herself seemed to have the ability to hex someone with bad luck by touch, by her nature, her very presence could influence events.

Deep in the celestial valley near a wishing well there dwelled a number of other luck faeries. Their close cousins, Wishing Faeries heard the desires of others, but it depended on their mood if they bothered to actually listen or not, as faeries themselves are selfish by nature. Luck fairies spent their time planting clovers, polishing mirrors, combing the hair of black cats or pulling the thistles from the feet of wild rabbits. Some were not very bright, and could only provide dumb luck from time to time, but they all were infused with the essence of something called *chance*.

Many people attempted to secure their magic through rituals involving sacrifice, omens or spells. Shamans and gypsies would capture and mash luck faeries to make bracelets, amulets and other such charms; which wasn't quite so terribly lucky for the fairy involved. Malevolent necromancers, witches and warlocks alike would grind the essence of certain 'bad' faeries of their persuasion to create curses to hex unwitting victims. Thus, when Ivy asked her companion about luck, she took it as a personal insult. In her own sassy tone, Ivy decided to dish back what she had been given.

"Well then, if you think so strongly about it; then with a little luck," Ivy spouted, as she walked up to the large entry and gave a light rap, "...someone might answer the door." Actually, Ivy was just acting haughty at the moment in an attempt to be rude back to the little girl. Much to her surprise, however, after a short twinkle of silence while Jinx sat there brooding at Ivy for her tone, a clank of hidden gears behind the door began to turn.

With a great groan, the dark granite doors heaved and a pressure of hot air burst forth when they cracked opened. Ivy and Jinx stood together, peering from behind one of the statues into the darkness beyond the doorway not knowing what to expect; but from the deep shadows stepped a single squat dwarf, burly and unkempt. He had long hair, an equally long beard of gray, and was carrying a large bucket; all the while grumbling to himself. Ivy and her companion stayed hidden behind the statue as they watched the stranger.

"Do this, do that, I can't believe you're so lazy ...blah blah

blah!" The dwarf grumbled out loud, "Making me come out here to get fresh rain water, gah! Women!" With that, he set down his bucket on the steps as the rain splattered within, but clearly at a far slower rate than he had patience for. Jinx whispered to the wood sprite that they should sneak in while the door was open, and Ivy agreed to follow. The dwarf grumbled again and snatched up the bucket with evident disdain and waddled out to the river, filling it up in the shallow stream as he peeked over his shoulder with a hint of guilt.

The two faeries tiptoed into the doorway and the shadows beyond, just as the little man was making his way back up the steps; a wide smirk crossed his face as that of someone who had secretly cheated. With the push of a large lever once within the doorway, the stone slabs slammed shut with a thundering boom. Dwarves can see pretty well in the darkness, as it was in their nature to dwell underground; but they still needed a bit of light, and preferred candles and lanterns. When he got to his candle and lit it with a strike of flint, it revealed the two faeries huddling against the wall. They were caught.

"Huh?" The dwarf stepped back in surprise, "How did you two get in here?" he asked with a growl, bucket in one hand, flickering candle in the other. Ivy was petrified, as this was the first time she had seen a dwarf, let alone been yelled at by one.

"Good sir," Jinx stumbled on her words, "Um, I mean, Hail to thee Dwarven sire." Jinx remembered the common tongue the dwarves who visited her grove had used as their greeting. "We request your assistance in finding something we seek."

"Oh, you do now, do you, fine and fancy that?" He answered with an air of suspicion. "Me really thinks yer sneakin' about all sneaky-like; coming to steal my precious gems from an honest working dwarf." He shot back with an accusing glare. "I'll have none of that!" he marched back to the lever and opened the doors once again as gears creaked and they began to slide open with a groan. "Come on ya pestering faeries ...out with ya!" The dwarf waddled back to boot them out with a crusty leather shoe, but Jinx was a good dodge.

"Sire, if you would just listen a moment..." she began, but was only met with the silencing huff of the dwarf.

"I don't want to hear your fairy chants, tryin' to charm me with your magic. Out, out, out, before ya make me get my hammer!" he snarled. It was Ivy who decided to take control of the situation.

"And so, is that bucket of water there for your wife per chance?" She inquired with a raised brow. The dwarf stopped short at the mention of his mate, the guilt of his petty crime welling up to the surface.

"Uh, yeah ...so?" He twisted his stubby hand to hide the sloshing bucket behind his back.

"Well if you don't let us stay we will tell her that you actually didn't get pure rain water in that bucket, but were going to substitute nasty river slosh instead and lie to her about it," Ivy dared to threaten, "what would she think of that, hmm?"

The little dwarf lost his nerve and became obviously flustered at the accusation that was, of course, entirely true. Now dwarves were known for their tempers, but slight a dwarven woman and it becomes a hundred fold. Dwarves were fierce in battle, and could face a thousand orcs; but there was nothing more imposing to them than an angry wife ...oh no. With a brief personal struggle of indecisiveness, he finally strolled back to the lever with a grumble and gave it a tug. With that, the stone doors slammed shut once again.

With a smile, Ivy turned to Jinx in the candlelight, who grinned back at her cleverness. The dim-witted dwarf never bothered to figure these two fairies had no idea neither who nor where his wife was, let alone that he could have simply locked them outside in spite of their bluff. But in his tiny mind the fear of a wrathful wife eluded all wisdom, and was worth every caution. The three of them strolled through the dark carved tunnel within the cone of light from his candle.

"Thank you so much, sir ...I mean, sire." Jinx corrected herself.

"So, what is it you so desperately need that I can trade for your silence?" the dwarf asked with a sigh of resignation. As they made their way through a maze of tunnels and steps, the sound of chisels and hammers echoed through the earth. "My name is Orin Shalestone, by the way; so you can make a proper bargain."

"Nice to meet you, Orin," Ivy extended the courtesy, "We are trying to find our way to a place called the Cliffs of Chaos to discover something called the Heart of Flames." she offered with a grain of honesty. Orin just gave a shake of his head and a suspicious glance to the dark haired girl.

"Well if it's the Cliffs of Chaos yer lookin' for, ya found 'em," he mentioned to the relief of the two fey, "but what is it you need with the Heart, I need to ask?"

Ivy and Jinx looked at each other for a moment, not realizing that the elves had not enlightened either of them as to the details of their quest. With a shrug, Ivy followed behind as they made their way down a long spiral stair, as many of the dwarven folk they passed by turned curious eyes towards the pair of naked fey, while a handful of dwarven women moved to cover the eyes of their staring husbands. Ivy was as forthright as she knew how, for there was only one answer.

"Actually, in all truth, Orin, we really don't know."

* * *

Heart of Flames

The stout dwarf led them through the maze of tunnels alive with shops and crowded street markets. Here lanterns and glowing hearths lit the grand halls where they dwelled. Orin had to stop by his hovel to drop off the bucket of water to his wife, who was busy chopping an array of cooking herbs in her cramped kitchen. A bubbling pot hung over a central flame, the room thick with the smell of hickory and sage. She was as stout as Orin himself, and to Ivy's surprise, bore a beard woven into a thick lock.

"Oh, ah, dearest ...we have guests." Orin announced as he walked in with a timid smile. "This is Brecca Feldspar, my lovely wife." he introduced his partner to the two fey who peeked in behind him. Brecca seemed a little shocked by the look on her hairy face, almost as much as Ivy did; who wondered for a moment how dwarves could tell the sexes apart.

"Greeting milady," Jinx bowed, as she glanced to Ivy to follow suit. Brecca cleaned off the oversized cleaver she had in her hands on her soiled apron, and set it aside with a hack into the cutting block where it quivered.

"Picking up strays now are we?" she glared with suspicion at her husband, who grimaced under his scruffy beard. "Did you get the rain water I asked for?" she demanded as Orin placed the worn bucket upon the table with slight hesitation as he gave a hasty glance at the two fey with worried suspicion.

"Yes, he did milady Brecca, he took great care to catch every drop." Jinx chimed in with a wink to the nervous dwarf. Brecca gave a suspicious glance to the tiny girl and took a sniff at the bucket, though she seemed barely convinced. Orin patted his sweaty hands with false bravado, trying not to let his wife see the look in his eyes; being married for over 500 years, she could read him like a book.

"Hmph." she gave a second sniff with her large nose over the bucket and gave Jinx a light grin. "The recipe calls for the purest water, its a medical ointment for my delicate skin." she claimed while patting her fat cheeks with her thick fingers. Ivy almost laughed out loud, ...just almost; but caught herself.

"We apologize for the intrusion, but your fine husband is escorting us somewhere, and won't be long; as a gentleman keeps his promise." Jinx advised as she fluttered her wings slightly, giving Orin a quick glance. He shrugged his shoulders with guilt, knowing they had him by the beard; as the dwarves would say.

"Oh, a gentleman are we now?" Brecca gave an astonished look to her mate, who was avoiding eye contact with her at the moment, "Cavorting with faeries none the less, I'll have a word or two with you when you get back *your lordship*!" she answered to Orin with a condescending tone and a threatening wave of her stubby finger. Orin gave a sigh with a tired look in his puffy eyes and wrinkled face; apparently his marriage to Brecca had aged him beyond his years.

"Yes, mum," he responded obediently with a shade of resignation to his fate.

Stomping out the doorway, they made their way down the busy tight streets to the curious turned heads of the locals. Ivy was a bit astonished by how well Jinx was handling herself, considering the strange environment. Orin led them past the quarters of the market and into the open mines where crafters were busy chiseling out hallways and ornate pillars from the living stone; right beside the dirt covered dwarves who tapped out nuggets of glittering gems and veins of silver they collected in large piles.

Tiptoeing closely behind, the two winged girls kept a close tail on the dwarf through the maze of tunnels and stairs until they were eventually led into a large chamber filled with thick steam and smoke. Here fires burned and hot coals glowed as hammers clanked on massive anvils. It seemed like the perfect setting of a dwarves smithy Ivy had been told about in fanciful tales. Within the center a great cauldron of iron sat, bubbling with hot liquid metal the color of warm amber. At this, Jinx and Ivy took a cautious step back, as iron was a fatal poison to their race. As long as they didn't touch it, they would be fine.

"And here we are." Orin announced to the confusion of the two girls. They dared to walk about the room, not knowing what they were looking for. Orin seemed bewildered by their conduct. "What is it you're seeking little ones?"

"Where is it?" Ivy asked, as she scanned the steamy chamber.

"Right there in front of ya..." Orin announced, with a hint of mockery, "we have many crucibles throughout the mountains, each ancient and forged by the Dwarven Lords long ago, back when the earth and sky were young." Orin relayed as he tapped the iron cauldron with a rod, "Each one has a personality of its own, individual as their given names; this one here is the Heart of Flames."

The two companions were flabbergasted, why would the elves send them to seek out something so deadly to their kind? Ivy dared to take a closer inspection, picking up a nearby lantern which she held over her head. The cauldron was massive, incredibly thick and speckled with age. In the flicker of the firelight, she could see it was adorned with intricate carvings around its rim. Dwarves bearing hammers and swords fighting fierce fanged creatures. She followed the relief around its entire circumference until it met at a central figure of something that seemed out of place; three teardrops embossed into the central band that joined the ring of figures on the relief. Ivy turned to Orin to inquire of it.

"What is this around its edge?"

"Its a story every dwarf is told as a child before they pick up their first hammer," Orin explained, "Each of the crucibles tell a different tale, to remind us of the long and glorious history of the Dwarves." he grinned with pride. Following the band around the edge, he enlightened the two fey about the story it told. Many ages ago when the elves and dwarves were once comrades at arms, they battled the dark beasts back into the shadows from whence they came. There came a time, however, in a distant battlefield when the promised aide of the elves never came, and the lone army dwarves were outnumbered by their foe; and the entire company was slaughtered to the last. The emblem at the edge was known as the Tears of Sorrow, a memorial to the lost lives created by their grieving kin.

It began to make sense to Ivy now; long ago there was a battle between the elves and the Craven with the aid of the Dwarven race, but there still lingered a grievance between the two races that lasted to this very day. A tarnished grudge of injustice hinted in their furred brows whenever the Dwarves spoke of Elves, passed down throughout the ages of their kindred. Ivy counseled with Jinx on what the meaning of their find was, and came to an agreement.

"Orin, where might we find this Dwarven monument known as the Tears of Sorrow?" Ivy inquired, considering that this iron crucible was not the final object that they sought, but an important clue to direct them in their quest.

"Oh, now, it isn't exactly a place," he replied with a raised brow, "the memorial was a jewel that was shared between the dwarven kingdoms as a reminder of our loss." With a thought, Orin pondered on the relic they sought, mumbling to himself as he tried to remember the story. "If I recall it correctly, the jewel is worn by the royal messenger of the dwarves whenever they must meet in council with the Elven lords; so as to remind them of their slight against our kind."

Apparently, dwarves weren't exactly the forgiving kind, Ivy realized. There was no way the Elves could have expected her and Jinx to snatch away this enormous cauldron of iron, so by common sense, it was possibly this gemstone mentioned upon it they sought. Perhaps they would find a few answers to their mysterious quest when they found it.

Orin informed the two companions that they needed to request passage to meet with the dwarven council by route of the silver swamps, beyond which was a bridge to their hidden realm. The king dwells in a palace of stone, and it was there they would find the royal messenger that does his bidding. Orin himself was willing to show them the way, but was on a short leash by his bearded wife; thus, could only offer them a second choice. Following him down to the gravel pits that were notably dank and dingy with soot, Orin introduced the two young girls to his strange pets.

Enormous worms lay grazing on the filth and loose dirt dumped there among an excess of rotting debris. They were off-white with semi-translucent skin, and moved in a way that made Ivy's stomach churn. As repulsive as they were, they had an air of innocence to them. They were simply gigantic beasts used to eliminate their garbage. They did, however, have the advantage of being able to tunnel through the earth.

"This is Uck, and Eww; my pets." Orin chimed proudly as he showed off his prize beasts. "Grew them from tiny little hatchlings me-self." the dwarf grinned while flexing his stubby little pinky, "They will take you through the disposal chute to the edge of the swamp, and you'll be on your own from there." he advised.

"And you want us to ride these ...things?" Jinx asked with a disgusted look at the abnormal steeds. Ivy would have elbowed her for her rudeness, but was wary of making any contact with her after what happened last time she did. Orin gave a nod of approval, seemingly oblivious to their repulsion to the slimy beasts.

He called them over with a whistle and stomp of his boot. The worms had no eyes to speak of, but found their way straight to their master. The dwarf grabbed a coil of rope and lashed a length each around the two worms, handing the ends to the girls. Their wings were fairly dry now, so Jinx suggested that they could either walk or fly their way instead, but Orin only chuckled at her suggestion.

"Trust me, there are areas of the chute that only these beasts can traverse. If you try to flitter about or climb your way through, you will surely meet your end." he advised with a stern look, "My pets will keep you safe, so long as you stay with them," Orin warned the two girls, "they didn't get to be this size by being careless; and there are a great many nasties lurking in these tunnels, so stay with your mounts until you reach the swamps." he advised.

Jinx was clearly unhappy with the ordeal, but realized they had little choice in the matter. Climbing up the rope, the worm squirmed and wiggled beneath Jinx as she tightened her grip on the leash. Ivy wasn't too thrilled either, but had once ridden a large fish beneath the waters of a lost jungle, and knew it was an experience she wouldn't soon forget. With a little assurance, she showed Jinx how to sit astride it safely. The worms writhed within under their crinkled skin in a very queer way that was quite nauseating to endure.

"Ewww..." Jinx whimpered in disgust, thoroughly revolted by the way it moved.

"Actually, that is Uck, dear. She is riding Eww." Orin corrected Jinx with a scowl as he pointed over to Ivy, apparently insulted by her error.

With a whisper to each giant worm and a pat on its side, Orin sent them on their way. With a lurch, they surged forward down into the dark tunnels beyond the warm lights of the dwarven town. Only when they entered the gloom did the worms give off a soft glow, much like faeries do in the dark after exposure to pure sunlight. Great arches of jagged rock swept past them as the worms slid forward at an ever increasing speed, climbing in fluid motion over steep barriers of boulders and stone. Truly these beasts were in their own element, able to stretch and curl over fissures and rifts like no creature Ivy had ever seen. As loathsome as they seemed at first, she realized they had an affinity with the earth; a special magic of their own.

With a gleeful "Woo!" and a "Wee!" it was clear that Jinx was beginning to enjoy the ride as they coasted up and down through the tight tunnels. There were a few moments when Ivy felt as if she was going to faint, not quite used to moving at these steep curves and angles. Flying was far different than being swept along beyond her own control. As the worms coursed through the dim tunnels, she could feel the dull drumming grind of the rock beneath them.

With a shock, they breached their confined tunnel and shot out across a chasm open to the sky above. Great waterfalls poured from all sides as a flock of birds squawked in alarm and dispersed to avoid the passing of the giant mounts. In a flash of the daylight from the stormy clouds above, they landed in another tunnel across the void to continue their wild ride through the maze of tunnels. Every so often Ivy would catch a glimpse of abandoned mineshafts and tools lying about at the foot of hidden pitfalls and forgotten passages. Truly, they would have been lost without the guidance of these large beasts.

The thrill of their ride came to a sudden halt when the worms reared at the entrance to a cave of crystal. Shards of glowing amethyst sprouted from the walls lined with clusters of raw ore. Over the large round heads of their mounts, Ivy could see the source of their unease. Before them a swarm of armored beetles, a hue of dark green, enveloped the entire cavern. Pairs of hooked pincers clacked as they scurried towards the worms, heaving in waves like a thicket of living thorns. Each bore a long spiked horn upon its domed head, sharp as any dwarven lance. These were horned scarabs, natural enemies of the worms.

Common among the caves as they fed on roots and fungi, a few would be of no concern to their huge mounts; but a swarm of thousands was another matter. Uck and Eww began to backtrack in an ungainly manner as the swarm of bugs shifted towards them, sensing an easy meal. Their long sharp horns proved to be an impassable barrier to the worms, as effective as a thousand jagged teeth they dared not tread upon. Ivy thought of abandoning her mount to fly back to the wide open chasm they had just crossed to escape this horde, but gritted her teeth with unease as she remembered Orin's words of caution.

Looking across to Jinx, she seemed just as worried about the encounter; and her welfare was also of Ivy's concern. Their eyeless mounts squirmed in reverse, away from the crawling tide of living thorns. In haste, the worms made their way back to the gorge among the roar of the waterfalls, but apparently lacked the speed they required to breach the gap they had hurdled before. With little hope of escape, the faeries could tell the worms had no where to go but down into the depths far below. Shrouded in the thick mists, they knew they could not possibly survive a fall lashed to the worms as they were. As they army of hungry beetles snapped at their heads, the worms became ever more agitated, and Ivy had to make a choice.

"We have to jump for it, take flight!" Ivy called out to her companion. With little hesitation, Jinx obeyed, despite the stern warning Orin had given them. Free of their burden, the worms were able to seek their own escape and wiggled their girth out into the waterfall with a score of beetles still latched to their tails. Having no skeleton, the fall would do them little harm, but the two girls were left hovering there as they watched the Dwarf's slimy pets disappear into the depths below. The sky high above was dark and brooding with storm clouds, a curtain of rain still showering through the deep chasm.

With the rain above and the mists below, the two faeries knew they had but moments before their wings became too wet to keep them aloft. Adjacent to the tunnel where the beetles now swarmed en masse was another corridor that would have been too narrow for the worms to enter. The two girls had to find solid ground, or they would soon flutter helplessly into the void below like autumn leaves in a storm. Ivy pointed the way, and Jinx hovered over, barely able to keep up with her.

With a puff of exhaustion they landed in the mouth of the corridor, now lost without their guides. They would have to find their way to the swamps on their own. From across the chasm, the voracious beetles eyed them hungrily with their beady little eyes, but were held at bay by the rushing waters between them, and soon vanished back into the shadows of the cavern from whence they came.

"Well, that was close." Jinx huffed while catching her breath, "Do you think we should try to go back?"

"I doubt we could make it across that gap in this storm," Ivy surmised as she looked out the dark tunnel to the churning clouds high above. This place was far too wet for forest faeries to move about. With a nervous tap of her foot, Ivy peered down the gloomy tunnel they had entered. If they could soak up some daylight, they would be able to see their way by their own fairy glow; but the sky was overcast with errant streaks of lightning flashing through the clouds. Jinx seemed to be especially afraid of the dark; the stories of moving shadows that snatched her friends away was festering at the heart of that fear.

"Orin said there were all sorts of *nasties* lurking in these tunnels; do you think there are any in there?" Jinx whispered as she pointed into the darkness. Ivy feared she would scare the girl with anything close to an honest answer, so she chose to ignore the question.

"There's no use in waiting here, we might as well explore this tunnel to see where it leads." she added, as she felt her way along the rough stone walls.

Jinx was used to tall grass and open fields, not cold and dreary caves as Ivy was. Though she was a wood sprite, she had spent a great deal of her childhood in the Undergrove, a small community of fey at the very edge of the Faerylands in a collection of mushroom huts set deep underground. A century ago Ivy had set out on a whim to find the Tree of Life, birthplace of the Faerie; but her adventures led her to the sullen reality of the world outside the veil of the Evermore. As an Elvenborn, she had a duty to the elven lords, to protect her own kind if nothing else. The Elves watched over the fey, but in reality, they were far more powerless than the faeries had known.

The passageway was full of dirt and dust, and in all respects seemed to have been abandoned for quite some time. The roar of the waterfalls echoed through the narrow hall, but faded as they delved deeper into the shadows. Though the corridor ended in rubble, there was an antechamber lower down by way of several well worn steps. Here the rushing of water could be heard, another vein of the underground rivers fed by the roaring falls.

The two girls followed the dim lights ahead, mouths open in amazement as they stepped into a shallow stream which glowed brightly from the inner light of dozens of tiny fish that fought against the rushing current. The bed of this stream followed a curved hall, which had clearly been a dry passage at one point in the past; but was now flooded by the shifting waters. Jinx was the first to notice something of concern in the tunnel.

"What are those, Ivy?" she asked the forest sprite who turned away from the tickly little fish that swam around their feet to look where Jinx stood gawking. Above them great webs hanging in tatters canvassed the ceiling; within them large sacks glittering with dew and grime bound to the walls above.

"They appear to be cocoons." Ivy thought out loud, but Jinx was the one to worry.

"Oh, I hope they're not spider cocoons. Please tell me they're not." she pleaded to her friend; hands clasped together to steady her unease. Ivy had seen many such webs deep in the forests and tunnels of the earth. But by themselves, it wasn't easy to tell what had made them.

"Hopefully whatever had spun these were silkworms instead of big nasty spiders." Ivy added with intentional dramatic flair, as she tried to spook Jinx. Ivy felt she deserved as much for making her plant her face in the dirt earlier. "Though, in honesty, they look to be quite old and abandoned," Ivy added to ease the frightened look on the little girl's face.

With a flutter, she hovered above and grabbed an open end to take a peek inside. It was quite empty, less the matting of leaves layered within its thick threads. With a tug it came loose from its anchors and landed at their feet with a splash as the tiny glowing fish bolted out of the way. It was then the two faeries noticed that the cocoon was quite watertight as it nearly floated away from Ivy's grasp.

With an inquisitive glance at one another, they could tell what the other was thinking. This wasn't a rough cave tunnel, but had been carved by the dwarves long ago; so it must certainly lead somewhere. That and the fact that these tiny fish must have swum upstream from the outside. The cocoon was well padded, and would protect them from the eyes of any nasty critters they might pass along the way. The girls also realized that if they tried to fly down these winding hallways, they might very well get themselves ensnared upon more of these hanging webs. There was just one problem, it was quite cozy in the cocoon, and there was little chance that Ivy could keep from touching Jinx; and would have to face the unpleasant wrath of her magic. It was certainly not something Ivy wanted to experiment with a second time. Jinx just gave a sarcastic pout as she tried to explain away their current dilemma.

"It doesn't work like that silly..." she noted to Ivy, "I have to actually mean to touch you." she sighed, as her inherent hexes were something she's had to live with her whole life. "No, really," she tried to convince Ivy who gave her a doubtful glance, "if I cross my fingers and hands and feet, apparently that annuls the magic somewhat," she added with a shrug, "...I don't know why, it just does."

With a hint of mistrust, Ivy let Jinx scoot in first, so she could complete all her hoodoo crossing of fingers and toes, hands and feet; before she crawled in. With a grimace, she felt her legs touch hers, and Ivy waited for the curse to pronounce itself as she gritted her teeth. But after many long moments, nothing unpleasant happened and she gave a sigh of relief.

"I told you so..." Jinx called out from within, "now hurry up and get inside." Ivy let go of the stone step she had anchored them to as she wiggled the rest of the way in, and in moments the quick current whisked them away.

Jinx made a mix of ill and gleeful sounds as the calm waters washed their tiny boat down the chute; bumping lightly against the walls, but keeping upright due to its unique shape. It was actually quite soft within their webbed canoe, its thick construction kept the two companions from harm. With an unexpected rush, their stomachs sunk as they fell several feet over a break in the river; but they were none the worse for wear.

After a long and harrowing ride they floated into a large ornate chamber filled with broken statues of Dwarven heroes of old. The pool beneath them glowed brightly from a school of hundreds of the tiny luminescent fish dancing beneath the waters. Jinx took her turn to poke her head out of the cocoon, and looked about the room with awe. Great columns adorned with stern faced gargoyles stood as sentries alongside ornately carved steps and decorative pillars, all streaked with age.

Jinx had never before left her enchanted grove and gone into the world, but she could almost hear the memories that still lingered here; etched forever upon the stone. Their silken boat gently drifted to dock upon a set of stone steps that rose out of the water from its drowned banks. Beside the rubble stood a high arched doorway from where they could hear the call of crickets and frogs.

With a smile of delight, the two girls crawled from their woven canoe; though unnoticed behind the two unwitting fey, a pair of heavy scaled eyelids slowly lifted to peer at these two intruders who had stumbled upon its murky swamp.

*   *   *

Skullgrinder

The fearsome eyes of the drake were speckled with ribbons of emerald green and subtle hues of red. It was a large lumbering beast who preferred to hunt during the night, but these two morsels arrived just before the break of dawn. It lay motionless, half submerged within the dank waters of the swamp; perfectly camouflaged by the texture of its rough scales spotted with strips of moss that clung to its hide. The schools of glowing fish were far too small a meal to catch, tiny enough to wriggle between the gaps of its large pointed teeth.

This was a beast of ancient dragon blood, though far removed and diluted from its noble ancestors who once soared the skies; masters of all the heavens. Drakes had no wings, bearing short stout legs with dense jagged claws; but they had retained the family lineage of a long and powerful tail. Their scales were formed of an impenetrable ridged armor that no other predator could pierce. This drake was very old and its sheer girth was evidence that he had eaten well enough in years past. Every wild beast of the swamp knew to give a wide berth to the monstrosity known as Gnaw Skullgrinder.

Gnaw had lurked these swamps for more years than anyone could remember. His eyesight was not as keen as it once was, and he hadn't seen a fairy in so long, he had forgotten what they looked like. Dwarves, though, he had seen aplenty. They were thick and tasty, ripe with the flavor of ale; and were worth savoring when he caught one foolish enough to enter his domain. Over the centuries many of those short pudgy men had tried to end his days, to collect the head of old Skullgrinder to show off in their great hall. But nothing could hurt old Gnaw; his hide was thick, his tooth sharp, and a lash of his powerful tail could bring down the tallest of trees in the swamp. His claws could gouge through steel, and his stare could drain the will of any beast or hero of lesser heart. His name was carried in the tune of many songs and countless tales throughout the

Dwarven Mountains; though in this day and age his visitors were but few. There wasn't much sport in being a vile and terrible brute if your reputation as a monster was all but faded and forgotten, and nobody remember your name.

For many years now, no dwarves had come seeking glory, and his black heart felt heavy in their absence. His current diet of frogs and snakes was less than satisfying. Every now and again he would snatch a crane or grandfather fish, but they presented little challenge and weren't as gratifying as those fat and meaty little men.

Since they had retreated into the depths of the mountain, he encroached upon their abandoned ruins; wondering where they had gone. Their glowing hearths and drums were now silent, and he no longer heard his songs echo through the swamp. Those were good days; when he had dwarves to fight, skulls to grind ...and his life had a measure of meaning. The swamp had been quiet lately, boring in fact, until these two fey trespassed into his lair.

Jinx and Ivy were simply glad to have made it from the cliffs and off the mountain to the edge of the swamp in one piece. Now if they could only cross its murky waters and find this bridge to the Dwarven council beyond its borders, they could find this messenger they sought and be on their way.

The cool light of dawn began to shine through the drowsy mists that hung in the air. The wetlands were heavy with the scent of dank mold and rotting mud. Among the chirp of crickets, the croak of toads and hopping frogs, there was the fragrance of swamp flowers and the buzz of dragonflies perched on lotus blossoms that floated on the water's edge. This was a jungle of reeds and willows and creatures who preferred to dawdle and drone to a lazy way of life. Even the air seemed unwilling to carry a breeze, or the drooping leaves to sway; a sluggish serenity slowed their breath. All in all, it was a presence that made Ivy feel quite sleepy.

The fact was they had both been through a harrowing day, and a rest would do them good. Here mushrooms grew aplenty. Besides berries and nuts, mushrooms were a wood sprites meal of choice; but Jinx would have none of it. She preferred the nectar of honeysuckles, and the pollen of flowers; though Ivy couldn't imagine how she could satisfy herself on something so insubstantial.

The two girls sat upon a great deck of glazed stone, a grand entryway to a time worn temple hall whose once polished grandeur had been all but swallowed by the encroaching swamplands.

"We should get some rest here, and try to find that bridge later in the day." Ivy suggested, and her weary companion agreed.

As the two young fey lay their heads down to sleep, something malevolent stirred beneath the dark waters. The ancient drake slipped beneath the surface around the wide stone steps, eyeing his prey as his girth lay hidden below the surface of the murky waters. He had grown fat over the centuries; and though the reptile moved with ease in the wet swamp, on dry ground, however, he was ungainly and tired easily.

The old drake noted that his prey had wings, and if he missed his chance to snatch them in his great jaws, they might very well take flight beyond his reach. His snout slowly broke the surface of the pool with practiced control, so as not to raise a ripple. These two creatures smelled queer, untouched by the taint of the swamp. Neither did they have the musk of smoke and sweat from the forges of the dwarves; they had a pureness to them he had almost forgotten that bordered on blandness. A meal was a meal, however, and his gut would be none the wiser once it passed his fat bloated tongue.

Jinx sighed with restless dreams, of a trellis of white stone laced with spirals. Below it sat a circular well with waters of the deepest blue, where wishes were whispered in exchange for token gifts dropped within its depths. A chant and a sacrifice was how this special magic was made, to conjure into being a secret hope or prayer.

Wish faeries, though, are the lazy sort, and are mostly deaf, if the truth be known. Nevertheless, once in a great while a wish is heard upon a perked and pointed ear. Wishes rarely if ever turn out in the way they were wanted; their words are garbled, turned and twisted until they are a pale distortion of what they once were. Jinx, however, was wise enough to see wishes for what they were, and such incantations for impossible desires never passed her lips. For luck or wish faeries, either blessed or cursed, would snuff out of existence if they dared to call upon such ancient and sacred magic themselves.

Each creature that ever lived, be they good or evil or any flavor in between; be they great kings or field mice, each was allowed a single wish within their lifetime to be granted by the very essence of the Evermore. It was safe to say that most beings never knew this fact, and unintentionally wasted away this precious gift on a frivolous whim. So many creatures of old from bygone eras had abused the magic in the belief they were owed a thousand such wishes, their feverish chants and prayers were but empty words that fell upon deaf ears; diluting its sanctity beyond any recognition or meaning. They say one should always be careful what they wish for, for you never know whether it be a good or evil fairy who might be listening.

Skullgrinder had no desire for wishes, never had any use for them. Since he was a hatchling he had seen the world change. Across many mountains and deserts, jungles and windswept plains he had traveled. This vast swamp with its pungent smells and misty shores was the place he now called home.

There was a time when dragons ruled the world, but no more; not for untold ages, a time long before even the race of Elves existed. Huge beasts of stark eyes, scales and fang roamed the edges of the earth; from the hot fiery caldera of volcanoes to the vast icy tundra at the end of the world. Dragons were gone but not forgotten; such was the power of their reputation and purity of their magic, that even the spirits of the earth once bowed to their will.

Now all that concerned Gnaw was his hunger, to silence the grumbling of his round stomach; a growing chasm created by his own lush indulgence over the eons. He once used to feast upon entire armies, now here he was, reduced to stalking a pair of skinny meatless damsels who were merely as thin as twigs. He would be almost embarrassed at his situation, but his appetite had turned notably less finicky in his old age. His plan was simple; wait until the girls took one step into the water, and he would gobble them up whole.

As Jinx dreamt of her home, so did Ivy, who had spent most of her years in the mushroom town of Undergrove among a generous variety of fey. The lessons she had learned on her adventures to find the elves had matured her in many ways. She now dreamt of blue skies and green forests from the time she was just a child, before even her wings had fully sprouted. Now the world above was tainted with a strange venom; stained and corrupted by the race of mankind long ago. Slowly, the Faeries were healing the land ...but she feared things would never again be the same. When she slept in the form of a tree, her dreams were timeless, as if she could see the world drifting by like a gentle autumn breeze. In doing so she also shared her magic with the earth and soil around her, and the melody of the wind through her leaves.

There were certain faeries that spent their entire lives as a rock in a stream, as an evergreen in the forest or a single drop of rain in a storm; experiencing the world in a way most creatures could never understand. Ivy was frightened when she first discovered her ability to transform, and it had changed her perception of everything around her. She could speak to flowers and trees, even hear their songs in the breeze. But here the willows that draped the dark swamp whispered coldly, and her troubled dreams told her to beware.

Ivy woke as the light of dawn broke through the thick canopy, sprinkling the weary girls with dabs of sunshine that filtered through the leaves. An eerie mist rose from the waters of the marsh, climbing and curling like living threads of smoke into the thick air. The song of strange birds came whooping from the trees, along with the mournful cries of cranes and the croak of frogs. Within a few hours of rest, they had gathered the strength to continue on.

The thick mists hid a maze of islands that lay scatted across the quagmire, but appeared fairly negotiable with a bit of effort if one was determined. Waking Jinx with the tickle of a long blade of swamp grass, Ivy addressed her partner on this trek.

"Let's be on our way, shall we?" she gleamed with a smile, as Ivy tiptoed out to the very edge of the bank. There among the floating water lilies and reeds sat a peculiar large rock half submerged beneath the surface; camouflaged just enough to be unnoticed among the drab greenery of the swamp. Slits of large eyes slid open ever so slightly at their movement, watching and waiting. Though Ivy held a personal displeasure for the dank and humid marshlands, she admitted they did hold a certain tranquility she found mildly captivating.

Jinx got up with a stretch and a flutter of her wings, and strolled over to snatch a lily for breakfast; it was then that Ivy noticed something strange that had almost passed her keen ears. The buzzing of dragonflies and the croak of the frogs, even the chirp of nearby insects suddenly ceased. It was as if a cone of silence enveloped them where they stood, and she didn't quite know why. There was a queer tension in the air that prickled her senses.

"Hold still," Ivy ordered just as Jinx began to reach out over the water for the flower, "...and don't move." she whispered. The little luck fairy turned to Ivy with a curious glance, but saw no obvious cause for her concern; so after a still moment she shrugged and turned back to pluck the lotus blossom from among the floating lily pads.

This pause did not go unnoticed by Gnaw; as most prey he ambushed seemed to sense their demise mere seconds before the end. The girl who leaned out over the waters was so small, he could swallow her up whole; hardly worth the effort really, but his grumbling stomach spurred him on. His diet of fat dwarves had diminished over the years, leaving him famished. He was left to feed himself on salamanders and herons and drudging for mire shrimp; but such paltry meals left him gravely unsatisfied; he had grown so fat over the centuries that he had become a slave to his belly.

It had been a long, long time since he had tasted the two-legged people, though these maidens didn't smell of dwarf. With a mindful sigh he realized he might only be able to catch one of them, and a coarse grumble from his empty stomach urged him to act. In his desperation, the great drake nearly miscalculated the quickness of his prey as he broke the surface of the waters with a violent lunge.

Jinx saw a great dark maw open before her eyes, dozens of

great jagged teeth stained with aged lined a set of wide jaws that loomed forward to engulf her. She wanted to scream, but the fetid breath of the beast caught in her throat. Ivy turned to watch in horror as a giant creature of scales and teeth swallowed her companion up in a snap of its jaws and swiftly withdrew beneath the dark waters.

"Oh no," she cried as she jumped to the waters edge calling out to Jinx as the waves of ripples the drake had left, subsided. Her fairy friend had been gobbled up.

Gnaw Skullgrinder sat at the bottom of the bog, feeling satisfaction at his fine catch; but something still troubled him. Annoyed that his belly still rumbled in complaint, his tongue felt peculiar as a curious sensation began to fill every inch of his putrid gullet. There was something on his tongue that he couldn't quite swallow. His stomach began to toss and churn, and for the first time in ages Skullgrinder began to feel quite ill.

With a kick of his tail, the drake broke for the surface in haste. Ivy fell back in fear as the great brute lunged up onto the stone steps beside her just before he gave a great belch. Jinx spewed forth covered in black slime, rolling out on the floor at Ivy's feet. In distress the monster heaved yet again, as a spray of vomit soaked the deck with a ceaseless litter of metal helmets and bent shields and bits of armor disgorged from the rancid bowels of the beast.

The stench was nearly unbearable, and Ivy herself began to feel sick. Though, to her joy, Jinx began to squirm as she lay there beside the stinking pool of debris; with a flutter of her eyes, she peered up at Ivy with a look of utter disgust. Foul spit and slime covered her from head to toe, yet she found the mind to back away from the enormous monstrosity who now appeared quite distraught. Gnaw's eyes rolled in grief, his stomach purging in dry heaves to his agony. The great swamp dragon wasn't used to feeling such pain, especially such intense suffering from his own belly.

A nauseating hint of nectar and pollen stained his tongue, the flavor was disagreeable with his palate; the great and fearsome Skullgrinder had experienced what its like to be jinxed. After the heaves subsided, for the first time in a millennium the great dragon's bowels felt at ease. Peering down at the putrid bile he had emptied from his gullet, he understood why. Countless bits and pieces of indigestible armor of every make lay steaming in a pile, dripping with pungent slime. A notable collection of forged steel that had been grating and scraping together in his fat stomach for centuries. With a sigh of relief, the beast finally spoke.

"You are not goblin nor dwarf, nor of fur or feathers, what manner of creature are you that defies my appetite, little one?" He growled, the deepness of his voice shook the very stone beneath them. The two small fey were aghast, as they cowered back against the broken temple wall away from the horrid beast.

"It speaks?" Jinx breathed, shaking the stinking slime of the drake's spittle from her hands.

"It ...IT!" The old dragon fumed, "I am Skullgrinder, master of the silver swamps! Dwarven lords have cowered before me, their hearts stop at the sight of me, their children wet themselves at the mention of my name." Gnaw rumbled in anger, yet the light faded ever so slightly from his tired eyes and his voice softened as he contemplated his bruised ego, "Ah ...but that was a time long ago," he added in self pity, "perhaps everyone has forgotten my name."

"We are of the Elvenborn, great beast." Ivy dared to answer, with a nervous flutter of her wings, "...we mean you no harm." Ivy's statement was so ludicrous to Gnaw that his entire girth rocked with a deep cackled laugh. Slowly his chortling subsided, as he had to admit this small creature had actually done him a great service.

"Tell me you fear me, and I might spare you," He demanded with a serious glare, "and cower well, or I will make a breakfast of you both!" The two girls agreed as his large piercing eyes shifted between them.

"We do, we fear you ...sir Skullgrinder." the two fey trembled. The great beast sighed with satisfaction; it was good to hear his name spoken once again.

"Hmph, I have not seen faeries for as long as I can remember," he grumbled, "children of the elves, bland and tasteless as chaff. Though your magic has rid me of this burden," he nodded his scaly head towards the grisly pile of steaming bits of armor, as the two girl noted with certain dread, many helmets, gauntlets and grieves still clung with half digested bones and shreds of discolored flesh from their previous owners. His stomach no longer turned in knots, now lightened from the impassible refuse that had chafed his ribs for so long. He took a deep breath through his great snout, and for the first time in ages his ribs did not hound him with their chronic aching.

"What mischief brings the race of the Faerie to my humble bog?" Gnaw grumbled in suspicion, the rancid vomit that pooled in his throat presently lulling his voracious appetite.

"You spoke of dwarven lords," Ivy mentioned as Jinx stood at the foot of the steps, washing the drakes slime from her skin, "we seek the bridge to their kingdom that was rumored to lie beyond the edge of the marsh."

"Ah ...yes, it rests beyond the moors." the drake answered, his head turning to the dense swamplands, "Not even I venture there anymore; for it is but a lifeless desolation shrouded in perpetual fog."

"If you're not going to eat us," Jinx added with a hint of doubtful concern, "...could you possibly point us the way." Ivy, too, wondered, giving a look of agreement to the beast with a plea in her emerald green eyes. The drake grumbled to himself, for he had actually never shown any mercy nor aid to another creature before; he was old and selfish, and had always been so. But he did feel relieved to be rid of that abrasive knot in his gullet, and felt better now than he had in ages.

"It's been a long time since I have crossed into the moors, but who knows, perhaps I might find a tasty dwarf or two along the way," he added with a grin, "What you seek is the Bridge of Time, and I will lead you there ...should you choose to follow." the drake added, so as not to appear to be providing charity; he had a reputation to uphold after all.

The two fairy girls seemed indecisive for but a moment, but quickly came to admit that a guide through these murky swamps would be preferable and save them from getting lost. Though still wary of the scaly beast and the score of sharp crooked teeth that lined his great maw, they readily agreed to accompany him.

With the drake's permission, he let them mount upon his wide back, the leathery ridged scales made easy handholds as the swamp dragon lurched into the dark waters that rippled in his wake, as fish and birds of lesser size dispersed from his presence. The waters of the swamp glittered with a tinge of silver in the morning light as the faeries headed out into the thick eerie mists, embracing them in its shroud as they rode astride an old grumpy dragon, who had never before had reason to show an ounce of kindness to anyone.

*   *   *

Tears

Ogres and mountain trolls frequently roamed the lower valley beyond the cliffs near the edge of these forsaken marshlands. Storm clouds churned in the skies above the great mountain that pierced the heavens with their dark granite peaks. The silver swamp was also home to a great many of other vile beasts nearly as loathsome as the elder drake. On their journey through the swamp, they passed many fanged creatures that would have made a shredded meal of the two faeries, but respectively gave the swamp dragon itself a wide berth.

As they weaved their way through the swamp, dozens of glowing eyes peered through the canopy with upon the strange intruders below. Thick tentacles rippled by them in the warm waters, snakes slithered and freakishly large toads sat brooding from dark shores. The girls quickly realized this swamp was an unwelcome place for their sort, and would last nary an instant if not for their lizard guardian. Skullgrinder chose not to tarry with the other lords of the swamp, as each had their place in this murky realm.

Life had turned quite boring for Gnaw these past few centuries. He had collected quite a trove of dwarven weapons, though of little use except as hollow trophies to enamel his pride; trinkets which he kept piled in his dank underwater lair at the center of the marsh. Dragons loved to collect such things, it was in their blood. There was a vanity to it that their kind would find hard to explain, in light of the fact that the mystical dragons were the most powerful creatures that ever lived. It was believed the royal line of pure blood dragons had long since died out. True dragons had, of course, all been hunted into extinction; though they were still spoken of in legends, and in a such a nostalgic tone that it almost seemed as if the dire beasts were truly missed. Old Skullgrinder himself, had his pride and his appetite ...but not much else in his miserable life.

It took a full day to reach the edge of the moors, their borders enveloped in a dreary fog. Both Ivy and Jinx felt a chill as the drake crept out of the murky waters and onto the peat bogs of the shore. Here the vegetation was blackened and dying; spotted with dead skeletons of trees reaching out of the deep mud. Cries of strange beasts could be heard echoing through the mists, making the two girls jump with fright. The giant drake slunk forward on his great webbed feet, moving deep into its dense haze. Out of the water and back on land, Gnaw was again free to speak with the two fey.

"This place used to be lush and green, but became suffocated in this vile fog centuries ago. Now nothing lives here, the trees have withered and died, and only the worms now squirm through this poisoned quagmire." the drake grumbled.

"What happened here," Jinx suggested, "appears to be the same slow death that was engulfing the forests around my home in the celestial valley," she noted while giving the wood sprite a worried glance. Ivy, too, had seen such darkness; this place reeked of the Craven.

"The dwarves no longer venture out beyond the bridge," Gnaw informed his passengers. "There was once a time when herds of sheep and livestock and other delicious morsels roamed these lands; but now it is nothing more than a blackened rotting waste." He sighed to himself, missing such easy pickings from his early years. A fat calf or lamb always made a good snack before bedtime; but now its been so long, he had entirely forgotten the delightful taste of veal.

Howls in the wind distracted the two girls, who shifted about nervously on the drake's back. Skullgrinder warned them it was the cry of the lycanthropes that now dwelled at the edge of the mists, werewolves that had retained their feral form. The dwarves once had deep silver mines in these parts eons past, but they became flooded and were swallowed up by the swamps over time. The taint of the precious metal still stained the waters, thus the lycanthropes were held at bay by their banks. Silver was a renowned purifier, and ate away at their corrupted flesh like acid.

It was cold and dank here, a place reserved for nightmares. Faces of phantoms dissolved in the fog, attempting to suck the very life from the two girls. Thick mud and dead grasses clumped together into mush beneath the drakes webbed feet, clods of filth sticking to his jagged claws. Gnaw had seen worse, as many such areas began to spread beyond the swamps; a foul and unpleasant presence that smelled mildly of death. Old Skullgrinder feared little in this world, but this place made his black heart shudder with a deep unease. There was something in this dark and smothering place that seemed to choke the senses; and he felt a welling desire to return to the protection of his swamp.

The girls looked up in awe as a towering cliff loomed above them out of the mist; they had arrived at the steps to the ancient bridge.

"I must leave you here, for though I am at home in the waters, I cannot climb such stones," Gnaw advised the pair. Ivy and Jinx slid off his leathery back and into the shallow mud near the thick granite steps that wound its way up to the bridge high above, reaching towards a great crack in the rock face which beckoned them to enter. Ivy's keen eyes saw a pair of armored dwarves standing guard far above upon its balcony, long spears with tapered flags hung from their pointed silver tips. Their armor, too, was of silver, a bane to the werewolves that roamed these parts.

"Thank you, Skullgrinder," Jinx offered at their parting, having forgiven him for almost eating her. The drake was abashed, having never before received a mark of gratitude in his long years.

"Oh now, you can thank me by telling the dwarven folk horrifying tales about old Skullgrinder, and to make sure they still fear me," he grinned with his vicious teeth, "and remember to tell them how dire and terrible I am!" he added with a faked snarl.

"Oh, I will." Jinx offered, as did Ivy, who nodded in hasty agreement. The drake slithered back into the fog and watched the two fey depart up the great stone steps, making their way to the sentries above. Gnaw had never helped anyone before, and thought perhaps he should try doing it again sometime because of the funny way it made him feel to act so out of character.

It took a long while for the tiny fey to trudge their way up to the fissure, the moist fog having left their wings far too damp to use for the present moment. Once they neared the entrance, the two guardsmen stationed there eyed them with their furry brows, and crossed their spears to block the path.

"Who are ye that dare enter the king's domain?" one of them demanded as the other huffed suspiciously at the two naked fey who appeared alone out of the thick fog below. It wasn't as if they got many visitors this side of the bridge, as they were appointed to guard the passage from unwelcome visitors or nasty creatures that would dare to trespass. Most fiends would meet the sharp end of a spear.

"We are of the Elvenborn, and seek audience with the king's counsel." Ivy noted to the guards with a degree of authority. Elves weren't exactly loved by most dwarves, but they were far more tolerant towards the Faerie folk. The guards mumbled between themselves; it wasn't as if these two stark naked fey bore any weapons of harm, and they must possess some degree of notable magic to have protected themselves on their dangerous passage through these dark and dreary moors. These two guardsmen were no strangers to the vile beasts that lurked below, and anything that could fend them off was worth a measure of respect.

"The king's counsel you say?" the patrolman offered with a tug of his beard, but finally nodded to his comrade to let them pass. The Faerie were allies after all, and not a danger to the dwarves. He stepped back to let the fairy girls come forward, and tapped a large ornate box that stood in the middle of the path. Its aged wood was cracked and splintered in spots among the deeply stained carvings that decorated its panels; and with a pop of the clasp, its cabinet doors swung open. Within stood a tall slender hourglass.

"Turn it once, and you must cross the length of the bridge before the sands run out." he cautioned, as he motioned Ivy to take it from the box. It was elongated, nearly the length of her arm, with twisted spiraled rods as handles which felt oddly like a mixture of ivory and wood; a texture Ivy had never felt before. "Give it to the guards stationed on the other side, and do not dally; ye have been warned."

Jinx looked at the hourglass and wanted to hold it, but dared not, lest it break from her touch. Ivy turned to the fissure and into its black depths; noting the planks of a tattered bridge at its edge. Ivy turned to Jinx once with a tilt of her head to follow, and her companion indicated she was ready.

"Well then, let's give this a go." Ivy shrugged and turned the hourglass over. Strangely, the sand in the glass stuck upright within the top bulb; it wasn't until she took her first step on the bridge that the sands began to run. A moment behind her, Jinx turned to the burly guardsman and thanked him for his help, offering a shake of her hand in gratitude. With hesitation, the gruff guard accepted the gesture and she bade him farewell as Jinx skipped along to catch up just a few steps behind her companion on the bridge.

With a sarcastic snort, the two dwarves turned to see the faeries had disappeared into the void of the magical bridge, and went back to their posts to continue the duties of their watch. It wasn't long after that the smug guard who had shaken the luck fairy's hand felt sleepy and dozed off for a moment while leaning on his tall spear. With a twist of a speck of gravel, his spear slipped loose from his hands, causing the drowsy guard to lose his balance and the poor little man tumbled headlong down the length of the steps into the fog below to the utter shock of his alarmed comrade. The unfortunate guard's day ended on a sad note, as a crunch and grinding of teeth could be heard from beneath the thick haze, and Gnaw Skullgrinder gave a satisfied grin for the tasty morsel before turning back towards his home in the swamps.

Back on the rickety bridge, the two fey beheld a strange sight as they crossed through the strange fissure. They treaded carefully, aware that below them a vast darkness and jagged rocks awaited should a rope or rotted plank snap beneath their feet. The span of the bridge was long, stretching out into the darkness between the edges of the fissure. Here no sunlight shone, no wind blew, nor echo sounded. It was a bridge between realms divided by time. The hourglass they held was the passport that allowed safe passage.

"I wonder what would happen if we turned the hourglass again?" Jinx wondered out loud to her companion, "Or what might happen to us if we were still on the bridge when the sands ran out?" she inquired once more with a curious glance. Ivy, though, didn't share her level of reckless disregard.

"Maybe this is your first time away from home, Jinx, but I've come to learn that it's not wise to trifle with ancient magic," Ivy warned her sternly.

"I was just asking..." Jinx pouted back, "You don't like me much, do you, Ivy?" she dared to inquire as they trotted along the worn planks. The end of the bridge could not be seen, and extended beyond their vision into the darkness of the rift.

"I never said that," Ivy responded after an awkward pause, "why would you say such a thing?"

"Because of the way you treat me," Jinx blubbered as she turned her eyes away, "...it's okay you know, a lot of faeries don't like me." she finished with a dramatic sigh. Her claim made valid sense to the wood sprite, who could understand Jinx scaring others away with the curse of her touch or being hexed by her presence. It was an unfortunate type of magic she possessed.

"Certainly you must get along with the other faeries back home ...don't you?" Ivy queried with a half smile of hope, not knowing what the little girl's answer might reveal. Jinx took her time to respond, still picking at bits of dried slobber from the drake that had been left smeared upon her wings that she had somehow missed before. After a moment, Ivy regretted having asked, thinking that she had brought up a painful subject for the cursed fey. With a shred of guilt, she opened her mouth again to change the subject, but Jinx finally broke the silence.

"Most fey either hound me with insults to no end or avoid me like a plague," Jinx gave a serious but short giggle, "the faeries with beneficial influence are always invited out to all the parties and picnics or games," she added, but gave a noticeable slouch of her shoulders, "but ones like me are shunned and made fun of most the time." Jinx finished with a painful short glance into Ivy's eyes. The woodland sprite felt sorry for the little girl. Truly, she couldn't pretend to imagine how it really felt to be cursed so.

"It must be horrible, I'm sorry, Jinx, I truly am. Maybe the Elves can help you somehow once we get back." Ivy offered with a lighthearted smile. On another note, Ivy was starting to become worried, as the sands in the hourglass were beginning to run out, yet the end of the bridge was still nowhere in sight. In desperation, Ivy began to walk faster, and Jinx had to do double-time just to keep pace with Ivy's long legs.

"Maybe," Jinx asked between short huffs, "...we should try to fly there." she finally got out with her tired breath.

"This thing is too heavy." Ivy advised, as she tried with a flap of her long green wings to no avail. She simply wasn't strong enough; faeries weren't built that way. The faster they went, the quicker the sands ran, and the girls wondered if they would be trapped here in this limbo once the magic of the sands ran dry. But just as the last inch was about to sift into the bottom of the glass, they saw the posts in the distance.

Her heart beat faster as she yelled back to Jinx to keep up. Ivy ran, trying to be as careful as she could with the awkward object, to keep the heavy glass upright. She honestly didn't think they were going to make it, but miraculously stepped off the last plank just as the last tiny speck of sand bounced around the edge of the funnel and fell.

The two girls mouths dropped open as they stood looking upon the wondrous sight that lay before them. They were standing upon a stone balcony encompassed by a raised railing, and off the ledge were great steppingstones of various shapes that led to a grand and fantastical floating mountain. High towers and bold sculptures lined its exterior, lush with trees and vines that clung to its sides. Like the floating steps that led to it, the bottoms tapered into shadows, hanging in the open nothingness upon which they drifted. The sun above hid behind thick glazed clouds that filled the void beyond.

"Annnnd, I'll take that Missy." A dwarf in silver armor waddled up to snatch the hourglass from Ivy's hands as they stood gawking. She leaned away quickly from the guard who reeked strongly of ale, his hair in a tuft and beady eyes red and puffy; only visible because he had left his helmet tossed to the side of the rail. There were other guardsmen there, singing out of tune and drinking from fat wineskins. A burp and a belch soured the air as the girls turned their immediate attention to the balcony around them. All these dwarves were drunk as skunks!

The one sentry that took the hourglass set it into a box, identical to its brother on the other side of the fissure, and closed its lid. He then promptly waddled over to grab a mug of ale while half its contents sloshed to the floor as he raised his hand, "Welcome to the dwarven kingdom, *urp* * ...kingdom of the dwarves." he burped. "And what's you're business here, young lass?"

Ivy was aghast at their behavior, but Jinx just giggled the way she always did. She knew more about Dwarves than Ivy did after all, so the wood sprite turned to her with a look of dismay.

"Dwarves like to drink..." she offered to her companion with a smirk, which quickly turned to a disgusted grimace as one of the intoxicated guards turned to puke over the side. The beauty of their surroundings was diminished by the drunken louts surrounding them. Though one of them had presence of mind to put down his tankard to be of slight service to the visitors.

"We are here by appointment of the high elves to seek the king's counsel." Ivy responded with a tight lip, not approving of the state of the watchmen. The sentry teetered there from one stubby leg to the other, staring back at her with a stupid grin on his fat hairy lips.

"Oh right, now then ...what's the password?" he blubbered, but was apparently serious about the request. Ivy turned to Jinx with a bewildered look, but she shrugged her shoulders just the same in response.

"Um, well ...we weren't informed of any password." Ivy answered nervously as she noted all the guards turned their eyes to her, with hands on spears and hilts of swords. The guard in front of her cozied up close to the girl, looking her square in the eye with a suspicious glare and gave a low growl. Both faeries took a cautious step back, wondering what they were going to do. Seeing that they were scared, the dwarf's attitude took a turn and he gave a roaring laugh as he grabbed his thick belly. All the other guards also broke down laughing so hard they fell to the floor, a few even managed to snort beer through their nose at the joke.

"Haw haw haw, oh, you should'a seen the look on your face, haw haw haw." The dwarve nearly tipped over. "There is *no* password!" he chuckled, patting a nearby comrade on his armored back so hard it left a dent. "Go on, be on your way ...the royal court awaits." he chortled with a hint of sarcasm.

A little perplexed by their sense of humor, Ivy weaved her way around the drunken guards to the great floating steps. With short flits, they flew from one floating stone to the next as it led them to the great mountain. Around them there was nothing but clouds and sky, and Ivy realized they were now in a realm far removed from the world she knew. Perhaps the bridge of time took them to elements beyond the Evermore altogether. The thought of it tickled her brain.

"Do dwarves always get so drunk?" Ivy asked her companion, "The ones we met under the cliffs seemed hard at work, and not at all like this." as she waved a thumb back at the stumbling guards at the bridge.

"I've only met a few that came to our valley, but they are stern and serious most of the time; I've never seen them so cockeyed and slobbering drunk before," she added, "they're kind of funny, actually." Jinx giggled, but Ivy didn't share her opinion.

The steps led up to a tall archway of stone, carved from the living rock. Great halls were filled with pillars so high they could accommodate titans, and were so vast they could house an army. Steps led up through the fortress and passed through grand cathedrals and decorative chambers. Lifts strung with ropes and pulleys aided where great loads needed to be transported. Ivy had heard countless legends about the Dwarven Kingdom and all its glory, and certainly the setting met its reputation, but her high expectations were quelled by the inebriated residents that roamed the halls.

She had heard tales of their songs and merriment, but the sheer excess of drink and squalor presented here bordered on repulsive. There seemed to be no strict sense of obedience, as every single dwarf she saw was either drunk, drinking or passed out cold across the floor, dreaming about bubbly pints of ale no doubt.   Lining the halls were inebriated dwarves with half strapped armor quaffing rum from barrels and wineskins. Ivy had never seen so many cups and goblets of every shape and make, strewn about the tables and floors. Drinking horns sat toppled next to empty jugs in mess halls that were an orgy of food and swill. Dwarves mumbled songs and joined in frequent toasts as they slapped tankards together in loud 'hoorahs' as foamy ale rained down around them.

Ivy didn't know what to think. Her dreams about this place were crushed by the reality of what she saw. Jinx, on the other hand, wasn't judgmental in the slightest, and just tiptoed around the pools of stale mead splashed upon the rough stone floor. The dwarves mainly ignored them, except for a few who gave them somber stares. Out of the crowd, Ivy noted a drunken dwarf dressed in noble garb and went out of her way to approach him. He eyed the two fey as they drew closer and let out a call, with a golden gem encrusted goblet in hand.

"Look, fairy folk, a toast to the faeries!   Hoorah!" His companions at the table stood all and slapped their cups together, splashing ale and wine onto the girls in their careless mirth. They all sat and gulped down their drinks, grabbing fistfuls of bread or greasy meat lying on platters within reach. Apparently, they were all in the midst of a grand celebration that had already long since reached its peak.

"Excuse me, sire, if I could take a moment of your time, but my companion and I are looking for the king's counsel. Perhaps you could guide us in the right direction." Ivy had to fight to be heard over the loud voices and clamor at the table. The noble seemed to have at least heard half of what she had said.

"The king's counsel you say?" he smiled, "Ah, well, the members of the royal court aren't doing much of that at the moment, I presume. Why don't you have a seat and join us for a drink?" he offered, changing the subject; but Ivy politely declined.

"I don't drink, thank you."

"I do!" Jinx butted in with wide eyes, eager to try what they were having. She drank nectar from flowers, how much worse

could this be? Ivy just gave her a disapproving look as Jinx
was offered a full goblet nearly twice the size of her head. She
took a sip, scrunching her brow as she took a gulp; and wiping
the cherry stain of wine from her lips with a lick. All the
dwarves at the table were watching her.

"Mmm, not bad." She finally said with a quirky smile. All the
dwarves laughed heartily at her remark, and bashed their cups
together in a loud toast of approval. It was very different from
elvish elderberry wine, or the sweet nectar of honeysuckles.
This stuff made her feel funny, much like the way it felt at the
border of falling off to sleep. Her head swam with colorful
bubbles, and Jinx gave a gleeful laugh. The poor girl had
always lived her life with a measure of depression, but the
fruity wine seemed to make the weight of that fade away.

"So, what is everyone celebrating?" she asked with a silly grin
on her face as the hairy dwarf next to her refilled her cup past
its brim. All the dwarves turned to her with a light smile,
though some of the smiles appeared awkwardly sad, as much as
a sad smile can be.

"You mean, you haven't heard?" the nobleman asked, with an
air of surprise, "we've been observing this celebration with food
and drink for the past three moons!" he gave an incredulous roll
of his eyes.

"You mean three whole *months*?" Jinx blurted with surprise
and disbelief, though with a glance around her, she began to
consider the truth of that claim, "but why?"

"By order of the king," he affirmed with a raised goblet and
strident tone, "...to celebrate his death!" he said loudly so all
could hear: at that all the dwarves in the room raised a cup or
goblet or bowl high above in honored toast, "The king is dead,
long live the king!"

*   *   *

Tower of Madness

The dwarves formal toast didn't make any amount of sense to the two girls; if the king was dead, how could he live any longer? Dwarves were just plain weird!

"What happened to him?" Jinx asked in all innocence. The nobleman turned his bubbly smile to the girl, and he answered with a measure of candor.

"Oh, the stone smiths are still recording his story in the great hall with hammer and chisel: about his grand and heroic deeds and his untimely demise ...much of which is still slightly under debate." he replied to her confusion, "Many dwarves voted to have the records say he was mortally wounded after battling off a horde of goblins, or defending the sacred treasures of our ancestors from a wave of banshees," the nobleman added with dramatic flare, making a face at the girl in his attempt to be scary, "but most of us chose the runes to say he was trampled while hunting ice mammoths from the northern frosts ...or some such." he ended, as several of the drunken dwarves at the table nodded in agreement.

"What exactly do you mean," the small fey asked a bit bewildered, "...he died three times already?"

"Oh, no, no, no dear," he answered in unison with a round of chuckles by the rest of the company at the table, "one night three moons past he was having a wee bit of drink, as most kings are inclined to do, and accidentally stumbled and fell on his own sword after a bit of showing off at the end of a very tall tale." he added with a note of humility, but quickly cracked a smile to the jeers of the guests at the table, "But as a lesson learned, I'll wager he'll never do that again! ...Ho, haw haw!"

Ivy flashed a morbid look of shock at her companion, but finally relaxed and joined the jovial laughter of all in the room.

"So ...you just make up a false story to cover how he actually died?" Jinx inquired with a hint of trepidation.

"Well, of course!" the nobleman added while rubbing his

greasy fingers from the leg of mutton upon his soiled sleeve, "You can't believe every fairytale you hear. The stories and legends of our ancestors that are told over campfires on cold nights, or recorded in these halls account for how well we can weave a colorful yarn." he admitted to her surprise. "Have you ever heard tales of dwarven warriors fighting dragons who sleep on giant mounds of shining gold, and believed it?" he asked with wide eyes.

"Well, yes." she answered with a slight pout on her lips.

"Ridiculous! A dragon's breath would melt gold into a formless piles of slag." he retorted, "And have you heard stories of dwarves facing hill giants that use uprooted trees as clubs?" he asked again while waving his leg of mutton like a maul.

"Uh-huh." With a slightly guilty look, Jinx agreed.

"Ludicrous!" he snapped again with a bite of the meat, "In height, we barely come up to their knee, couldn't hurt them a bit if we tried. Not like they've got any reason to fight with us either; those filthy creatures are as dumb as nails." he slammed down his meat as he took another swig from his cup, "If a dwarf and a giant got into a real fray, we would get squashed." the nobleman smashed his goblet down on the table on a chunk of meat as if to accentuate the point; which made little Jinx jump with an 'ooh!'

"You mean all of the stories we've heard weren't true?" she added with a sad look of disappointment. The dwarves next to her patted her on the back to lighten her unhappy mood, but it was the nobleman's childish smile that lifted her spirits.

"Maybe, maybe not, little fey, but likely they're just fanciful tales from the crafty tongues of our storytellers." he grinned as he refilled her large goblet, though Jinx had truly had her fill. On another note, she couldn't understand why everyone seemed so happy that their king was dead and she had to ask if he was such a horrible a person that they were glad he was gone.

"Oh no, little lass," a dwarf beside her corrected, "Lord Fellforge was a good king, and as all kings he had the right to order the manner of his funeral, and how his subjects are to properly mourn his passing according to his command," the red bearded dwarf informed her as he reached for another pint of frothing ale.

"It was his wish that we celebrate in remembrance of him for a full season," the nobleman remarked, "though, come to think of it, he was also mighty drunk the day he said that." the dwarf gave a pause of thought, "...But who are we to argue?" He grabbed his goblet to be filled with a splash of wine, raising it again for the crowd at the table in toast once again. "To King Fellforge, though a bit clumsy, but so very wise in death! Hoorah!" Both Jinx and Ivy gave each other a tired look and a sigh as another rain of ale and foam came pouring down upon them yet again from the overzealous tributes to their former lord.

Through the loud merriment and overabundance of food and drink, they noted that a new king had already been chosen, but could not be officially crowned until the end of the lengthy wake. It took the two faeries a while to fully understand that all the tall tales they had heard about the dwarves were for the most part entirely untrue. Certainly they loved to scrounge in the earth for gold and trinkets, or hammer out enchanted weapons in the heat of a blazing forge; but besides that, after a hard day's work they did little more than boast and drink.

They wore armor most of the time because they were so small and usually on the menu for larger creatures that roamed the dark caves and rotting swamps. Their run-in with the drake, Skullgrinder, had supported that grim fact. From time to time, the drunken dwarves would weary of their infrequent barroom brawls. Filled with false bravado fueled by too much ale, in a drunken stupor they would take up arms for a scuffle with a local monster; most usually upon a bet or a dare. After being thoroughly thrashed they would run home with their hairy tails between their little legs, only to make up eccentric stories about their bravery in the face of certain death.

After a bit of sobering up by the dwarves involved, the hazy circumstances of such altercations would be generously elaborated upon with a wag of their silver tongues; especially when having to confront the widows of any fallen comrades with exaggerated excuses and brazen lies about their demise. Thus is how dwarves truly were, though they tended to hide their guilty expressions under their thick hairy beards. That's why sober dwarves always appeared so irate most of the time, it was just a naturally defensive reaction for a dwarf to appear angry and disagreeable so as to conceal what pitiful little liars they really were.

It didn't take long for the two faeries to realize the daily life of a common dwarf was fairly dull. They drowned themselves in alcohol to relieve their boredom for the most part, because most other races were repulsed by their obnoxious behavior and avoided them altogether. Their kind knew how to brew a good mead, however; but as dwarves usually do, they selfishly hoarded the very best batches for their own self indulgence.

Finding a moderately clean rag, the two fey wiped off the sticky ale and wine they had been showered with during the revelry. The fact that the king was dead was of no real consequence to them, as it was the king's messenger they actually sought as the jewel was reputed to be in his possession. With a great deal of lost patience, they inquired with several drunken dwarves as to where they might find this royal messenger. It wasn't until they got to the kitchens they found at least a few of the dwarven women setting out stacks of dishes and barrels of ale to be of mind enough to provide the girls with some helpful information towards that end.

"The messenger, you say?" One of the cooks in the steamy kitchen replied; wiping sweat from her brow upon her grease stained apron. She was a large woman with matted blond hair and her curly beard wrapped in a tight braid tucked beneath her blouse, "You must be looking for Ogle, he was the counsel's envoy last I heard." she babbled as she grabbed a great cleaver chopped this and that upon the cutting board while vigorously churning a pot of stew, "You girls can find him out near the upper courtyard most days; wears a yellow tunic." she advised, "Now if you don't mind; I've got a thousand mouths to feed, and no time for quaint conversation."

With a shrug, both Ivy and Jinx realized they were in the way, and scurried out of the kitchen that was alive with the bustle of cooks and servants somehow making sense of all the madness brewing within. Sidestepping jeering dwarves arm in arm, their thick beards kept the two fairy girls from telling between the sexes except by their dress. With little effort they found a grand stairwell that led to the upper chambers, which they took instead; not entirely trusting the contraptions of gears and pulleys that raised the heavy elevators the dwarves had built. Curiously, the two fey saw a few other races of beings besides the dwarves milling about the halls, but weren't quite sure what kind of creatures they were.

Above in the courtyard, through pillars of worn stone they found a sparse garden open to the sky. Here at least they could flit about with their wings, though the abysmal drop off from the side of the floating mountain was a powerful intimidation for them not to breach the edge. With a little wandering, they finally found an old balding dwarf wearing a worn and tattered robe the color of sunflower petals. The giggling dwarf seemed distracted, busy peering at something through a small crack in the supporting wall at the end of the garden foyer.

Jinx got up to him first, but as the girls flitted to his side, their bare feet made little noise in the soft grass and their presence went completely unnoticed by the dwarf. His face still pressed up against the wall, and was mumbling to himself with a stupid grin showing through his scraggly white beard; clearly preoccupied by whatever he was looking at. A set of thick stained glass windows were set deep into the wall beside him and looking through them, with a little effort, Jinx discovered how Ogle had earned his name.

With a hushed gasp, Jinx backed away from the window, and turned to give the old dwarf a seething glare, and Ivy leaned over to see what her companion had spied through the warped glass of the window. The room beyond was a wash room where several nude lady dwarves were bathing. To the lithe faeries, the dwarven women were squat and bulky, and not too attractive considering every one of them sported mustaches and thick beards; though their femininity was still obvious with them bathing naked. Apparently, Ogle liked his women that stumpy and hairy; though now wrinkled and balding, his attractiveness to the younger dwarven maidens had long since expired.

Ogle's lusty grin quickly subsided when he turned his eye from the hole in the wall to see the two angry faeries glaring at him, standing there with their arms crossed as were their thin pointed brows.

"Oh, for shame, you dirty old man." Jinx snapped at him. A look of guilt washed over Ogle's face like a tide of disgrace crashing upon a rocky shore. Ivy thought Jinx was being a wee bit harsh with the little man, as she understood it was only normal for a male of his race to have such carnal desires, but faeries still adhered to a sense of common decency. To the Elvenborn, nudity was only natural, as all wild beasts of the lands and forests were. Jinx seemed to think his actions were shameful; though, personally, her older and wiser companion ended up finding it all a bit funny.

Needless to say, true faerie passion greatly paled in comparison to most living creatures. It was their influence that birthed the very essence of romance, the creation of poetry and songs among other races that endeavored to express their feelings on such untamed emotions. Ogle though, was a willing victim of his own sensual pursuits; there was nothing remotely romantic about being a peeping-tom.

"Are you Ogle, the king's messenger?" Ivy asked, trying to change the subject to keep this poor dwarf from piddling himself under the burning glare of the tiny luck fairy for his shameful voyeurism. Pulling his attention away from Jinx's seething eyes, the old dwarf patted his tunic nervously in a vain attempt to regain a slight measure of composure.

"Why uh, yes, I am Emissary Ogle, the court's royal messenger." he gave a half curled grin to Ivy, who wasn't chastising him with as much a prosecuting look in her almond-shaped eyes as her little friend. Ivy was glad to hear that; she'd had to suffer through the past few hours of obnoxious and loudmouth revelry of many a dwarf to find him, and her hair was still sticky from the shower of ale. Hopefully, she could convince him to abandon his peep show for a few moments to help them.

"My name is Ivy Elvenborn, and this is Jinx," she smiled, "we are on a quest from the High Elves."

"And how may I be of service, Milady?" Ogle bowed, trying to impress Jinx with his courtesy, in an attempt to soften her glare; but his integrity had already been soiled in her eyes. Ogle seemed to be keenly aware of that.

"Actually sire, we would like to examine something reputed to be in your possession," she added as he gave her a questioning look, "We would like to see a jewel you carry called the Tears of Sorrow." Ivy inquired.

"And what might you want with that ...*Elvenborn*?" he replied with suspicion, pointing out her heritage with his end comment, tying its relation to the purpose of the relic. Ivy did happen to catch his sleight of tongue, and wondered how she was going to iron this out considering the history involved with the jewel.

"We are simply following clues, and merely wish to see it for ourselves," Ivy pleaded. Ogle, however, seemed a little reluctant to comply, and even a tad eager to get back to his afternoon distraction presented through the hole in the wall. Jinx made sure to cut him short of that thought.

"Or, maybe I should just flit in there and tell those ladies about the depraved little man who's been peering at them all afternoon; hmm?" the little girl threatened. At the mention of that, Ogle's face turned such a deathly shade of white, that it nearly matched his age bleached beard.

"Oh, oh, now dear, we wouldn't want that," he stumbled over his words, "...they would have my hide!" he confirmed the likelihood of his fate to himself in a scared tone.

"Needless to say, the controversy it might create, if the king's appointed emissary were accused of such lewd and lascivious conduct which would most certainly be frowned upon by the royal court..." Ivy trailed in with an approving nod from Jinx. At that, Ogle became unraveled. These two little obnoxious faeries certainly had him by the scruff of his beard; and could expose him to face the embarrassing consequences. With a sigh of defeat, the old dwarf agreed to cooperate.

"Oh my, that would be a horrible mistake and would soil my reputation," Ogle blabbered with a wave of his hands in surrender, "...we certainly don't want to get ahead of ourselves now; I was merely asking why you two beautiful young fey would be so interested in the gem." he lavished them with hollow praise. Ivy knew full well that Dwarves didn't find female faeries attractive in the slightest. To them, fairy girls were pretty much repugnant, with their stick thin bodies, lack of bulging muscle, their thin eyebrows and almond shaped eyes, and their lack of facial hair made them especially repulsive to any Dwarven male.

"We would really just like to examine this jewel, and we will be on our way." Ivy offered to convince him of their intent. "...And of course, there would be no reason to mention this little ah, *situation* to anyone." she promised with a wave of her hand to Ogle's peep hole.

The old dwarf seemed to be more than happy with that offer, and showed them the way to the upper chambers of the keep. Ogle escorted the two fey through the winding staircases and across a narrow stone bridge to a tower poised at the outer banks of the castle. Behind a thick wooden door laced with ornamental metalwork, he led them into a round room sparsely decorated with worn rugs and faded tapestries. There were several glittering trophies collected by the royal court set on pedestals and velvet covered tables.

Knightly helmets and scepters carved with intricate designs inlaid with fine gold and precious gems the Dwarven folk so valued, sat about the room for presentation. There were many decorative swords and shields, battle axes and spears among other shiny items used in the pomp of regal ceremonies reserved for the nobility. Jinx so desperately wanted to pick them up and examine them, but knew her touch might coerce a gemstone to pop loose, or a priceless sword to snap in two; so she just surveyed the room with her hands cupped behind her back. Unfortunately, quelling her own curiosity was simply something she had become rather used to.

Ogle directed them to a display case and opened up the lid to show the two girls. Within sat a thick silver necklace with a large solid back-plate mounted with three large tear-shaped gemstones of the purest aqua blue. Though the polished gems shimmered with an ethereal hue, the necklace itself was rather unassuming. Upon a closer look, Ivy noticed there were glyphs woven within the pattern imbedded in the silver backing, and inquired of Ogle as to their meaning in search of some sort of hidden clue.

"The dwarven script is pretty plain actually," the envoy explained as he glanced over the markings, "it simply gives the name of the island of Tyre, which is where a great siege was waged and an entire clan of Dwarves were abandoned by our Elven allies to meet their doom." he mentioned with a notable grimace, "Every last one met their bitter end that day, as every honorable dwarf fought to the last."

"I'm a little confused, was this memento named after the island of *Tears*?" Ivy asked, trying to decipher the meaning of this piece of the puzzle they had been led to. Jinx edged herself closer to take a better look, though like Ivy, she couldn't read the markings either.

"No, no, young Miss," he shook his head, "though it may seem like a play on words, the tear shaped gems were meant as a symbol of the sadness endured by our race that day we suffered such a great personal loss that struck the hearts of every Dwarve like hammer to a forge." he noted with sincerity, "The Tears of Tyre remind us and the Elves of our sacrifice and the price that we paid in the battle against the darkness known as the Craven." Ogle finished with a sigh as he set the necklace gently back in its case. Ivy was slightly perplexed by his puzzling choice of words.

"Don't you mean the Tears of Sorrow?" she blurted out, trying to figure out what she was missing.

"Hah, no young lass. The royal court refers to this relic solely as the *Tears*," Ogle noted, as he paused to rub his scruffy chin in deep thought, "...though the Tears of Sorrow is what the peasant folk call it outside the kingdom, so I've heard; which by golly, is another play on words if you think about it." he proclaimed. Jinx and Ivy exchanged bewildered glances; truly, the little luck fairy was just as confounded as Ivy was.

"We don't quite understand..." Ivy replied.

"You look a wee confused, lass; so let me shed a little light on this for you," the old dwarf offered as he turned away from the glass case, "Sorrow, is a person."

Her mouth fell open in surprise; but that revelation only sprouted more questions than answers. Who was Sorrow? In short length, Ogle explained that Sorrow was the artisan who created the necklace for the dwarves, as a symbolic gift to their race for the great loss they had suffered. Sorrow herself was a priestess from the Isle of Tyre and of a strange race of dark elves know as the Drow. After learning this, Ivy gave a tired shrug of her shoulders, realizing that their quest had taken yet another turn. Apparently, they would have to travel to this mysterious island to look up this drow elf.

"Oh, now, lass, you should really rethink what's drumming through your head," Ogle gave a concerned glance at the two faeries, "the Drow are not the kind to be trifled with, and better left alone, I'll tell ye."

"I believe we have little choice in the matter." Ivy explained as Jinx gave a glare of impatience. The high elves could certainly make life complicated for a little fey. Ivy learned long ago to tolerate the Elves natural skill at being so notoriously indirect, as there were lessons that could only be learned through self-discovery. Truth was, faeries themselves usually failed to retain anything they were told outright because of their lack of attentiveness; and like children, they usually always had to learn from their own experience. It's not like you could hold it against them, as most fey were not the intellectual sort. It was known that Faeries were called *flighty* for more reasons than one.

Jinx had the old Dwarf under her thumb, so he finally agreed to take them to the central map room where several hundred parched scrolls lay piled upon narrow shelves. As each were bound with ribbon and twine, it took a while for Ogle to find the map of Tyre. An elaborate sketch of the island was drawn in faded ink, great serpentine beasts were shown in the waters around the small isle. There were two large coves and several shrines shown within its borders. Directly to the East was an odd line along with a crest of the sun marking a road from the swamps off the mainland. It was all rather confusing.

"Ah, yes here it is," as the white bearded dwarf spread out the fragile scroll on the central table, placing heavy lumps of gold ore at its corners to keep the parchment open, "The shaded area between the two bays is where the massacre took place, and to the west in the center of the isle shown there is the temple of the sisterhood." he explained.

"The sisterhood?" Jinx asked with an inquisitive glance at the map while straining to stand on her tiptoes so she could see onto the table.

"Yes, little one ...the Sisterhood of Blood." he replied as Jinx gave a gulp. "An unpleasant bunch if the name tells ya so."

"And what does this mean?" Ivy inquired while pointing to the crest and the line across the water.

"There lies a sandbar beneath the ocean that is only exposed at a seasonal low tide. There are all sorts of nasty critters that roam those waters, so I don't recommend trying to swim or boat across; and the coastal winds there might keep you from being able to fly your way across," Ogle clarified for the two fey, which led to their next question as to how they might reach this strange island.

With a great deal of scampering, Ogle grabbed a stool and snatched a large rolled map from a high shelf. He laid it out upon the table to point out where they were.

"We are many leagues from the island, so you must take the bridge of time to get closer to your destination, I'm afraid." he advised with a worried rub of his chin.

"Do you mean that bridge we came across from the moors?" Jinx butted in, "What was that all about with the hourglass ...and what would have happened to us if the sands ran out?" she added out of curiosity. Ogle just gave a casual grin, realizing the extent of the young fey's confusion.

"Oh, nothing much. In a way, the hourglass is used as a ticket of passage across the bridge, but its magic is a type to impress the traveler with a sense of urgency." He gave a slight chuckle, "Whether you walked ten feet or ran an entire league, you would still have stepped off its end when the sands ran out ...if you ask me, I just think that bridge really hates people walking on it."

"But, it just leads back to the moors from where we came, how would it get us to the shores of Tyre?" Ivy asked, a bit perplexed by his instructions.

"The magic of that bridge also spans many points of distance, you were led here because that is where you asked to go, and the bridge obliged," Ogle gave a wave of his stubby little hands, "When you cross the bridge again, take it to Thieves Gate, which is here..." the dwarf pointed to the south of the map on the mainland below the island. "Then you will have to wait until the first new moon after the summer solstice when the sandbar is exposed. Be warned that you will have to cross before the lapse of the new moon; or else the monster infested waters will swallow you up!" Ogle lavished his tale with a quick motion of his arms as they come together, giving Jinx a slight jump.

"And, where might we find this elf named Sorrow?" the woodland sprite asked with a tilt of her head as she studied the map. The dwarf gave a disconcerting shake of his finger at the tall citadel drawn at the isles center.

"There, at a place they call the Tower of Madness," his voice dropping to a whisper, "I would warn you against traversing upon that accursed land, but I can tell you're not in the mood to listen." he finished.

With a loud sigh, Ivy realized their journey had taken yet another spin. They would have to find this lady Sorrow to discover the next step in their quest; but at least this was a real person to talk to, rather than a giant cauldron or a scrap of jewelry; and would hopefully lead them to some true answers they could count on. The high elves had entrusted her to find a way to awaken the Undying; the spirits of their world to aid them in their time of need, or face the scourge of the Craven with what little hope they had left. Ivy felt the weight of her task more so than her companion, who seemed to be along for no more than the adventure of it all.

Ogle escorted them from the upper chambers back towards the central courtyard. Ivy cheerfully bade the dwarf farewell, though Jinx still gave him a silent and accusing glare to behave himself with a short shake of her finger. Making their way through the castle, they passed many intoxicated dwarves stumbling about in their drunken revelry.

Ivy huffed once again as they exited the castle door, her hair sticky yet again from the splashing broth of ale. The jovial melody of song and cheers from the hall faded away behind them as they crossed the floating path of stones. The dwarven guards at the bridge gate were still rummy from their swill, but able to be of enough assistance to hand them the hourglass from the thick wooden case.

"Ah, ye leaving us so soon?" The drunken guard belched as he led them to the foot of the bridge.

"Yes, we have business to attend to." Ivy answered with a pause, as she reminded herself of the long journey ahead. Ivy had heard about the Drow before from stories her mentor told her, but it was something the woodland elves dared not speak about openly. They were a mystery to her, and secretly she was anticipating meeting them. Ivy had always had a fascination about the dark side of magic, though she didn't know why.

"Ah, well, you know the rules; state where yer off to and turn the glass before you take your first step on to the bridge." he advised.

"We need to get to a place called Thieves Gate." Ivy declared, and the guard lowered his spear out of her way. As Ivy turned the hourglass, both faeries stepped out into the creaking planks of the enchanted bridge, wondering where it would take them.

*   *   *

Thieves Gate

They knew this time that there was no true rush to reach the end of the walkway, but watched the sands of the glass dribble away as they pressed forward. As the last grains funneled from the upper sphere, a great howl of wind welcomed them as the end of the bridge suddenly appeared. Stepping off the path, blowing leaves churning in the harsh wind ruffled through their hair as the sky grew dark above them. Several dwarf guards in studded leather armor stood forth from their protected booths of rough stone to take the hourglass from them.

Ahead, a great arched gate of blackened steel towered in the distance. A thick storm brewed with flashes of lightning and threatening booms of thunder overhead, though it was devoid of any rainfall. Tall stark trees nearly bare of their brittle leaves lined a twisting path towards the distant structure.

"Is this Thieves Gate, near the isle of Tyre?" Ivy had to shout over the roaring wind to the guard standing before her.

"Aye, it is; though not a place for two unescorted fey I'll add." he answered in kind. He walked back with his garrison to a small hut built of thick stone slabs and led them within. Here many a sour faced dwarf sat in the flickering candlelight, not sharing in the jovial mood of their fellow dwarves back at the king's castle. The sentry promptly placed the hourglass in a familiar casing like the others, which made Ivy wonder if perhaps they were actually all the very same item; but existing in different places at the same time. It was certainly a curious thought. Once inside, they were able to speak at a reasonable level, though the wind still buffeted the shabby wooden door as it rattled on its hinges against the angry storm.

"If I may ask, why is it called Thieves Gate?" Ivy asked as she brushed her hair out of her eyes. The dwarf just gave a snort as he closed the cabinet on the magic hourglass.

"Because of all the thieves, I presume!" He responded in a gruff tone that actually brought a rough chuckle from a number of the soldiers within earshot. The watchman strolled over to a rack of weapons and pulled out a thick rust pitted axe, and held it out to the wood sprite, "You can have this," he offered, "you shouldn't go in there unarmed." But Ivy politely refused.

"What is beyond that giant gate on the hill?" Jinx asked, as she hopped up onto a worn stool beside them.

"A cesspool of hoodlums and thugs, a city of thieves and cutthroats; and it would mind you well to take a sharp blade if you truly plan to breach their walls into that vile pit." he warned with a scowl as he hefted the axe into the thick doorframe beside them where it stuck fast.

"Actually, we only need to get to the island of Tyre, if there might be any way around the city itself we will certainly heed your advise and avoid it entirely." Ivy offered with hope.

"Nay, the western edge of the city borders the high cliffs of the coast; only a raging sea and jagged sheer rocks awaits you there, and makes any hope of passage impossible. The coasts writhe with foul serpents that no ferryman will dare cross, and ye cannot travel through the east fork of the petrified forest where no living thing may tread," the guardsman forewarned, while taking a seat at the old table stained by age from the dribble of dark oil and candle wax.

If Ivy was to guess, these sentries were not stationed here by choice, as the present accommodations were more than lacking. The weather was disagreeable and the wind befouled with the stale scent of the salt from the sea spray upon the distant cliffs. This land held no joy of sprouting flowers or the chirping of birds, but was heavy with twisted trees embraced by thistle and the cry of tormented beasts that echoed upon the angry breeze. Looking around the room, she could see the grief that weighed in the guardsman's eyes.

"If there are no other roads, then why do you stay here?" she dared to ask.

"By royal decree, we've placed guards at every entrance to the enchanted bridge; but a full garrison is stationed here to keep the miscreants that dwell in the city beyond that foul gate from using the bridge for their own ill means." the sergeant of the guard replied. This still boggled the two faeries.

"Well, why not just wall it up and be done with it?" Jinx suggested in a smug tone, as if the answer to their woes was obvious.

"Lass, it is an ancient magic we protect. A bridge must lead somewhere, and minds not who crosses it." he snapped back, "Ages ago, the city beyond was once a grand and vibrant port of trade filled with the noblest of people; the seas were calm and the land green and full of color and life ...but no more as ye can clearly see."

"What happened here?" Ivy inquired as she took a stool next to her companion, as the other dwarves in the bunker resumed their somber existence and blank stares with worn glazed eyes.

"Shortly after Tyre fell those long years ago, the scourge of the Craven besieged these shores. The good and decent folk fled for their lives as darkness fell across the land, and in their place villains and knaves and other breeds of miscreants blossomed as law and order quickly crumbled away. The depraved citizens that remained wallowed in corruption, devolving into thieves and murderers for their own survival," the guard relayed with hardened eyes, "Stricken with dire poverty, they sneak and steal to fill their bellies."

"But ...why don't they just leave?" Jinx asked in all innocence, suggesting logic to their dilemma.

"There is nothing but the great marsh to the north, and we bar any passage to the south. Since the forests to the East turned to stone, they have nowhere to go, and nobody wants them. They are liars and vagabonds, crooked as gypsies and unwelcome among common folk." the guardsman sneered, "It's best to keep their kind safely walled up here where they can only plague their own kind," he grimaced and spat with a mumbled curse.

Faeries simply do not believe in, nor could even conceive of imprisonment with their innocent little minds. Certainly there had been stories of witches or demons or dark spirits bound in confinement, but those were by the hands of warlocks who practiced necromancy. A fairy would most certainly prefer death than being forced into captivity. Though understanding its perspective, the fey simply did not view death in the way most others did, and thus, failed to heed the principles that most other creatures held as their deepest of fears. Then again, they did not detest others whose actions might seem mean or evil to others, as they were merely being what they were meant to be in the eyes of a fey. Thieves thieve, and crooks, steal, killers murder, and swindlers cheat; it all made perfect sense to a fairy, for they saw the world in different colors than most.

The dwarves, however, knew the hoodlums were a bad influence among their kind, as trust and honor were the backbone of any dwarven hall. Pride was a standard they lived by, and they frowned upon those that had none. The guards realized full well there were women and children beyond those walls that lived in poverty and squalor, among many others who were merely victims of their environment. There were all manner of beasts and races within the shabby walls of the decrepit city that had fallen into ruin; now they were nothing more than pathetic parasites tainted by their brush with the Craven who had poisoned this land.

The sergeant cared not for the reason of their journey, for his duty was to protect the bridge from trespassers who bore ill intent. He cautioned the two fey to stay to the road, for wild and hungry beasts prowled within the shadows. He handed Ivy a copper coin, one with a symbol of a hammer and anvil stamped upon it; mentioning she would need it as a toll to pass the gate into the city. As he led them out into the storm on the windy road towards the distant gate, he shook his head with pity, knowing no one would likely ever see them again.

The two girls held their wings tightly against them to keep from being torn in the harsh wind as they made their way down the path of broken cobblestones. Unfriendly eyes peered at them from under the thick brush and dark branches in the trees. It was a long and winding path until they reached the edge of the city. Many a bandit and highwayman roamed just out of sight, but noting these two naked fey carried nothing of value worth their time.

The gatekeeper was dressed in dirty black garb. He was a large and hairy brute, with a wide jaw and short yellowed tusks that protruded from his thin cracked lips. His eyes were big and black as midnight, except for the ring of mottled green that speckled their rims. Ivy had never seen one in person before, except for the fairy tales she was told as a child; she was quite certain this was a bugbear. They were reputed to be voracious creatures that were born for battle and took pleasure in torturing their victims, however, this one seemed a bit past its prime.

"Your toll!" it grumbled through its tusks at the two fey who seemed so out of place in this accursed land. Ivy produced the copper piece she had been hiding in the palm of her hand, and the bugbear held out his matted hairy paw to take it. He sniffed the token and bit onto it to make sure the coin was real, for he knew faeries were not to be trusted. As a young bugbear, he too had been told tales of conniving faeries as the tricksters and liars they were, who took delight in cheating others through their use of enchantments and illusion. Once satisfied it was authentic currency, he grunted and opened the large gate that groaned upon its rusty hinges.

It wasn't the gatekeepers concern as to what business the two fey had in the city walls, The bugbear's sole interests was in his occupation to jigger loot from anyone passing through. He had seen many a hero in shining armor come this way, eager to cleanse the riffraff and hooligans from within and bring order back to this town. Exercising such noble intentions usually ended badly, with their shining armor and coin purse being divided among the brigands who ended their sorry lives. These delusional-minded good Samaritan's never stopped to realize that there was actually no one in the city worth saving. Even the smallest child would turn on them for a crumb of bread; you couldn't trust anyone.

Ivy had never been in a city like this before, homes and shops were packed together like crates. Broken masonry and chipped wooden rails lined balconies where dozens of wary eyes looked down upon the two little fey as fresh victims. The streets were running with filth and garbage as the rank smell of sewage filled the air. The people themselves were dingy and unkempt; with rotted teeth as crooked as the buildings around them. The tightly packed buildings bled a sense of claustrophobia, and gave no room for the wind to come in. Ivy couldn't believe how anyone could choose to live this way.

As they passed by each tavern door a drunkard would be tossed into the street, or someone was being beaten and mugged in a darkened alley. There were yells of haughty laughter and screams of pain, it was all a familiar chorus to the inhabitants of this wretched city. Though a storm brewed overhead, it seemed not to bother the citizens who dwelled below its oppressive gloom.

An old beggar with withered legs and one dead eye rattled an empty cup, pleading to every passerby. A small boy their size stood at the edge of a stair, twisting a sharp rusty knife in his hands, giving the girls an uncomfortable glare. Old ladies in torn stockings raised their noses and whispered insults behind their backs. There were races here from every culture from what they could see, but they all held one thing in common; a spark of malice that glimmered darkly in their eyes.

It was a horrible place to visit, and Ivy just wanted to get out of here and straight to the northern gate so they could reach the island beyond the western shore.

"Ivy, I don't like it here, these people are weird." Jinx complained, and rightly so.

"I second that, let's just find the far gate and be on our way." Ivy responded, and took off with a beat of her wings, as her companion began to follow; but once she reached the rooftops, the stormy winds nearly sent her into the nearest brick wall. Jinx had even more trouble as her wings were far more delicate than Ivy's. Settling back down to the cobblestone street, the wood sprite gave a sigh with a disappointed look at her companion, "Well, it looks like we will have to find our way there by foot," she grimaced as she shook a lump of blackened slime off the street from her slender foot. The filth in the streets was very unpleasant, and the numerous balconies, lanterns and signs thrust sharply out into the narrow alleys, made it far too dangerous for them to safely flutter above the dirty streets.

The angry call and hiss of feral cats echoed from garbage filled alleyways, as distant shouts and violent quarrels pricked their pointed ears. Ivy was disgusted by the horrid stench that wafted in from every turn, and the dark cramped corridors of brick and stone where no sunlight could get in even if there weren't gray storm clouds swirling above. The little fairies couldn't understand how anyone could wish to exist like this, and they were struck with a horrible feeling of being somewhere they didn't belong. It was something so unnatural they could almost feel the misery wash upon their skin. Jinx rubbed her arms to ward off the tingle of goose bumps from the unpleasant sensation.

"This place is like a maze, and it smells bad, too," Jinx whined as she wrinkled her nose, "How will we find our way there?"

Ivy let her mind linger on that thought. Jinx had a point though; this city was a confused jumble of crooked buildings and winding streets. Had it not been for the storm overhead they could have avoided it completely by flying safely above the rooftops; but Ivy knew things rarely went as she'd like them to. She gave a short glance to Jinx and wondered for a brief moment if she might be the cause of their woes. It wasn't entirely her fault she was a bad luck fairy, but still; there was a precedent to lay a measure of blame on her.

Distracted as she was while contemplating their situation, Ivy failed to notice the group of young ruffians who stepped out of the shadows to block their way. Jinx came to a halt with a scared look on her face, and Ivy cursed under her breath for not hearing them sooner.

There were four of them, children almost. There was one boy skinnier than the rest who had the features of a ground mole and carried a short club he slapped in his clawed hand repeatedly with an intimidating smirk stretched upon his animal face. Beside him stood a girl with pale white skin and blood red hair, whose face was wide with almost elvish eyes which made Ivy suspicious about her race. Another behind her seemed to have boyish traits, but his head and face were all scrunched together like a shaved dwarf that had been dropped on his head from a great height. His eyes were unpleasant, and his balled fists shook slightly with unease. In front of the three stood a tall boy with a notably dirty face who bore a torn knit cap upon his scraggly head. He flipped a sharp knife in his hand casually as he spoke.

"Ah, look, Bella, we have tourists come to visit our fine city," he gave a false grin to the girl beside him, "Couldn't help but overhear that you needed an escort, which we can provide for your own protection ...for a price." he finished as the flipping of his dagger came to a sudden halt and he wiped the sharp blade on his ragged shirt.

"Actually, we can find our own way, thank you." Ivy blurted after a tense moment; but the boy stood forward to block her way as she tried to step by.

"Oh no, I insist." he stood in front of Ivy, their noses almost touching. Now, it was obvious the two naked fey had nothing of value on them that they were used to thieving. No jewelry or coins nor trinkets as they were accustomed to collecting whenever they orchestrated a mugging; but faeries were a rare sight in this part of the land, and had a reputation of their own. When Ivy's green eyes began to glare, the boy took a step back; but kept her crowded enough to keep her from passing.

"Hey, we're just trying to be friendly, offering to help a couple of tourists to our little town," he gave a condescending smile back to his friends and down to Jinx, "and it would be awfully rude for you to refuse our hospitality." his smirk flattened into a thin line upon his lips. "Now, that would be mighty unfriendly ...wouldn't you agree?" He flicked a strand of loose hair from the front of Ivy's face, in a casual effort to bully her.

Jinx gave a glare to him, but had a respect for the weapons they carried and realized their willingness to use them should they refuse.

"We don't have anything of value to give you, so it would hardly be worth the trouble," The small fairy offered as she tried to stifle a scared stutter.

"Oh, but I think you do," the boy responded curtly, "we heard that faeries can grant wishes and all sorts of things. And since we'll be doing something for you by escorting you to the north end of the city, we want you to do something for us. A favor for a favor, so to speak." he added with a tilt of his head, and a stern look as if daring either of the two girls to refuse.

Now, Jinx knew she could likely curse one or two of these thugs by her touch alone, but the result could be any number of things that might be something so harmless as to be of little help to escape this situation; let alone the retaliation they would likely suffer from their associates. Ivy could turn into a tree, but that would be of little use and leave her vulnerable to harm; besides the fact she could not possibly root herself within the hard cobblestones that lined the streets and walkways. Some faeries had the power to turn into wisps of light and spirit away; but neither of the girls possessed such magic. They would have to accompany these hoodlums for the time being until they could think of a way to escape.

The boy pressed the faeries to introduce themselves before they turned back into the darkness of the alleyway and down a flight of age worn steps into the dank sewers below.

"This here is Bella Blackwidow," he motioned to the girl with the white skin, her oversized eyes turned a nonchalant glare to them for a second at the mention of her name, "she has a thing for spiders," he whispered back to them with feigned secrecy as if attempting to be personable, "I probably don't have to tell you which one is Grunch," as the deformed punk with the mashed features grunted, "and of course Shrew who is hard to miss," he grinned, waving to the boy with the rodent face, "and you may call me Ash."

"And what is it that you do here, Ash?" Jinx spouted with a hint of attitude while they were led down the dark tunnels lit only by a small lamp that Grunch held aloft. The boy whose face was covered in soot played along with the little girls bravado, not realizing he was playing with fire.

"Oh, my friends and I are entrepreneurs. You might say we indulge ourselves to make a living by exploiting business opportunities that pass our way from time to time," he added with a smug grin, "but we've had something special in mind recently that we believe you may be able to help us with."

Down in the dark winding tunnels littered with rats and rotting filth, the two faeries had to cover their noses to ward off the overpowering stench of the sewers. The rancid odors fumed from the river of stagnant green water and rotting feces that bubbled from beneath. It was something beyond the farthest repulsion that any forest fey had ever seen. They couldn't understand how any living beings could lower themselves to such a disgusting habit of collecting their own putrid waste. Molting rats with beady black eyes peered at them from the shadows, only to scuttle away into hidden cracks at their approach. Through the maze of tunnels they came upon a small rotting door Ash opened by a hidden lever.

The interior was an old forgotten pump chamber used as a gate room for the sewer channels. Thick chains hung from the high walls on notched pulleys, long since rusted solid. The quarters were by no means livable, but once shut, the thick door did help block out the stench. There were several lanterns and makeshift chairs, and a small collection of crude hand made weapons of knives and clubs and other tools of their trade. Around the small room were stacked barrels and crates upon which sat small cages that protected crusts of bread from the hungry rats that roamed these tunnels.

Ash took the small lantern from Grunch and set it down on a splintered table in the center of the small room, illuminating a hand drawn map filled with lines and scribbles. It was a diagram of some sort of building, but Ivy couldn't decipher the details from the glance she stole. The thugs motioned the two girls to sit near the far end of the table, while the mole-boy watched over them with his dark glossy eyes. Ivy was a little nervous about being brought here, and dared to inquire of the purpose.

"You said you were going to take us to the gates at the north end of the city..." she led with a suggestive tone.

"Ah, yes, we will escort you there; but we had a little detour to show you our headquarters. I wouldn't want to be rude to our guests by being in such a rush, and failing to extend some small measure of hospitality." he chastised her, "Besides, there is a little matter of your fee for safe passage for us to attend to."

Shuffling the shreds of paper around on the table, Ash finally pushed a few scribbled sheets within view of the two fey, while noting their disinterest.

"And what might this be?" Ivy dared to inquire.

"My comrades and I have been working on a scheme to relieve a certain aging wizard of a few of his worldly possessions, which is where your assistance comes in."

"A wizard?" Jinx spouted suddenly, as if both curious and suspicious about the matter and their motive.

"Yes, a Magi of certain repute who is the last living member of the once esteemed wizards guild at the center of the city," Ash admitted while spinning the map on the table, "This is the layout of the lower chamber of an ancient temple they used as a foundation to build their guild upon. The place has been a subject of tall tales and rumors for centuries I've heard, but that was when the guild was at its prime and well protected from say ...unwelcome guests." he smiled.

"And, exactly what is it you had in mind, pray tell?" Ivy responded with a tilt of her head, noting this scenario might offer an opportunity to relieve themselves of their present company. Ash was a bit encouraged by her sudden interest, though slight as it was. The girl with the fiery red hair spoke up from behind to enlighten them.

"An ornery old goat named Meridian is the last of his kind, but still maintains the enchantments that protect the wizards' tower." Bella noted as she used the tip of a long rusty stiletto to point on the diagram, "Warlocks collect all sorts of arcane relics in their studies of the magical arts, but this old geezer has been recently seen selling off anything of value to keep the wards in place around the guild. The wizards themselves used to be a wealthy lot, wearing flamboyant costumes and robes of crushed velvet, assorted jewels spun with lace of silver and ribbons of gold. But there is something far more valuable there that we want to get our hands on..." Bella chimed as Ash interrupted.

"The Eye of Omens," he pointed to a rough drawing of a circular object decorated with ornate curled base, "It's a relic that is said to lie within the upper tower, an object of immeasurable value."

"...And you want us to steal that for you?" The wood sprite assumed.

"The tower is magicked with glyphs and charms; those who were brash enough to have tried to break in before ended up dead, very dead!" Shrew added from over their shoulders with his raspy hushed voice.

"And what possibly makes you think we can acquire this item

for you?" Jinx retorted with astonishment.   The thugs just
glanced at one another as if it was obvious.

"You're faeries, creature of pure magic.   You can disenchant
the wards or even wish the relic here to us." Bella responded.
At hearing that, Jinx nearly burst out laughing, leaving the four
street punks wordless, but scowling nonetheless.

"What kind of fairytales have you been listening to?" she
giggled till she realized they weren't sharing her mirth, "If we
could wish away anything we wanted, don't you think we could
have gotten out of here on our own?" Jinx noted with a certain
level of logic. That statement didn't sit well with the thugs, as
they clearly took it as an insult. Ivy could realize that growing
up in this decrepit city must be hard, and living in these squalid
conditions even more so to cause them to be so ill-mannered;
but was aware that Jinx was about to make them lose their
nerve, and any possible chance to part company from these
thugs on their own terms.

"We are not the type of faeries that grant wishes," Ivy
intervened quickly, "but we might be able to bypass any
enchantments to get you this *Eye* thing you so desire ...as long
as you promise to let us go afterwards." she added to buy them
time. Ivy wanted to give Jinx a swift kick under the table, but
was a bit wary of what the repercussions of the curse of her
touch might bring when it materialized.

Ash and Bella and the other two thugs nodded to each other,
confident they had the upper hand in the situation, not knowing
that Ivy was far more conniving than she appeared; as beautiful
fairy girls usually are.

Now, most wizards and enchanters and conjurers of every type
know full well to use a fair deal of iron in their locks and bolts
and the bars on their windows not only to keep out sneaking
faeries of every type, but also to keep them in. Faeries were
dissected for their pieces and parts just as roots and herbs and
other magical ingredients. They collected eye of newts, toes of
frogs, wool of a bats, or tongues of dogs; no creature was truly
safe from the arcane experiments of warlocks. Sometimes their
enchantments were strong enough to capture fey so they could
collect their essence, and those faeries usually, if not always,

came to a very sticky end.

After assuring the two fey girls that the lower temple area was made of stone and devoid of iron, Ivy played along to see what kind of side plan she could conjure up on her own. Jinx seemed a little muddled at Ivy for cooperating with their captors, but thankfully continued to bite her lip and not provoke them any further. From what she gleaned from their idle chatter, it seemed the wizard Meridian spent the majority of his time in the very top floor of the high tower built atop the temple.

This relic known as the Eye of Omens was supposedly a type of crystal ball that sees anywhere and anything, and circulating gossip was that it had once been used by the wizards guild for those clients willing to pay the exorbitant fee for such knowledge. The drawing they had of it was designed from several rumors about the relic itself. The four thugs voiced that the relic was their prize target; once they seized it, they could leave this city and live like kings, or so they frequently touted among their colorless boasts of grandeur.

Ivy hoped she and Jinx might be able to give their captors the slip and evoke the wrath of the lone wizard upon them, but it was taking a chance that the warlock might also do the same to them or worse. It was well-known within the race of the fey that no love was shared between faeries and wizards, and their decision to come here was turning into a sticky situation for them both.

*   *   *

The Eye of Omens

Meridian sat in a rather worn leather chair reading from an old thick book by the light of a thick melting candle propped within the eye socket of a Orc's skull ornately covered with runes. Reaching high above the city, his tower loomed above all else. For lack of servants, this room, including the entire Wizards' Guild had fallen into ruin and disrepair. Meridian had been a member here for quite some time, centuries in fact. He had seen young mages come and go, off on valiant quests where it was usually the knights and other sword wielding buffoons who ended up stealing all the glory, and the wizards, whose mastery of magic had saved the day ...were all but forgotten.

He had seen his cohorts disappear over the decades, ending up as victims of the thieves and cutthroats that had overrun the city as of late. He was the last wizard left, and he knew his time, too, was fading fast. Countless centuries of research and spellbinding had been stored within these walls, and it was more important than ever to keep their collection of valuable and arcane knowledge safe from the uneducated brigands that roamed the streets below. Once there was a time when the affluent guild of mages made a hefty bag of gold selling their services to the townsfolk. They were able to hire guardsmen to protect their gates and inner sanctum. But as the city fell beneath the curse of the Craven, so did the livelihood of their profession.

There were fewer and fewer herbalists in the markets to buy ingredients from, or robust young acolytes to gather elements for their spells from the countryside. Few in the city even remembered how the petrified forest to the east had been turned to solid stone. It was a very long time ago, he recalled, while sipping on a mug of goblin teeth tea; that the mages guild was recruited to fight back the scourge of the Craven in the epic battle that befell their homeland. Dwarves from the hidden kingdom once marched through their city in their shining armor.

Though obnoxious drunkards they could be in the taverns, there was no denying they were fierce adversaries in battle. Elves too had stepped foot here, bringing skilled archers in woven greens from the ancient forests; and the very speech of the animals to aid them.

Meridian reminisced as he clinked the goblin molars in the bottom of his cup; few if any remember what had happened here as well as he. This city was once a shining spire on the western coasts, merchant ships from far reaches of the emerald oceans to the craggy snow lined peaks of the winter lands came here to barter and trade. Oh, how he missed the laughter of children who had played in the oak shaded streets and concerts in the green rolling pastures outside the city walls. But over time, those walls had grown thicker as the threat of the Craven encroached upon the borders of the Faerylands. Once dragons had also roamed the clear skies here, misunderstood creatures of such immeasurable power and wisdom that it would be unthinkable that there would come a day to pass when they would be wiped from existence.

Pure blooded dragons, the living essence of the Dracos, dwelled within the elements as did the Faerie. There were dragons of the earth, with armor of rock and steel, whose roar made mountains tremble. Akin to them were the red dragons of fire, who could spit living flame; yet little was it known they were not the fiercest of the drakes. There were the dragons of ice and snow who could summon lightening and frost in their wake. Then there were the peaceful dragons of the clouds and sky, their scales glittering warmly in the bright summer sun. The green sea serpents from the depths of the cold waves were as wild and untamable as the churning sea.

These elements were each brother and sister, giving balance to the world ...until the arrival of the Craven. By the nature of their profession, wizards study balance and acknowledge the existence of chaos. More so than most breathing creatures in this world, they knew that life itself rests upon the equilibrium of this very fine line. There were, of course, dark mages who in their selfish deeds tried to upset this symmetry to gain a windfall of limitless power. Foul and loathsome magic sprouted from such sorcery by necromancers who summoned the dead, animating phantoms and corpses to do their bidding. Such practice was an insult to all Masters of Magic.

The Elves themselves forbade all practice of the dark arts, and any who exercised such vulgar witchcraft were promptly put to death, usually in such elaborate and bloody methods as to prevent the conjurer from becoming one of the undead themselves by the black magic they were tainted with. It was one of these reclusive dark magi that managed to capture a young dragon and performed many horrible and unearthly experiments on the poor beast; twisting its nature into something vile and unnatural. As dragons themselves were sacred beings of creation, such an unforgivable crime laid consequences upon everything it touched.

A creature of rotting bone and sinew was all that was left of the once majestic Dracos, its essence now black and corrupted. It was the very night this foul beast was unleashed upon this land, that Meridian's world had begun to crumble. As his clouded mind remembered, he gave a sad frown for the lives lost and friends he once knew, now forever gone.

An acolyte who assumed the name of Odious Sihr had been secretly practicing the black arts in the shallows of a forest cave far outside the city. Although most wizards had a native curiosity about all forms of magic and their applications, it was the Elves who mandated their use. Regulations were set forth to sway magicians to practice beneficial magic that would do no harm; nor upset the natural order of things. As an example, death itself was a natural event to most every being; though extending one's life beyond its normal length was acceptable, raising the dead back to life, however, was not. There were, of course, many mages who wondered what it was the Elves were hiding from them by banning all experimentation into such strange and forbidden magics.

Now, curiosity can be a dangerous thing, especially to a magi. Meridian had seen a number of apprentices both young and old come to many a ghastly end because of their overly inquisitive nature. Some deaths were merely accidents, such as the bravado of one particular young sorcerer who jumped into the arcane arts utilizing spells he did not fully fathom, and came to an unfortunate end when a protection spell failed and had his arm eaten down to the bone in a vat of blood worms. Wizards were naturally secretive about their experiments to create new types magical charms and spells. Thus, it was not entirely uncommon for fellow magi to stumble across the corpses of these reckless few who were found with roots growing out of their skin, or their lifeless bodies fused with metal and stone.

Meridian, as most other wizards in the guild, wondered if the High Elves were trying to protect them, or as some suspected, keeping the most powerful magics to themselves. It was a subject of many a rumor to the point the mages themselves began to mistrust the Elves and their true intentions.

The reasoning was far more simple than the scandal it was made out to be. Elves were actually *a part* of nature, which was observed but misunderstood by many. Wizardry practiced outside the race of elves was truly abnormal. Shamans and Magi would fabricate magics they did not possess by nature, and through their abuse of charms and potions, magic became commonplace and abused as an object of novelty and commerce. The flight of a bird, or the invisibility of a chameleon, or potions of love could all be bought for a price; and thus, those wizards with empty pockets turned to greed and began to bottle lightning and enchanting scrolls that could be sold for a handful of coin.

Now the Elves didn't exactly approve of the stealing of magic for use outside of its natural form, but reasoned that the sharing of this essence would aide to enlighten those who did not possess it; who in turn, had previously frowned upon the Elves in envy of their mystical ways. There were but few wizards like Meridian who truly cared for neither power nor wealth, but simply to the study and understanding of the essence of magic itself. To him, it was like the great mystery of life, that gave a personal satisfaction and joy whenever a layer of its secrets were peeled away. He wanted to explore life, and how the world worked, nothing more.

However, the dark wizard Odious was another breed entirely. He had a deep seeded craving for power and wealth, driven by a feverish desire that drove him to a point beyond reason. One day in his youth, when he was out in the eastern forest gathering herbs and ingredients for spells, he had stumbled upon a dry well. Beside it, concealed behind a curtain of moss and brambles he found a hidden cavern that had once been used as a storeroom for grain during the winter months by settlers who had long since departed these lands. Instead of reporting the find to his superiors in the guild, he kept its location secret, and returned there whenever he could. With a few protective glyphs and incantations the surrounding roots and ferns hid this sanctuary from prying eyes, and he used charms to enlist a pair of rogue goblins to build him a stairway into the empty chamber of the forgotten well buried deep below the forest.

Over the years that passed, the natural cavity beneath was transformed by his slaves into a subterranean temple where the Wizard Sihr began to act upon his delusions of power. He began to pilfer items and relics from the guild and secret them away to his forest lair in the middle of the night, where he conducted his vile experiments. Certain that the Elven lords were hiding the most powerful of magics through their strict ban, here he was free to practice his dark arts here far beyond their sight. With stolen funds from the guilds treasury, he hired mercenaries whom he sent on arduous quests to scout the far reaches of the lands in search of legendary relics to use for his own sinister means.

His personality and demeanor changed dramatically, which had not gone unnoticed by the elder mages. When he was finally caught thieving from the vaults, he was dismissed from his duties and cast from the guild. The eviction from wizards sanctum was a personal blow he never forgave them for, and Odious spent many moons brooding how he would get his revenge. With renewed vigor he planned to prove to the high mages that the forbidden magics were the most powerful, and demand the respect he felt he was due.

When one band of mercenaries he had sent out returned with a rare tome of ancient and forbidden spells, he had found the means to pry deeper into the depths of the arcane and indulge his dark impulses. Having been cast out from the guild, and unable to pay the adventurers for their services, the unfortunate lot became the first of his victims. He stripped them of their flesh and let the worms feast on their wet meat. His studies exposed ways to reanimate their corpses as mindless minions under his control. It wasn't long thereafter until Odious began to rob the graveyards and turned to murder, and the citizens of the town learned to fear every shadow that passed in the night.

Soon the forest around him became haunted by dire wolves and the moaning shuffle of the undead. Even then, Odious could not see what he had become. With great effort and personal risk he had stolen the ethereal mists of a djinni, and with its use he summoned the spirit of a dragon and ensnared it. With the use of his archaic knowledge, he transformed the mystical beast into a nightmare.

While resting one dreary night he found himself staring into the shadows, and he heard their whispers. The thing that was the Craven had been watching, and in his mind they spoke; pulling the fine strings of his desires, tugging on the threads of his lust for power. Words that didn't make sense to the ears, but still weighed like lead in his hollow heart. Odious had been charmed himself by a force far older than the world, and was now a slave to its calling.

In the darkest night on the darkest hour he unleashed the bone dragon upon the world above as the catalyst to enact his petty revenge. Little did he know that the Elder Mages of the guild had been keeping watch on his every move. The brazen murders within the city walls and the taint of dark magic had led them to his lair by the use of a powerful relic called the Eye of Omens, offered to them by the High Elves.

When the dragon burst forth, they were ready. All the innocent creatures of the dark forest had left days before. Foxes with their pups, raccoons with their young, every squirrel, every bird, every deer and doe had been warned by the elves who could speak to the animals. All that was left were the dying woods and blackened leaves, stirred only by the wandering dead and murderous wolves.

His head full of dark whispers, by his own recklessness he had lost control of the corrupted beast which destroyed his subterranean temple as it escaped from its imprisonment beneath the earth. The entire grotto and surrounding chambers collapsed as the twisted monster surfaced. The relics that he relied upon to control the foul magic were buried under the dirt and rubble that became his crypt.

Meridian had been present that night those many centuries ago, decades before he began exploiting enchantments to prolong his natural life. When the vile dragon emerged from the subterranean grotto, his fellow wizards were ready. By use of the Eye of Omens, the relic allowed them to keep watch on the dark wizard Sihr himself; and predict the very night that the corrupt beast would be set free; and how to stop it.

A unique spell provided by the Elven lords was created using the ground backbone of a mountain giant, the plucked eye of a medusa, powdered flesh from a cockatrice and the dried blood of a basilisk. When the spell was cast, the evil dragon, the horde of undead, the blood fang pack of dire wolves; in fact every bush and tree and blade of grass in the entire forest had been turned to solid stone. Over time, the farthest outskirts of the forest began to grow back with life, but you could still find clumps of petrified wood hiding beneath the mulch of soil and leaves. The center of the stone forest, though, was never cleansed of the essence that once defiled it, as if the taint of the Craven had forever left its stain.

A score of vile and wicked beasts still lurk there to this day, drawn to the eerie woods by the corruption that lingers there. Through a strange series of events since that time, the Elves had never returned to retrieve the Eye of Omens from the guild, so the wizards kept the powerful relic safely locked away. The use of this Elvish device had garnered enough fame through the retelling of the story over time through generations so as to be an item of legend, to the point were many people simply huffed in disbelief that it ever truly existed. Even so, it was this valuable relic that Ash and his thieving cohorts had heard so many rumors about and chose to acquire.

The timing of their running upon the two fey presented an opportunity they couldn't resist. Lucky for them, they were the first party of rogues to accost the faeries who were foolish enough to enter the city unescorted. They led the two girls towards the center of the city via the twisting routes of the sewers, knowing every nook and cranny of the dark shadows to hide within to pass unseen. The group approached the lower temple walls at the very same time Meridian sat high above in his study, stirring a cup of his favorite brew of goblin tooth tea and reminiscing about the past.

The ruffians had been keeping an eye on the old wizard themselves these past several months, as the old mage had been forced to sell off many of the guild's valuable trinkets at the local fence in order to pay for the upkeep of the guild hall. Nearly all of the former wizards had fallen victims to a slew of fatal muggings in the past, but Meridian in his prudence, always took a different route, keeping one step ahead of prying eyes that meant him ill intent. With no more wizards in the city, there was, of course, no one else who could dispel the protective wards surrounding the guild.

The temple itself was a sight to see, far more ancient than anything else in the city which had been constructed around it. The building had been here for a millennium, sitting idle as the drama of countless generations play out around it. Unseen by others, in the eyes of the two fey, however, the temple itself was a different color entirely. They could see chiseled engravings scrolled upon the upper borders, runes written in a language long dead; and detailed murals etched upon every wall depicting breathtaking scenery. What magic they saw through their faerie eyes was cloaked from view by their company of mundane thugs. Even the ordinary round pillars that surrounded the temple appeared as intricately carved maidens with wreaths of leaves curled within their braided hair, drifting low into the gently flowing gowns that came to rest at the base of the temple's foundation.

Surrounding a single ornate etching was a door at its center. The thick wood stained with age, but still fresh with color. A great glowing glyph sat branded onto it, shining blue in the eyes of the fey. It was a lock to keep out those who possessed no arcane abilities. A simple key could be stolen or duplicated, but this lock could not be picked; that's why it had stumped every

would-be burglar as there were no handles. Any force met upon
the warded entry was only met with equal force back upon the
one who applied it. Those few robbers who were desperate
enough to take an axe to it were met with a sharp and
unpleasant surprise.

"And, so, here we are," Ash announced while flipping his long
dagger once in his hand and giving the girls a sly glance, "Open
these doors for us, and dispel any other enchantments we come
across." he ordered, as Grunch and Shrew hefted the bundles of
empty garbage stained sacks they carried, fully anticipating the
looting they were about to indulge in. Bella stepped forward
and little Jinx recoiled in disgust as a large white spider crept
out from beneath her hair, crawling out onto her shoulder. It
was obviously some sort of pet to her, and sat there peering at
them coldly with its numerous eyes.

The thugs stood waiting as Ivy stepped towards the door,
looking keenly at the glowing glyph. Now she wasn't very
good at reading at all, but had learned to memorize a few
simple letters and words. The blazing glyph seemed wrong
somehow, as if the stems of the words it represented was off
kilter. Logically, she gently reached out and touched the runes,
entirely invisible to the hoodlums watching far behind; and
moved the glowing lines into their proper place.

Jinx watched with interest as the thugs took a pause to step
back with a gasp as the door swung open. An ethereal mist
curtained the entry as the two fey stepped inside, followed
closely by the wary thieves.

The interior of the courtyard beyond appeared somehow larger
than its outer shell seemed to be, which seemed nothing but
dusty and bare to their abductors. Dim light cast in through
several upper windows, but the two fey girls, however, were in
awe of what appeared before them. Here, daylight streamed in
with the chirping of yellow birds that flitted about the inner
courtyard alive with tall green trees and flowering vines. There
was the scent of spring flowers as a great fountain splashed
from a large sculpture of a woman carved from marbled stone
holding a shell above her shoulder from which a torrent of
sparkling water flowed.

The company of thieves grumbled among themselves for initially seeing nothing of value in the dark, musty atrium, not being able to witness the lush garden magically shrouded from their view. Searching the area, Shrew noted another door near the back end of the courtyard, and Ash ushered Ivy over to it. She was just biding her time until she could find an opportunity for her and Jinx to escape safely, hoping they could find an open window or balcony somewhere along the way where they could possibly make their departure. Though the storm still brewed outside, they could still put some distance between their captors if they were able to make it outside and down to the streets below. All four of the thugs seemed very capable of doing the girls harm, and if their wings were cut or torn in any way, they would be left at their mercy.

Bella gave the girls a goofy glance at their strange behavior as the two fey skipped over towards the doorway; but Ivy and Jinx were simply making their way over the invisible stepping stones in the garden the robbers themselves could not see. At this door stood another set of glyphs, this time there were three. Ash held his arm out in front of Grunch, wary of any hidden magics, keeping his companion from stumbling into any unknown harm as the faeries stepped forward.

"How does this one work?" Jinx asked, curious to learn what Ivy was doing. Glancing back over her shoulder at the thieves, she whispered back to her friend softly.

"Try not to reveal too much to them if you can, just play along until we can find a way out of here." Ivy advised the young girl.

"Hurry it up, you two." Ash ordered from behind them as Bella set her pet spider down to the floor, while eyeing them suspiciously. Ivy turned back and nodded back to Ash, trying to be nonchalant; acting out her promise to cooperate. She dreaded the thought of running into the old mage they said lurked within, as he would likely turn his wrath on all of the intruders, including them. Ivy had heard many stories about warlocks; none of them good.

Sorcerers stole magic that wasn't theirs and used it at their command. She had heard horrible stories of how they killed unicorns simply for their horns, or clipped fairy wings to grind into powder. She heard tales of how they could cast fireballs and burn people to a crisp, or turn them into a pond frog for the rest of their lives. Faeries feared wizards as much as they hated them. Mages were highly unpredictable and were known for abusing magic on a whim, as they showed no respect for the natural order of things in their unorthodox pursuit to gain such mystical powers. Magi had not only earned a notorious reputation for being exceptionally egotistical and flamboyant, but were all-around dangerous.

Sure, there were tales told among the Faerie of good wizards who were helpful, but those were very rare. Any non-elven mage was not to be trusted, for they were commonly known for failing to have any regard for the essence of the magic they siphoned. The Evermore itself was whittled away bit by bit whenever a magician pilfered magic unnaturally to himself, weakening its integrity. There were some High Elves who were in tune with nature to the point they could see these wounds, even feel them; so they tried to limit what harm was being done. They found it near impossible, however, to explain to the other races about something they simply could not see for themselves. It was the black magic, the corrupted use of such witchery that left the deepest wounds in the Evermore; and this is where the darkness of the Craven had festered.

The three glyphs before them were simply placed out of order, but Ivy could only recognize the rune cluster that meant 'Enter'. Now she wasn't too terribly dim, and realized that it was very possible that these protective glyphs were booby trapped. Get a puzzle wrong and she would be sizzled with a bolt of lightning or burned to ash in an instant; and being a wood sprite, either possibility was naturally feared. Ivy stood in silence for a long moment, wondering if she should trick her abductors by lying that there was no ward on the door at all and let them trip any possible traps on their own. Then again, if the range of this trap was entirely unknown as to what it might do; including by chance if it snared only one of them, both she and Jinx would most certainly face the consequences for their deception. To her surprise, it was Jinx who stepped in front of her, noting her indecisiveness.

"Here, let me try this one." she offered to Ivy.

Behind them it was clear that Ash and his compatriots were getting a bit antsy. No thief had stepped foot within the threshold of the mages sanctuary for as long as they had could remember, and the rumors they heard of those that did were not very pretty; so they were naturally nervous. The little luck fairy couldn't read worth a hoot, but she was willing to take a calculated chance. Her aura of bad luck most usually worked in her favor, and she advised Ivy to take several steps back.

The glowing glyphs were just funny symbols to her, and she was eager to experiment with something new. She grabbed a hold of the top glyph and moved it down to the bottom, switching them. Still invisible to the eyes of the thieves, a line in the floor around her glowed red. Jinx realized she had gotten the puzzle wrong when vaporous snakes shot forth towards her and she let out a short but audible "Eek!" of a squeal as she froze in fear. There was nothing that Ivy could do but watch in horror as the glowing asps surrounding the small girl and struck at her. But just as they were about to bite, the glyphs on the door fell apart into a jumble.

Jinx had jinxed the trap, and it misfired. Ivy let out a sigh of relief as Ash approached from behind when the door swung wide before the tiny girl.

"Hah, she opened it," he waved his companions forward, "but why did you just scream?" Ash demanded, as the four thugs were completely oblivious to what had just happened. Jinx peeled her eyes open, realizing she was alright, and hadn't been harmed. The little fey gave him a guilty look, but quickly caught herself.

"Oh, um, I ...I though I saw a mouse." she lied. With a smirk at her apparent girlish stupidity, Ash hurried the two fey through the arched doorway and up the winding staircase beyond.

High above in Meridian's study, a skull sitting on a side table began to chatter in alarm. "Intruders in the lower sanctum! Intruders in the lower sanctum!" the tattooed skull babbled as the startled old wizard dropped his cup with a crash as several goblin molars scattered across the wet floor.

"Oh my," he grimaced in regret, "that was my favorite mug, too." The old mage was mildly shocked to hear the alarm go off as it had been many decades since anyone had been brazen enough to trespass upon his sanctuary. He wasn't too terribly concerned, though, as he had several snares in place around the empty halls of the guild; each deadlier than the last. He waddled over to the fireplace that sate before him and reached for a thickly twisted staff he tapped twice on the stone floor; whereupon a dull green flame immediately erupted from the fire pit.

"Show me our uninvited guests." he sighed as he gazed into the magical flame, expecting to see the remains of their sprawled corpses within the walkway of the atrium. To his utter astonishment, he witnessed a group of four thugs ascending the stairwell to the upper temple. What was remarkable is that the emerald flame also showed two ghostly figures that glowed with an inner light accompanying them. Their aura was so bright it was difficult to make out any details as to who or what they were. Meridian bit his lip, and with a raised brow of concern wondered who these trespassers might be?

Up the wide winding stair the thieves escorted the two faeries; gleefully sacking every jeweled chalice or golden candlestick they happened upon. There were cracked statues holding gemstones and amulets hanging freely on decorative plaques; each one was quickly snatched from its display and stuffed away into a burlap bag. Still, this was all small pickings to what they had dreamt about, expecting to loot wands and potions and eventually mystical relics and other such tools of the sorcerers trade. Ash held onto his scrap of parchment with the crude drawing of the Eye of Omens, so he would recognize the object should they stumble upon it.

Each of the thugs was used to burgling, finding most of their victims sound asleep at this time of night. They didn't know that wizards imbued with such enchantments to prolong their lives, rarely slept; it was a side effect of the bewitchment that could either be considered a benefit or a curse. Ash and his gang of cutthroats assumed the aging wizard would be sound asleep, snoring away in some oversized bed with his pointed hat sitting beside him on a pedestal. They had no real idea just how old Meridian really was ...nor how wise.

The old mage on the other hand was fairly intrigued to see who these trespassers were, and how they had gotten past his wards thus far. He plopped on his crooked hat and with staff in hand, made his way down the stairway from the high tower to the lower chantry; where there was a magic glass that would allow him to view these individuals more clearly.

There were several priceless relics still left sealed within the walls of the guild, but they were well-disguised through a chameleon spell to protect them. Wizards discovered long ago that the first things would-be thieves would attempt to break into were the obvious barred doors and any locked chests lying about; so as subterfuge they made it a habit to pepper their sanctum with several decoys, each laden with deadly traps. Some wizards took great pride in designing such traps; in fact, wizards had annual contests with one another as to who could concoct the most imaginative and devious traps of all.

It was common to hand out awards in the form of a brooch, which was worn as a badge of honor for those who created the best and most wondrous of traps. So, as a friendly warning, if you ever see a wizard or enchantress wearing a decorative pin of a blazing star on the collar of their robe, it would be wise not to steal from them.

There were all sorts of wondrous items and tools wizards used in their daily profession. Some items were skillfully crafted by the hands of a dwarven smith to custom designs, so they might be properly enchanted by experienced sorcerers; and a mages guild was full of such trinkets. Many such items required a knowledge of how they worked, however, and the seeing glass was one such object. Unlike the coldfire flame used in his upper study, the pool of slow glass in the chantry was a far more complex device to operate.

It appeared as nothing more than a rough pane of glass set in a twisted wire frame; in fact if anyone had seen it in a junk yard or abandoned house, they would not have given it a second glance. Beside the pane sat a deep copper bowl filled with the purest of water, distilled from a pool in the depths of a mystic cave. Many oracles and seers use such shallow bowls of water as a tool for viewing; but any real soothsayer can tell you it isn't the vessel that holds the magic, but the origin of the water itself that lay within.

Meridian walked down the long steps into the chantry, his unbalanced steps showing his age. He rolled back one of his wide sleeves and dipped his fingers into the metal bowl; wetting his fingers. With a wave of his hand, he flicked the droplets of water onto the upright glass. The ragged pane rippled like a pool of water as the droplets hit its surface, the magic of the slow glass awakened, awaiting his command.

"Show me our guests." the old wizard asked, and the pane shimmered yet again.

Instead of seeing from a fixed distance in the coldfire, here the pane showed a perspective from the very intruders themselves, shifting its point of view among them. Meridian raised a furry gray brow when he saw two unclothed girls in the company of the sloven thieves; their wings, however, were hidden from his view. "Interesting ...most interesting," was all that passed his lips as he viewed the strange party through the looking glass. They were about to stumble into the guild's largest collection of snares and traps. Many were the mementos from wizards who had left them behind after their untimely demise; some so complicated that even Meridian had no idea what personal treasures they protected. Wizards rarely bothered with another mages safeguards; for they were, of course, not only designed to guard the valuables from would-be thieves outside their own walls, but also from the prying eyes of other warlocks. As secretive as most wizards were, they were insanely protective of their own personal possessions.

Back in the stairwell, the four burglars continued to sack everything within reach that could fetch a silver coin, and loaded the bundles onto Grunch's wide shoulders. When they ascended to the upper floor, the odd group came across a strange site indeed. Here the floor was laden with several ornate carpets; each weave of a vastly different design than its neighbor. Some were so gaudy of pattern as to be of apparent bad taste. Lining the walls were several locked doors, many of which did not match in the slightest, and were a mix of different types of wood and varied in both shape and construction. These had been used as the personal chambers for each of the guild members, thus, each one was custom made; since wizards had the means to easily do so through enchantments.

Ash and Bella scouted the room looking for valuables as the mole boy rattled several locked doors until he eventually came across one that was open. Entering the chamber, he found a small simple room with little more than a cot and a modest assortments of furniture within. The only thing of true interest was a richly carved dresser upon which sat a small jewelry chest. Well, to Shrew, a jewelry box of course meant there might be jewels within; and since his companions weren't beside him at the moment, he figured why not pocket a few trinkets for himself without the petty annoyance of sharing this little find amongst his comrades.

With a toothy rodent smile brimming of greed, Shrew found the small chest unlocked, though slightly irritated that its lid would only open half way. Peering warily over his shoulder to make sure his companions weren't watching, he decided to filch a few petty baubles for his own; and could always later claim he had found the chest entirely empty if need be. Desperate to be quick about snatching whatever valuables were inside, he stuck his knobby clawed hand into the box, and felt something very strange. With a perplexed tilt of his head, he pulled his hand out to see what it was that created such an odd sensation; and to the shock of his companions in the carpeted room outside, Shrew let out a horrific scream. His hand was gone!

The fairy girls turned towards the commotion as did the thug's companions who rushed in to see what had happened. Ash burst in the door as Bella leaned back in surprise at what they witnessed. Shrew was holding his left arm by the wrist, wailing in torment. What was so incredibly odd was that there was no dreadful wound gushing blood as one would expect, but where his hand had been was nothing but a mere stub, as if it had never been. In fact Shrew felt no pain, except for the frightful anguish of his missing appendage; but for a career thief, a missing hand was a most traumatizing wound.

This particular trapped chest was ingenious, and itself won an honorary badge of award for its maker. Those thieving from it would be enticed never to steal again. It didn't cause any pain, but simply stole in turn from any unsuspecting crook; snatching from them the tools of their trade. Grunch himself waddled over to see the cause of Shrew's anxiety, as did Jinx and Ivy. What they all witnessed next was the most disturbing sight they had ever seen. None of them knew that the lone wizard stationed several stories above was also spying upon them during their companion's horrid ordeal.

Shrew began to babble about the loss of his fingers. The cause of his grievous injury was so strange that he lost all sense of reasoning and in his desperation, he reached back into the chest with his right arm to retrieve his severed hand. Feeling the unpleasant sensation yet again, everyone but Shrew noticed that his arm had somehow reached unnaturally far into the small box. In panic he pulled out his right arm which was now nothing but a mere stump at the elbow. A cry of hysteria escaped his lips yet again and his eyes grew wild with dread. His companions could do nothing as their distraught accomplice reached yet again back into the box in deranged desperation to retrieve what he had just lost; not being able to believe what was happening to him.

Shrew babbled incoherently as he thrust his left arm back in to try to find his amputated right, not realizing he had plunged his arm up to his shoulder into the small box. When he pulled away, that too was a void stump. In a last frenzied attempt to regain his lost limbs, he thrust the stub of his right arm back inside, so deep it came up to his neck. For a short horrible moment, Shrew pulled back and his entire head was missing to the gasp of everyone in the room; just before his entire body lurched forward and was consumed by the mystical trap.

The trapped chest wasn't meant to be so effective as to cause a fatality; as any logical person would have cut their losses, and avoided ever touching the jewelry box again. Shrew was gone, all that was left to prove he was ever there was his soiled boot that had pried off on the lid of the coffer as it gobbled the last of him up. Speechless, Ash finally walked over to pick up his companions shoe, clearly wary not to go too near the small chest. The astonished thieves had expected secret doors and even enchanted traps ...but had never in their wildest dreamed imagined anything so heinous.

"I think it would be prudent if we stuck to what we came here for," Ash uttered in a cold and cheerless tone as he turned to his fellow robbers, who nodded back ever so solemnly as he handed the empty shoe to Grunch who looked down at it with worry sketched upon his wrinkled face.

*   *   *

Meridian

The old wizard who had been watching through the gazing glass was mildly satisfied, though a bit surprised by the effectiveness of the trap within the chest. Sorcerers left glyphs and warnings on their personal items that anyone in their profession could clearly read. Meridian himself dared not rifle through any of the personal belongings of his former guild members that radiated such dangerous auras. There might be some very useful items within these halls he could sequester for his own needs, but he knew it was far too dangerous to pursue such folly. The vicious trap he had just witnessed devouring the thief clearly justified this precaution.

Ash grabbed Ivy roughly by the shoulder and pulled her to the center of the great room.

"You tell us if you notice enchantments on anything else in here, or I will feed you to that box myself." he warned the forest sprite, waving his hand towards the loathsome jewelry box that devoured his friend. Ivy nodded in agreement as Jinx came to her side for support.

"We can only view glyphs, we can't really *see* magic itself." she partially lied. Even here in this room, both the fey girls could in fact behold the raw magic lingering in this ancient temple that their abductors could not detect. Each of the chamber walls depicted several large tranquil faces sculpted from the very stone, all of which was entirely invisible to their present company; a fact which the faerie girls themselves had not yet fully realized.

Ash figured the rest of the doors here must be locked for a reason; and after the strange and horrific demise of his companion, he would rather not spend the rest of the evening here poking around blindly. He wanted to find that legendary relic and any other eccentric items of notable worth, and be on his way. Ash wasn't too terribly smart, but he wasn't entirely stupid either. One had to have street smarts to survive in this town.

The three thugs were noticeably more wary of what they chose to handle after realizing the grade of hidden and unexpected dangers within these walls, even from items that appeared harmless at first glance. There were small statues of pewter and gold, yet Bella withdrew her hand before touching them, for fear they might come to life. Dragging Ivy over by her arm, she ordered the fairy girl to reveal any dangers; not fully realizing that the fey could be just as conniving and simply lie about what Bella could not perceive. There were oddly shaped vases and lanterns and other items of value they were forced to examine; even though Ivy could, in fact, discern soft auras of magic around a few objects, she chose to keep quite about it.

"And what about that vase?" Bella Blackwidow shoved her over towards an inset shelf, but Ivy stuttered in her response. It wasn't until that moment that she began to realize that these hoodlums might not be seeing what she was; for the vase Bella was pointing at was not a vase at all; it clearly appeared to be a small pudgy idol. "Well...?" the thief girl shook her arm roughly for an answer, her nervousness masked by anger for fear of meeting an unpleasant fate similar to her missing comrade. Ash came over and eyed the wood fairy with a suspicious glare.

"Hold on a second, Bella, I'm a good enough liar to know one when I see one." he stated firmly to Ivy's dread. A look of guilt washed over her face as she turned her green eyes away from his. "What color is that vase?" he demanded, then grabbed Ivy by the chin to force her to look at it, "Answer me or I will carve your little friend." he threatened holding the shiny dagger in front of her menacingly while offering a searing glare over to Jinx who cowered back a step.

"Um, its ...blue-ish?" Ivy guessed while fishing for a clue, wishing for the moment she had practiced lying more often in life than she had. He callously pushed her away and was clearly upset, seething under his breath.

"But ...it's an old brown clay vase, it's not blue." Grunch grumbled like a halfwit, not realizing what was going on; that the fairy girl had been caught in her deception.

"You two got us in here alright; but since you're feeling like you don't want to cooperate, we are going to make you personally inspect each item by hand," Ash determined, "so if there are any more traps like that devouring chest back there, *you* will be the next victim."

Ivy realized that she blew it, but really didn't have much of a choice. In the eyes of the Faerie, they saw things that others could not. This temple was tainted with old magic; an ancient power with ties to the very bloodlines of the Elves themselves, which was why the two fey were attuned to it. Jinx was a little confused.

"Why do they think that statue is a vase?" Jinx whispered to her companion, "And why is he being so mean?"

"I would assume the mages that lived here had placed enchantments to disguise certain items," she explained, "I don't think they can see everything as we can, Jinx," Ivy pondered as she struggled to remember what her mentor had taught her years ago about the Craven, and how their presence drains and even neutralizes the essence of the Evermore; the very source of all magic. Considering that outside of these enchanted walls, the dismal conditions of this corrupted city and twisted morals of its suffering residents were the symptoms that bloomed from the lingering touch of the Craven. These thugs had become victims of their tainted environment, and could no longer see the magic in their world.

Grunch looked on as Ash and Bella pushed the faeries around by knifepoint to pick up several items of interest. When nothing adverse happened to them, after a pause they would hand each given bauble to Grunch for him to bag. This method worried Ivy, since she realized that the deadly jewelry box appeared quite ordinary to her despite the soft aura around it; which was quite similar to many of the other objects they had already been forced to handle. It was likely only a matter of time until they tripped another of these lethal booby traps.

As Jinx was also being made to identify any enchanted valuables, Ivy suddenly held out her arm in front of the small girl to block her way. Jinx didn't know what to think, but Ivy glanced directly down at the floor before them as unobtrusively as possible so the other three villains wouldn't notice. The thieves had only been concerned about flitching the small items they could carry out, and never gave heed to the large ornate area carpets covering the room. One in particular throbbed with a soft pulsating aura.

Bella snapped at Jinx for not following her orders to inspect a golden lantern she had found, instructing her to pick it up before Bella would dare to touch it.

"Get over here you little bug!" she blared at the tiny fey girl who turned to give Ivy a worried glance as to whether she should obey. Ash was used to her forceful attitude and tapped on a wall with the blade of his dagger as he waved Ivy back over to him. The wood sprite gave a short shake of her head with a glare to Jinx not to walk across the carpet to Bella. Jinx got the clue, and fluttered her wings to flit safely over mere inches above the floor. A few steps away, Ivy shuddered as she watched what transpired in the moments that followed.

Unlike the other enchanted items about the room, the rug had a slight pulse to it that made it stand out from the rest. She wasn't sure what it meant, but had thought it prudent to keep her petite friend from treading upon it. Bella launched forward in rash anger to accost the small fairy who she thought was making a break for it when Jinx suddenly took flight. There were no windows here, but she wasn't going to let the fairy girl get out of her reach above them. In her dash across the strangely woven carpet, her haste triggered a snare. At the outer edge, nothing happened, but as she stepped dead in the middle of the rug, it gave away as if there were an open pit beneath.

Bella floundered forward in surprise with a yelp, losing her balance. Both Ash and Grunch hurried to her, looking around the thick pillars within the room to see what had happened. The two fairy girls were nowhere near their comrade, who was now somehow wading waist deep in one of the large rugs. Astounded, they rushed to her aid, yet dared not step onto the carpet itself that had trapped her just out of arms reach. Bella's eyes were wide with fear, for she had seen what had happened to Shrew, and she began to panic as he had.

Ash stepped over to Grunch and grabbed an empty sack for

Bella to grab, hoping to pull her from the strange pool of thread now enwrapping her. Bella screamed in horror, struggling even harder to free herself from the bog of writhing strands. Like a thousand tiny tentacles, they crept up her torso, dragging her even deeper into the void of the rug. With the unrelenting tug of the strands grasping onto her arms, she fought to free herself from the nightmare she found herself in.

"Don't let me die like this, Ash!" she screamed to her fellow thief, who swung the end of the bag to her. Grasping it as best she could with one hand, she could not free her other arm. She gripped the bag like death itself as Ash pulled from the brink of the carpet's edge. To counter her escape, the threads from the rug itself snaked up her arm and enveloped the shoddy bag, whereupon its very weave began to unravel. Grunch stood gawking as the two fairy girls stepped back, and Jinx held her hands tightly over her eyes as Bella shrieked when the bag they held unwound and snapped in two.

Ash fell back on his rear with the shredded end of the sack in his hands, watching helplessly as the threads of the carpet enveloped Bella's face, muffling her screams and pulling her into its weave like quicksand. Her clenching hand was the last to disappear, testifying the little thief had fought to the end.

Having witnessed the entire event unfold, Meridian stood stroking his frizzy beard with a wry grin hidden beneath. The thief girl had triggered the passive trap herself, in her own haste running across, when a "no running" sign was clearly marked into the weave of the carpet itself in ancient runes. Had she not struggled so, the enchanted rug would have simply released her unharmed. He took a moment to considered that snare in the common room, and it was very likely the little crook was still alive even now, but would likely suffocate to death in the next few minutes as she drowned in the threads of the tapestry. The old wizard was glued to the pane of slow glass, quite interested how this predicament would unfold.

After the shock of the moment washed away in the following silence, Ash could still hear the echo of Bella's screams in his head. With a ruffle, the carpet ceased to be a pool of swirling threads and became a simple rug yet again; save for the dark image of Bella's shadow displayed in its weave as a horrid reminder of her fate. Standing, he threw the shredded sack to the floor and immediately grabbed Ivy harshly by the throat.

"You got her killed!" he yelled with an angry glare, as his spittle splashed upon her cheeks. Ash was livid, and she wondered if this was the end of their long journey as he drew his dagger forward with a threatening wave as if considering whether to stab her.

"I didn't know the rug was enchanted," Ivy squeaked from the pressure on her throat, "we were all walking on them this entire time. Maybe it was something she did or said." Ivy reasoned with a rasp. Her answer hardly satisfied Ash, who wrenched her towards the floor.

"I'm tired of you trying to pull a fast one on me," he growled as he pushed Ivy onto the enchanted carpet, "let's hear you scream for your life like Bella did, fairy!" he glared as Ivy stumbled back onto the rug, terrified as to what was about to happen to her ...but nothing did. The rug remained a rug. No tendrils of threads or consuming pool of strands drew her beneath the floor; she just stood there in her bare feet, in complete shock. Needless to say, so was Ash; which ended as an anticlimactic, almost embarrassing turn to his heated threat. Staring down at the motionless carpet and back up to Ivy, a look of broiling anger grew on his face.

"You little sneak," his face now quite red with fury, "you damn faeries were controlling the enchantments." he blared, mistakenly presuming that the magical trap was somehow a result of the two fey girls presence. The fearful look in Ivy's green eyes were completely missed by the angry thief; who surmised the wood sprite was in some way responsible for the demise of his two companions. Seeing that the quicksand carpet wasn't going to execute his revenge for him, he brought his rusty dagger forward to put an end to her himself.

Jinx, of course, would have none of that. Grunch dropped the loot filled bags he was holding and made a clumsy grasp for the small luck fairy as she dashed forward to intercept Ash's lunge towards Ivy. Pushing his arm away, it was obvious the desperate ploy only served to annoy the angry thug; and Ash swiped back his blade at the little fey. Luckily, as faerie hexes were at work the moment he hit her, she was only struck by the flat of the blade.

Ash stared in dismay as the trusty dagger he had used for years snapped in two at the hilt; he also couldn't quite contemplate how he had lost his footing as he fell backwards against a large stone pedestal; cracking his head. He felt dizzy, and slightly disorientated as he lay there on his rump, trying to recover his senses. Grunch hurried to his side as he shooed the small fairy away with a threatening wave of his arm. Jinx stood back as Ivy quickly stepped off the enchanted carpet for safety's sake. Their attention was quickly brought to the rolling sound from atop the pedestal, as a fat hourglass that sat upon it had been knocked askew by the crack of Ash's head.

Grunch himself was a bit too thick-headed and slow to catch the hourglass as it fell off the edge, striking Ash's skull for a second time. The weary thief moaned in agony from being clouted on his sore head, and gazed at the remnants of the shattered hourglass and the glass shards and layers of sand which covered most of his head and shoulders.

Behind locked doors many rooms above, the old wizard gave a grimace of undiluted remorse. Having watched the events unfold, he not only mourned the loss of a priceless hourglass, but also a slight tinge of pity for the poor fool who it broke upon. Any wizard worth his salt knew that sands in an hourglass were far from ordinary. The grains of sand in that particular relic had been collected by a distant caravan that had crossed the dunes of Morbia eons ago. The mystic sands in the broken hourglass had actually been collected from the side of a sleeping sand giant who rested at the foot of a temple in a strange and forgotten desert oasis that lay beyond the edge of a crystal forest, deep within the borders of the Faerylands.

The enchanted sand had particular qualities, which revealed themselves as grains sifted over the injured boy. Ash was speechless as he held up his hand to take Grunch's offer to help him up, only to see his fingers drift away like dust; followed by his arm and face, washing away the look of stark terror that froze there for but an instant. Like a wind swept dune, in moments his body transformed and his flesh turned to sand that piled upon the floor beneath his clothes.

Grunch, too, was speechless, having witnessed the horrific deaths of all three of his companions in short order. He gave one slow glance over to the two fey girls, and a low moan of pure fear seeped through his lips. For a moment, the two sprites thought the mutant thug was going to attack them like Ash had; but instead, he dropped every last bag and ran away with a hurried waddle towards the exit with his stubby hands flailing in the air. Down the steps and past the empty looted alcoves he scuttled, where just mere moments before he and his comrades had worn wide haughty sneers of greed across their faces as they ransacked the temple. Meridian watched through the slow glass as the would-be burglar sped out the lower doors of the atrium and triggered the trap that had recently reset itself.

Green wisps of slithering adders entwined the poor thief as he let out a short but frightful yell. The adders bit and bit until his face was flush with poison; his eyes glazed over like white linen, and Grunch was no more. In his room above, the wrinkled mage rubbed his scruffy chin; trying to make sense of what he had just seen. Grabbing his twisted staff once again, he tucked in his belt and set off to the lower chambers to deal with the two trespassers who were left loitering down in the guild's common room.

Ivy and Jinx suddenly found themselves alone after Grunch had run off to meet his end. In their hopes to escape the guild hall, they followed his trail until they found his stiffened pale corpse flush with an unpleasant shade of green. His body gave off a steam of rancid toxins as vaporous snakes slithered from beneath his clothing. Realizing the rune on the door had reset since Jinx had hexed it, there was no way they could try to jinx it a second time since the doorway was wide open, and the snare awaited anyone to spring it.

The two fairy girls made their way back up the stairway, stepping around the several bags littering the steps that Grunch had relieved himself of in his haste to escape.

"So, now what?" Jinx pouted, wishing they had never run into those crooks; but hid a smile at the thought of their unpleasant demise.

"Let's see if we can find a window higher up and fly back down out of here if we can." Ivy answered, referring to the violent winds of the storm brewing over the city, which would make their descent by air dangerous enough as it was. Any wind sheer could bash the small faeries into the tower walls, or plummet them onto the jagged rooftops below with lethal force. Faeries were delicate, and just weren't built for that kind of abuse.

They made their way back into the common room, avoiding the scattered loot and ominous pile of sand strewn upon the floor. With all due means, they also avoided the enchanted carpet with Bella's distraught shadow embroidered upon it. Though as sensitive as their sharp fairy ears were, they had failed to notice the entrance of the guild's custodian. An old wizard with a long grey beard, wearing a faded purple robe stood before them, holding aloft a gnarled wooden staff. In one dramatic motion and a mumble of incantations he slammed the butt end of the rod onto the floor, from which erupted a shower of blinding light that swept the room.

The two fey girls shielded their large eyes from the glare, only to look up at the mage in dismay; a feeling also shared by Meridian, who was boggled why these two thieves weren't affected by his spell. His old weary eyes weren't as keen as they used to be, and as he tried to focus on the two burglars he raised a furry brow to see two girls who were quite naked. Their almond-shaped eyes and fair skin, the large pointy ears, and with the ruffle of their wings; it took him a moment to realize these were true Faeries.

Jinx immediately cowered behind Ivy, who herself sought some direction to run. She wanted to fly up the stairway from where the old wizard had entered, but in the darkness any unseen overhang would knock her out cold. Faeries feared wizards because they had a habit of dicing up and draining fey as ingredients for their potions and spells; so the rumors went.

"Oh, I say ...you two are of the race of fey." he mumbled, and was a bit abashed by their nakedness. Jinx slowly poked her head out from behind Ivy to look at the magi, and nodded as did

Ivy. "What would a Faerie want thieving from my hall?" He began to growl angrily, not having any patience for unwelcome trespassers. Faeries after all, did in fact have a quite considerable reputation for being thieves as it were; though the faeries themselves considering their habit only as a forgetful case of *borrowing* things that weren't theirs.

"You misunderstand," Ivy broke out with her hand up in surrender, "we wouldn't steal from you; we were captured and forced here by these crooks against our will." she relayed, as Jinx nodded her head in agreement, but with a frightful look twinkling in her eyes as to what the wizard would do next.

"Please, sir ...don't grind us up." Jinx pleaded in a sad squeaky voice, looking as if she was going to cry. After a moment of tense silence, a crack of a smile broke across the wizard's face. He leaned on his crooked staff with both hands and gave the two girls a thoughtful glance.

"Ha, ha, no need to worry about that, little one," Meridian chuckled softly, "it's been so long since I've seen a fairy in these parts I had thought your kind had all but faded away," he admitted, turning to the side and motioning them to follow, "Though you two don't rightly smell like faeries I've ever heard of," he announced covering his nose as they drew near; as it was the rancid stench of the sewers still lingering upon them. A bit embarrassed, Ivy stepped forward with Jinx not far behind.

"If ...if you might have something we could clean off with?" she implored, noting the stinking muck caked upon their feet.

"Most certainly, please follow me ...and don't touch anything." the wizard spoke over his shoulder to warn them. With a word, magical candles lit up the stairwell with a soft yellow glow, all the way up past the chantry and into his study high above. There he gave the girls towels which he enchanted with the fragrant scents of lemons and honey to cleanse themselves. Meridian wasn't used to having company, so he tried his best not to be a grouch.

Looking out the narrow window, Jinx saw just how high they were, far above the dark city that twinkled with lights from a thousand lanterns. The sky above crackled with lightning and churning clouds as dry leaves whisked through the violent storm; yet she felt not the slightest breeze breach the open window. Offering them some warm tea, Jinx poked curiously at the molars clinking around at the bottom of her cup.

"I would never have thought that goblin tea would be so yummy." she smiled, as she closed her eyes to savor the pungent scent of its curling steam.

"Oh yes," he grinned in agreement, "it's a rare delicacy, not everyone knows that goblins have a sweet tooth." the wizard touted as he took another sip from his own cup.

The wizard's study was small, cramped even, compared to the rest of the guild hall they had seen. Ivy could tell he was a bachelor as the room was more than a smidge untidy. Her old mentor Grubroot had been the same way, and she saw the similarities in him. The walls were made of coarse stone, giving it an earthy feel, and lightly decorated with faded tapestries and dusty chandeliers. In fact, the study was quite ordinary and modest considering the elaborate layout and decor of the rest of the mages guild.

"So, young ones, tell me the story of how you fell into the company of common thieves?" he asked, sinking back further into his cushy chair. In what seemed an almost breathless response, Jinx rattled on to both Ivy's and the wizard's amusement. The island turtle, the dwarven mines, riding giant worms, and being gobbled up by a foul drake, crossing the swamps and into the foggy mires and tasting mead and wine with drunken dwarves, their searching for the legendary amulet and crossing an enchanted bridge to the point where they were accosted by their unsavory captors and dragged into the sewers.

"...and, here we are." Jinx shrugged her shoulders with a smile as she finally paused to catch her breath and took a deep sip from her oversized teacup.

"Oh, my," Meridian responded, a bit bleary-eyed at this point in her story, "you two *have* been through quite an ordeal." he said as Jinx nodded readily in agreement. "Now, could you repeat this part about what the thieves in your company were after?" the wizard asked, holding his hand up to calm the girl down.

"Something called the Eye of Omens or some such." Jinx

interrupted as Ivy was about to answer. At that, Meridian gave a noticeable grimace that quickly washed from his face.

"Ah, I thought that relic would be long forgotten. Apparently not." he groaned while pouring himself another cup from the tea kettle. "Your friends," he began as he caught the tiny luck faeries sudden harsh glare and sharp shake of her head, "ah, ...your *'not'* friends," he corrected, "would have been sorely disappointed." the wizard noted, realizing with a tickle they had actually ended up off far worse than being *merely* disappointed at the end of the day.

"And why is that?" Ivy finally got a word in.

"Because the Eye is not here. It had its use here at one time, but the Elves who lent it to us never returned to reclaim it, so we delivered it to a temple for safekeeping on the isle of Tyre centuries ago." he grumbled as he spit the loose goblin tooth that he almost accidentally swallowed, back into his teacup where it rattled. With a raise of her sharp brow, Ivy realized their meeting might be more than just chance.

"Oh, that's where we're going!" Jinx chimed in.

"And why is that, little one, do you also seek the Eye yourself?" he asked suspiciously, "It is a most dangerous device in the wrong hands, and not to be trifled with."

"Oh no, we are trying to find a lady called Sorrow." she blurted out, shifting a guilty look to Ivy for not knowing if she had just revealed too much about their quest. They really didn't know who this lone wizard was after all, or if he was to be trusted.

"Sorrow ...Sorrow, well, the name seems familiar, but I can't quite remember." he grimaced while rubbing his chin in thought in his usual manner, "Now why was it you were searching for this ...this amulet of tears you mentioned?" Meridian tried to recall the girls hasty blabbering moments before as she told her tale. Unfortunately, his mind wasn't as sharp as it used to be.

"Oh no, you misunderstood," Jinx corrected him, "we *found* the amulet, but we need to find the lady who made it; and *she* is on the island, so we were told."

"But, the question young fey ...is why?" the wizard repeated; realizing he was nosing into their business, but then again they had trespassed within his walls and he had the right to demand a few answers.

"We were sent by the High Elves to find someone who could help us battle the Craven." Ivy finally admitted, breaking the silence that had grown within the room.   With her answer, Meridian suddenly appeared tired, almost distraught.

"It has been a long time since I have heard anyone utter that dark name." he sighed, "Alas, the Elves in their wisdom have sent you to find this person on your own because you would likely go unnoticed by prying eyes or twitching ears that might be listening." the old mage enlightened the two girls. "If you do not find this individual you seek, then you may have no other choice than to use the Eye of Omens to aid you in your quest." Meridian suggested, not doing so lightly.

"Thank you for your advice, sire," Ivy replied with an air of gratitude, "but where is it located now?"

"The Eye was far too dangerous a device for us to possess, which put the guild itself at risk," Meridian noted, "so in lieu of being unable to reach the High Elves to return the relic, we delivered it into the hands of their closest cousins; the Drow."

Ivy shuddered at hearing that name yet again, for all stories she had ever heard of the dark elves known as the Drow; were that they were vicious reflections of the kind forest elves, and were to be feared. Dark elves were rarely tolerated when they were seen in the underworld, though they naturally dwelt in the caves beneath. When the faeries from the surface withdrew to the tunnels beneath the earth centuries ago, they commandeered many areas that were once home to the Drow. This, of course, led to high tensions between the forest and nether races of elves. The only short term remedy to the unease was their shared conflict with the Craven. Unaware of the details, Ivy heard that somewhere along the line the Drow withdrew to small pockets at the very edge of the Evermore, where no forest fey would dare tread.

"And, where might they be on the isle of Tyre?" Ivy had to ask, having to consider all avenues. The Drow were still elves, and would be inclined to assist them against the scourge of the Craven; no matter what personal grudges they still held. With a stroke of his beard, Meridian got up from his worn chair and fiddled through a few of his sorcerer tomes lining the shelves of his cabinet.   After shuffling through several thick books, he finally came upon one which captured his attention.

The wizard plopped back down in his seat and palmed through the worn pages, taking a moment here and there to skim through certain passages.

"Ah, here it is. A group of magi secretly transported the relic to the buried temple of the Drow located in a caldera near the center of the isle." he murmured as he skimmed farther on.

"Buried?" Jinx blurted, "So how are we supposed to find it? Meridian held up his finger in response and turned the book to face the girls.   There among the cryptic symbols and rich bordering was the sketch of a baleful tower.

"Upon the site of their sacred temple was built the Tower of..."

"The tower of madness." Jinx interrupted to the old wizard's astonishment.

"Yes, indeed, the Tower of Madness," he continued, "which was built to mark the territory of the Drow. As it is written within," Meridian noted in the passage, "those who were in sight of this tower should take heed that they were trespassing upon sacred ground."   The wizard gazed on through the following chapters, but found no other information of value.

"It is this very tower where we were to find Sorrow." Ivy admitted in afterthought, which gave her a thread of hope that they were on the right track; but they still had to get there.

"I must tell you, the isle of Tyre is not as it once was," Meridian cautioned the girls, wondering how these two fragile beings stood any chance at what they were about to face, "The island is a cursed haven for a slew of foul and unspeakable beasts, which care not of your affiliation with the Elves. They are afflicted creatures stricken by the Craven ages ago, and have only festered in their own darkness since that time."   He gave the two girls a look of gloom, "But first, we have to get you there, and that endeavor itself is a perilous task of its own."

*   *   *

Magic

The two faeries watched intently as the old wizard plotted the course of the seasons with a confused jumble of star maps and charts beyond their meager understanding. They would only have a three day window during the passing of the first new moon after the summer solstice. The two fey girls admitted they had nary a clue about calendar events, and relied solely on mage and his calculations. As it turned out, it would only be a few weeks away, and Meridian offered to let them stay safely within the walls of the guild while they awaited the waning of the moon.

But even as his guests, there were so many rules to obey that they only managed to discouraged Jinx, which brought a pout to her sullen face. First, the wizard had to clean up the mess left behind from the unfortunate thieves. The old mage had to take delicate measures to contain the mystic sand from the shattered hourglass; and took some convincing from him to show the girls that the jewelry box was quite harmless, as long as you didn't put your hand inside, of course.

There was little he could do about the enchanted rug with Bella's silhouette now woven into its design as Meridian had not created the magic carpet. As a precaution, he rolled it up and stored it away to their satisfaction in light of the fact the two fey found it quite eerie to view the dead girl's shadow embroidered upon it, every time they entered the room. Grunch's corpse was another matter entirely, and the faeries were a bit curious as to why the old wizard was quite adamant when he ordered them not to watch while the mage disposed of his remains.

He slaved over certain enchantments until he was able to create fresh mushrooms and flowers for the girls to eat, since they wouldn't touch the seared fish and breads the mage brought back from the market. He wasn't used to entertaining, so he had little more than books and scrolls to offer as a diversion to pass the time. This did not sit well with Jinx, who was dying for any type of amusement. Ivy, however, quite relished the thought of skimming through ancient tomes so she could look at the pictures and fanciful sketches inked upon their pages; despite the fact she could not read a single word of the cryptic language scrawled within the countless spell books and scrolls.

The runes on the magical wards, however, were etched in the common tongue, something Ivy's old friend from her years back in Undergrove had tried to teach her to read. But Ivy had been very restless in her childhood, and much more interested in gallivanting around the underworld to relieve her boredom and insatiable curiosity. Which, of course, was an affliction she readily recognized in her young companion, who from time to time, reminded her of the way she used to be in her youth.

Ivy had matured over the years, realizing the world was a much bigger place and her part within it; a reality she was still trying to understand. As an Elvenborn, she had certain responsibilities; and a higher sense to follow them.

Jinx herself seemed to become ever more bored out of her mind after each passing day, annoyed at the stringent rules the wizard had demanded during their stay. They were not allowed into the upper chantry, nor to attempt to open any of the locked doors; and manipulating any enchanted wards was strictly forbidden. They were also warned not to handle any of the items or relics lying about the guild hall. So, while Ivy skimmed through his library, Jinx was left with nothing to do. With a frown she flipped through a few pages of a book, but was quickly weary for lack of any engagement. She was used to flitting about the wooded groves and prairies, free to make her own discoveries, but being locked indoors and scolded not to touch *this* or *that* she found personally insulting. It didn't take very many days until Ivy noticed Jinx had become indifferent and glum; not at all her usual sassy self.

"I'm bored..." Jinx whined halfheartedly as she mindlessly played with a writing quill the mage had left on the table. Meridian had retired for the evening several hours ago; and even though he rarely ever slept, it was an old habit he found hard to break; and instead took the time to meditate on his spells while lying in bed.

"I could tell you've been getting antsy. It's only a few more days until we will be back on our way, since Meridian promised to guide us to the island." Ivy replied.

"No, he said it was like uh, twelve days away ...that's more than a few, Ivy." Jinx pouted in response, "I can't stay locked up in here that long," she protested, "I'm really, really, *really* bored!"

"You're going to have to learn some patience," Ivy scolded, "needless to say, it's not very safe outside; besides, we could use some assistance to get there safely."

"And then what?" the little luck fairy demanded, "He said he would only take us to the edge of the island, and then he's going to abandon us there," Jinx began to sulk, as she referred to the conversation the three of them had earlier that evening before the mage waddled off to bed.

"He has his own responsibilities to tend to here," Ivy relayed, trying to get Jinx to see the logic of their situation, "we should appreciate the help he's given us so far."

Jinx just had too much energy to be loitering around a dark temple, especially when most of the rooms were off limits. She couldn't even go exploring, let alone touch anything lest she break something accidentally by her vexing; or trigger some unpleasant trap. The fact was, there was really nothing for a child to do here. The wizard spent all his time reading or mumbling to himself while memorizing incantations. Jinx tried to keep amused and watched the mage when he was making potions; but when she once tried to help by handing him a scroll he had misplaced; to his unpleasant surprise her hex had made all the inked rune letters actually fall off the parchment only to scatter across the table. Ivy had to remind her of that.

"Oops..." the little girl mumbled.

"You've got to remember to be more careful, Jinx," Ivy declared without trying to sound too berating. Though there were times when she had to remind herself how difficult it must be for the young fairy to not be able to touch most things for fear of something breaking or going wrong; whether it was her fault or not, poor little Jinx was used to being the one who was always blamed. Ivy knew she would never truly understand what it must be like for Jinx, having grown up being criticized at every turn. It must create a level of pressure that caused her to be so defensive, especially if she was constantly being blamed, even for something she didn't do just because of her presence; it must be entirely frustrating.

"Well, I could try to teach you how to read," Ivy offered, "...although I really don't know too terribly much in the way of words." she admitted.

"Nah," the girl muttered back with a sigh, "He would probably kill me if I touched one of his precious tomes and all the words fell out onto the floor." the little fairy gave a pout; and as if on cue, the quill she had been playing with fell apart as the vane crumbled away. She gave a shocked look for just a moment, then slammed down its bare stem onto the table; making Ivy wonder momentarily if perhaps one of the table legs might also decide to give way at any second. With a growl, Jinx stormed out of the room as Ivy looked on helplessly. There just wasn't much she could do to comfort her.

Jinx stomped down the stairway to the lower rooms, and took some time to sulk in a corner. Why did she have to be a bad luck fairy? Where was the fairness in that? Everybody in the grove avoided her, and they were probably glad she was gone. Nobody would truly miss her she realized; she was just a disaster waiting to happen ...nothing but a nuisance. Sitting all alone crouched up in a dark corner, little Jinx began to cry.

Ivy wasn't the motherly type, and didn't rightly know how to handle the constant sassy attitude of her companion. It seemed like Jinx only got disagreeable when they weren't out gallivanting around. In reflection, she did seem to have a bit of fun when they were in the dwarven kingdom while everyone was drunk, or when they were out adventuring on the open road.   But, whenever things slowed down, her personality would turn ever so slightly, as if she was hiding something inside. There wasn't much she could do about it though, as Jinx wasn't the easiest person to talk to. So Ivy figured she would just give her some space.

There were plenty of strange and interesting pictures scrawled in the wizard's books, and his library was extensive. Meridian seemed friendly enough, but he was still a wizard, and that was something to be wary of. Wizards stole magic that wasn't theirs, and it was no secret that was something the Elves frowned upon. They simply tolerated it for fear of reprisal, as they had suffered at the hands of the huskmen so very long ago. A mistake that had arguably led them to their demise and the situation all of the Faerylands now suffered for.

There were countless races and beasts in their world, but none truly understood the Elves, except the Elves themselves. Even Ivy, a true blood Elvenborn, was mostly left in the dark as to their methods. The lady Dawn had trusted her enough to show her the Tree of Life. A mere fragile sprig barely higher than her knee, but pulsating with a magic she couldn't dare to understand. It was kept safe and hidden within the center of a colossal illusionary world tree, that served as the symbol of strength to all Faerie kind.

Ivy had been privy to secrets behind the silent truth upon which the dignity and honor of the High Elves drifted, barely kept afloat by their perplexing; and sometimes irritating wisdom. She realized they were only trying to keep balance in the world, and somehow, at this point in time, she was a mere pawn, a counterweight in their mysterious plan. Ivy pondered as she sat at the table, realizing for a brief moment just how deep her thoughts had run. There was a bigger picture, things she herself could not quite see; much like the former thieves who could not see this sacred temple as it truly was. The magic was gone from their eyes, because they were drowning in their own personal concerns and their individual worlds had grown so very, very small.

"Still awake I see..." Meridian noted gently, stirring Ivy from her train of thought. She hadn't even heard him walk in, "Where is your little friend?" the wizard inquired as he snapped a finger to light a magical flame under the fat kettle and picked through a pottery jar of goblin teeth and herbs to make a fresh pot of tea.

"Jinx? Oh, she wandered off, likely to get some sleep I

suppose." Ivy got up to look out the single narrow window in his study. It was difficult to tell if it was night or day because of the perpetual storm clouds that hung over the city. "Does the sun ever shine here?" she had to ask, gazing up towards the murky clouds churning overhead.

"Not for over the past hundred years. The curse of the Craven that has overshadowed the isle of Tyre has slowly spread out across the entire coast and beyond." he answered while inspecting a stained molar before plopping it into his teacup, "I fear this city hasn't much time left to it before it is overrun by the afflicted. There have been reports in recent years of foul and unnatural creatures roaming the swamps to the north, who venture ever closer to our walls."

"So, why do you stay here, Meridian? I mean, you don't seem like the other riffraff that reside here; just pack up everything and leave while you can." Ivy offered, showing relative concern. After all, if she was in his shoes, that's what she would have done.

"Things aren't quite that easy, little sprite. I'm far older than I look, and don't have the energy for such an endeavor. Needless to say, there are far too many costly and dangerous relics in this place to clean out. My tired old bones wouldn't be able to handle the strain ...besides, where would I go?" he muttered while pouring water from the kettle, "The Dwarves won't let us leave, and there isn't another guild for more than a thousand leagues. I believe my place is here, young girl."

He offered Ivy a platter of fresh mushrooms and walnuts he conjured up, along with a bouquet of flowers for her friend Jinx.

"Maybe you should go get your companion to come join us for breakfast." the wizard inquired lightly, but Ivy seemed reluctant.

"Actually, I'm a little worried about her," she admitted with a hint of sincerity, as her thoughts were not often shared with others; but the wizard had a kind face worthy of her trust, "I'm not quite sure why the High Elves sent her with me along on this quest; I mean, I'm not really used to having to watch over someone, and she would get herself into all sorts of trouble otherwise." Ivy confessed.

"Ah, not used to looking out for anyone but yourself hmm?" Meridian noted, seeing right through her words. Ivy reflected on his wisdom, and realized that was actually what she was trying to say to herself all along. It was strange how our own personal dignity tends to twist the meaning of our true intentions once they pass our lips, and interpret into something else entirely. Ivy shook her head on how silly it all was.

"What I mean is that I truly worry for Jinx, too. The task set to us has been fraught with danger, and I don't know what I would do should anything happen to her," Ivy conceded, "I mean, I used to be much like her once, and..."

"And the world is a cruel and unforgiving place." Meridian finished her sentence for her as he settled back into his chair. "I take it the burden of responsibility must be a heavy weight to bear for one of the Faerie, who usually spend their lives frolicking about without a care." he twiddled his fingers in a mock dance, then struck a serious grin, "The Elves are held in such high regard among the rest of the races of the world, because of their ability to commune with nature, so to speak." the wizard enlightened her, "They are like no other beings, and are envied among every other race because of the chaos and turmoil we are infected with, and so desperately wish we could shed. The Elves seem to be immune to that sense of unbalance that everyone else seems to feel in their lives; that is why they seem so alien and misunderstood." he offered.

What the mage said made a lot of sense to Ivy. In her youth, Ivy cared not for the rest of the wide world, but only the things that amused or were of benefit to her. She did feel an inherent affinity towards the forests and trees, but not much else. It wasn't until the revelation of her previous adventures that she realized the grand scope of the world and her part in it. She had matured, and that was not a small thing for a fairy.

"I just don't understand fully why this burden was put upon me," Ivy sighed, "I'm just a little wood sprite, nobody of real consequence, and neither is Jinx. I mean, I don't know why the Elves didn't just send their own elder priests on this journey; I'm sure they would have done a far better job than I.

"As a woodland fey, you must have certain magical skills they thought would be of importance. So what was it you were doing before you were dragged out on this grand adventure?" the wizard inquired.

"I was sleeping, actually." She gave a slight giggle, "I can turn into a tree." Ivy relayed, describing that she had rooted herself in the Grey Forest before the elven priestess know as Dawn had awoken her a century later.

"You don't say?" the wizard showed a curled mark of astonishment, "And what is it like being a tree?"

"Oh, how can I explain," Ivy's mind wandered, "...it's like a quiet dream, where everything flows around you in deep fluid tones. A squirrel may climb your branches or a bird might flit past, touching you like the song of a flute carried on the wind until it fades away with no proof that it had ever really existed at all, yet the haunting memory of its tune still lingers in the back of your mind. And the trees all sway in dance and sing upon the breeze, with my roots deep within the soil; it makes me feel safe ...and content." Ivy added as an afterthought.

"Quite interesting." the wizard responded, as he sat back trying to imagine what it was like, "You are very lucky to have the ability to change your perspective and see the world in different colors than most." He finally declared, but Ivy just gave a shy modest shrug of her shoulders in agreement.

"And, so why did you become a wizard?" Ivy dared to ask, turning the conversation, "It does seem to be a bit tedious." she noted while nodding to the countless volumes of books and scrolls and piles of paraphernalia mages uses for their studies.

"Oh now, there's a question," Meridian gave a heavy sigh, his brow furrowed as if to pick a specific explanation rolling through his brain. "Every one of us in the guild had a separate reason that led us on the path in our pursuit of magic and all of its wonderful intricacies. A majority were mainly interested in power, and for others it was merely a hobby for intellectual pursuits. Some, I would say, were only interested in attaining a level of respect or monetary gain; but there were the few, who, like myself, simply sought answers to the mysteries of life..." he finished as his voice trailed off in thought.

"So, you were just curious?" Ivy hit the mark. The old mage nodded in agreement with a note of enthusiasm.

"Yes, yes, you could say so. There are beings such as yourself with magic that runs through your veins, no matter how slight it may seem; it is the very essence of the Evermore itself you are blessed with." he gave a wave of his hand as sparkles flittered from his fingers, "The Elves are a purer form of this attunement with nature, the magic of life itself!" he stated, and Ivy caught the weight of his words. "You see, young fey, many of us are dying inside ...that is why we age far more quickly than those born of the Faerie. The life within us is tainted, diluted." his voice raspy with age as if stressing his point.

"As it was with the huskmen?" she whispered out loud; remembering what Dawn had told her about the human tribes. Meridian nodded his head in agreement as he lazily levitated the kettle to pour him another cup of tea with a slight motion of his hand; though the pot was clearly shaking from the strain.

"Ah ...the race of men, almost entirely forgotten after all these years if it wasn't for the poisoned stain of the inheritance they had left blistered upon this world," he groaned as the kettle fell back to the table with less than perfect grace, "The life within them was thin indeed, so much so they could not even perceive the Evermore. They perverted wizardry into a thing called science, in an effort to spell out and explain everything in the universe, no matter how unexplainable, in their relentless quest to reach for what they could not possibly attain. Stubborn they were to the very last," the old wizard gave a sad gruff, though Ivy was still confused.

"What exactly was their connection with the Craven?" she ventured to ask, hoping that the old scholar held such knowledge. It was a dangerous question she dared not ask the High Elves.

"It was the race of *mankind*, they called themselves, who became empty vessels for the Craven." the old wizard began while he set down his cup and pressed his hands before him in deep thought, as if dragging forth a painful memory he would have rather left buried. "The Elves know more than any other breathing creatures among us, that the world is more alive than rest of us could ever hope to perceive. The race of men were willing victims to the influence of the Craven, and turned a blind eye to how corrupted their own depraved people had become by its taint; only to end up suffocating on their own folly and selfish greed as their society spiraled downward into the abscess of their self-inflicted destruction."

Meridian got up and strolled over to the narrow window so he could look down upon the twisted rooftops and dark crooked streets swarming with swindlers and thugs in every shadow, "This rotting city below, with desperation so thick it spreads like a plague, is in all truth but a pale shadow of what the lives of men had become. Mankind was so utterly shallow, so petty, and had drifted so far from nature; in the end, they had nothing left to live for ...no meaning to their existence."

"And the Evermore withdrew, leaving them to their fate; and ours as well it seems." Ivy concluded. The old mage shuffled back over to his chair as the forest fey considered the bigger picture, "But even without the race of men, the Craven still linger ...how is that possible?"

"Interesting ...in your innocence, you don't quite understand, do you?" speaking his thoughts out loud, "Good and Evil is merely perspective, young girl, nothing more than that. Some beings regard others gently, with kindness and respect; while some choose to torment others and even themselves. It is all a matter of choice, a weakness or strength of character bonded by the essence of life itself. Some grow more attuned to it, while others ...others stray so very far that they choke off every root, every fertile touch they may have once had with the essence of what life is and the blessing it was meant to be." he finished as Ivy realized the integrity of his words, remembering that the degenerates that had accosted her and Jinx had been unable to see the temple as it truly was. Slowly, things became a bit clearer for her.

"So, the Craven is Death...?" Ivy threw into the conversation for the magi to confirm.

"No, you still misunderstand," Meridian countered, "it is something else entirely; it is the absence of life's meaning, nothing less than a twisted abomination that poisons and corrupts all that it touches." relating what he had learned about this faceless scourge over the centuries. "I can't pretend to be an expert on the subject, nor on how to help you battle the Craven; but perhaps you will find those answers on the isle of Tyre, once you find either this lady Sorrow, or through the Eye of Omens, should it come to that." As the wizard went back to reading one of his thick books, "Keep in mind, though, that using the Eye to gain such knowledge comes at a price," he warned.

"What do you mean?" Ivy asked, truly perplexed.

"I am only repeating the words of the Elven priests who presented it to us those eons ago." Meridian admitted, "I myself have never used the relic, only participated in its safekeeping for a short time before it was ferried off to the isle of Tyre."

The subject having been drawn to its conclusion, the wood sprite turned back to the platter full of thick spotted mushrooms and fragrant bouquets of yellow honeysuckle, thinking she should take a moment to look where Jinx might have wandered off and disappeared to.

The tiny luck fairy sat huddled in a ball in a corner, her sobs echoing softly through the dark halls of the guild. Jinx tried to act tough most of the time as a facade to ward off her feelings of self pity and doubt; wondering why she had been cursed with such a hapless and graceless form of magic. Other faeries avoided her when they could, and her annoying hex made daily life truly miserable at times.

Wiping away her tears, they sizzled and turned to glitter as her teardrops fell upon the cold stone floor. Had Meridian known, he would have dashed to bottle them, as fairy tears are rare indeed. They were rumored to heal wounds and cure the sick, or even bring forgetful bliss. Jinx didn't care, though she knew as every Faerie does that such deep sadness was dangerous for a fey to show. Such depression and anguish suffered by a fairy could cause them to fade, and if the regret about being alive ever became too strong, it could physically snuff out their existence. It was known that a fairy with a broken heart could not live; and thus, few fey ever shared true love for fear of its most mortal peril; and sinking to little more than wallowing in self pity can drive one to do unwise things.

Strolling though the passages, Ivy called out her friend's name into the labyrinth of columns. With a hint of guilt, Jinx poked her head out of a lone hallway. Flitting out of the alcove into the main hall, she spotted Ivy near the foot of the stair.

"Oh, there you are. Why didn't you answer me?"

"I was um, distracted; just thinking about something. That's all." Jinx blurted sadly, not wanting the wizard to find out she had been creeping about down here all alone.

"Well, I just wanted to check in on you, and let you know there's something up here for you to eat if you're hungry, Jinx," Ivy offered with a measure of concern, while trying not to sound too motherly. The little fairy shrugged her shoulders in acceptance and followed Ivy back up the stairs where her platter of flowers awaited. Finding Meridian in his worn chair and reading as usual, the little luck fairy dug into the flower petals and stems she savored while licking nectar from the tips of her tiny fingers. They tasted a little funny though she decided, since enchanted flowers seemed to lack any flavor of pollen.

"Well, since I have you both here, we should probably start planning for our trip to the island." the wizard mentioned as he slapped his thick book shut and puffs of dust shot from the pages.

"But it's over a week away..." Jinx sighed, anticipating the grinding boredom that awaited her in the meantime.

"Yes, well, I want you to be prepared and give you time to learn how to use a few weapons." he declared while rolling back his sleeves. Both the girls stopped stuffing their faces to look up at him in surprise while he grabbed a gnarled wand from a cupboard that closely resembled his tall staff, and whirled it in slow circles in the air until a ring of light started to emerge from its tip.

Humming a few mumbled incantations, he picked up a stick of wood from the fireplace with his free hand and touched it to the glowing circle of light with care. There was a slight flash, and the stick began to grow, twisting and winding upon itself as the wood hardened and a shining string snapped into place. Now gripping it in the center, he stepped over and handed Jinx the magical bow. She just looked at it curiously, and, of course, waited for it to crack in two at any moment.

"Don't worry about your hex, young girl; the bow is woven with an enchantment to keep it from breaking," he assured her as he turned his attention to Ivy, "And now for yours," he offered, while proceeding with the same ritual. Touching another twig to the circle it shot out in both directions from his hand and the wood began to lace upon itself. Its end hardened into the tip of a spear that shone with a silver hue. Handing this to Ivy, she inspected the gift as he noted to them both, "Where you two are going, you will need to protect yourselves."

*   *   *

Tyre

The two fairy girls spent the next several days learning how to use their magical weapons proficiently. With a little foresight, the wizard set up an archery range for Jinx to test her skills within the lower atrium. Jinx was a bit tickled to actually own something that didn't disintegrate in one form or another at her touch.   Her hardwood bow had an iridescent string that materialized a flaming arrow when pulled taut; that way she didn't have to bother with carrying a quiver or running out of ammunition. Meridian chose this element to imbue onto the bow, as they would be facing creatures particularly vulnerable to fire, making the fiery arrows even more practical.

Ivy, on the other hand, had been given a short spear with a pair of hidden blades that folded out into a trident. Both ends were wrapped in silver tinted bronze, and the wizard took a moment to demonstrate its special properties to her. Taking it from her gently, he took a stance while he formed a dark cloud in the atrium with the wave of his hand. Holding the spear above him, he spoke a single word, and the fairy girls jumped back in fright as an arc of lightning flashed out from the rumbling clouds; striking the spear. The weapon sizzled and danced with fingers of electricity across its shaft until they nearly faded away.

"You will be faced by beasts of snow and frost who can wield such elements at their own will," Meridian warned her as he handed the spear back to Ivy. "This is a defensive weapon that will block and absorb such powers used against you, which you can then redirect at your foe. Just keep in mind that the energy of such a chaotic element will quickly drain away from the weapon."

He grabbed the handle in the middle of the spear between Ivy's delicate hands, and thrust it forward to guide her. In an instant, the two blades swung out and electricity coalesced at the head of the spear; a bolt of lightning flashed out with a kick, striking a distant pillar in a shower of sparks. Of course, Ivy flinched, nearly dropping the short spear from her grip; as she also noted the strike wasn't very accurate. Jinx giggled in glee beside her with a clap of her hands in applause, though realizing she would likely break the spear if she ever tried to use it herself. Actually, she was quite happy with her bow of flames.

"Keep these items well secured, and remember that they can also be used against you if you should lose them." he noted, "There is no armor I can create that would be of any benefit for your slight frames, and would only serve to overburden you, for those rare skills are of the dwarven smiths. I do, however, possess a bracelet that will serve as a token to the Drow, should you find them. It will act as a sign of your affiliation with the guild, and may serve to aid you in safe passage among them." Meridian offered Ivy a gold bracelet embedded with a large clear gemstone, which interestingly enough, slowly turned a shade of emerald green when he clasp it around her small wrist, the magic of the stone revealing a window of her true essence.

Apparently, the spear was also designed for close quarters combat, but Ivy was the first to admit she was no warrior. The enchanted pole arm was light enough to fly with, so at least it wouldn't become a burden in an emergency. The bow was a new toy for Jinx to use, and she wore herself out practicing with it to relieve the boredom that had been taunting her since their arrival. Several days before the phase of the new moon began, the wizard packed a satchel so they could be on their way to the northern coast when the time came.

Meridian had not ventured beyond the borders of the city for many centuries, and he was eager to get back to looking after the safety of the guild after seeing the two emissaries of the Elves were safely on their way. Ivy realized that the wizard could be of invaluable assistance to aid them in reaching the tower of the Drow, but there was also a missing chapter in the story of Thieves Gate he thought she should be made aware of. After departing the wizard's sanctuary and making their way through the dark alleys towards the northern gate, the mage set his staff aglow to push back the shadows.

"It is a dangerous path from the outer gate through the northern swamps, and I want you two to be ready should the need arise." Meridian advised as he hastened them along, his thick robe fluttering in the night air. Thieves and scoundrels eyed the strange trio from among the dim shadows of the street, though wary of the wizard's power; they withdrew from the revealing ring of light emitted by his staff.

"We could always use your help in crossing the island to reach the tower, should you wish to join us." Ivy offered, trying to make her request not sound too desperate as the plea it was.

"I have truly considered accompanying you both, as I, too, share your burden of the blight of the Craven upon our lands," he sighed with shortness of breath as they wound through the labyrinth of streets; distant screams and shouts echoing from the narrow alleys, "however, in all these years, the Elves have never returned here to aid us; nor applied their influence to save those of us who were left trapped here." the wizard divulged to the two fey following closely in his wake.

"So, I take it you must no longer trust them because of that?" Ivy presumed, yet understanding the lack of faith their absence had earned them.

"Sadly, the people of this land had misplaced their sense of responsibility, and began to rely solely on the intervention of the Elves to save them at their every whim," he answered her, "an unfair expectation that led us to this current state," he waved his hands at the filthy trash-ridden streets of their city, "instead of taking action by our own hands, we had waited too long for the Elves to be our saviors yet again; a mistake that had cost us dearly."

Ivy understood what he meant, as the lady Dawn had admitted the failures of the High Elves and their inability to spread themselves so very thin. Everyone in the Faerylands had held them in such esteem, they had not realized what a burden it had become to the gentle elves, whose willingness to assist others had grown to be so terribly abused.

The relic known as the Tears of Sorrow had led them thus far; its very existence was created by the Dwarven race who themselves held a seeded grudge against the Elves for neglecting to assist them in a time of dire need. Ivy could see now just how heavy a burden the races across this land had placed on the shoulders of the Elves, who had feared to reveal their dwindling numbers either out of concern or sheer pride.

Meridian had been right, Ivy reflected, individual choices were made based on nothing more than arrogance and secrecy had created a rift among the many tribes of beings across the world. Hopefully, it was a blunder that could someday be cured. Peace among the races was a fragile thing, maintained only as long as expectations were fair and balanced. Ivy was no diplomat, but she understood the dilemma created by a series of poor choices from those in power who call themselves kings and chiefs and high priests across the far lands. Now everyone was at the mercy of the Craven and the threat it now posed.

Across an open courtyard though a street lined with dead trees, the three companions approached the tall northern gate. It was an imposing structure that had been reinforced because of the frequent assaults by several breeds of strange and vicious beasts that had encroached upon their borders in recent years. Those few guards left here no longer patrolled the streets to enforce order, but were left to defend the walls from the foul creatures that threatened to overrun the city. With the Dwarven army guarding the southern gate, the people here had nowhere left to run. Few had ever seen the lone mage so far from his tower.

"Halt there," a burley guard wearing a mismatched shamble of armor dared to step forth, while warily eyeing the glowing staff the wizard held. Magic among these parts had become a rare sight ever since the members of the mages guild had dwindled away into obscurity.

"We require passage to the northern road," Meridian stated while the two faeries stood safely behind him. His brash statement brought a doubtful chuckle from among the few guardsmen present.

"You really want to go out there?" the bearded soldier laughed, "maybe you might want to donate your valuables before you march to your death, I'll make good use of them ...I promise." he blabbered in jest as he swaggered over to take the staff from the old man. Meridian would not tolerate the lack of respect, and stomped his conjuring staff once upon the ground, causing arcs of electricity to shoot forth, just short of scorching the sentry who nearly fell over as he stumbled back out of the way. This brazen show of force rightly changed the attitude of the patrolman.

"The gate!" Meridian demanded once again, while flipping a gleaming gold coin onto the man's chest as he lay there prostrate. With a quick eye to the valuable token, he scampered up to his feet and ordered his men to remove the thick barrier that braced the lower gate. Curious dark eyes glared at them from beneath rusting helmets as they cranked the taut ropes to swing the heavy doors wide with a piercing creak. Once opened, a foul wind blew upon them, as the tarnished land greeted them with its sour kiss.

The two faeries covered their noses from the noxious smell, an odor so strange and putrid that it was beyond naming. Stepping forth into the harsh wind, they fought their way past the safety of the gate that slammed shut behind them; its echo drifting across the bogs along the bottom edge of the trail. Making their way down the wide path, it wasn't long before the road itself began to fade into the overgrown weeds of the northern bog. After lack of maintenance for centuries, this route to the northern borders of the coast had all but vanished.

Meridian led them directly west towards the coastline, not wishing to linger too long in the overgrown marshlands that had encroached southward over the years. Scores of glowing eyes peered at them from distant shadows, and a ceaseless noise of clicking broke the stillness, permeating the pools of drifting fog. The faeries could tell this was an unpleasant place to tread, and had no desire to wander far from the wizard's sight.

Stepping just off the path, Jinx cut her tender feet several times on sharp spines jutting through the coarse sand. They weren't from any type of plant she could tell, but appeared to be made of a type of hardened shell. With a strip of cloth, the mage bound her feet as best he could, advising the two girls they should hover off the ground when they were able, for lack of protective footwear. This part of the marsh was eerie: a meld of sand and rock and overgrown ferns. Moss hung heavily off dying willow trees and jagged boulders that littered the border between sea and swamp. Still, there was life teeming here, though the trio couldn't help the overwhelming feeling of being someplace they weren't meant to be.

Even flying here was dangerous, curtains of moss hanging from the limbs of trees left a sticky residue when touched; and picking it off their wings was a nightmare. Everything here had a rancid stench to it that permeated the air, making it hard to breathe. The two girls were eager to get to the shoreline, though the wizard seemed apprehensive about wandering into the full clearing of the open beach. Large black stones worn by time and the molding hands of the ocean waves clumped near the shore. A wide stretch of the coastline marked the fringe of where water and earth each struggled for control.

The odd barbs in the sand were plentiful, and the two faeries had to rely on the moss covered boulders to rest upon as they followed their escort across the sandy grass filled dunes. The lapping of waves was to their left, and the air heavy with the smell of salt hammered at them. The ocean was cold and grey, frothing with foam as the waves lashed upon the shore; embracing it only for a moment before withdrawing again into the churning sea. Jinx wanted to be thrilled for seeing the ocean for the first time, but the waters here were harsh and violent as the frigid wind, and murky as the bleak and foreboding horizon.

To rest, the trio made a modest shelter out of branches and bundles of grass to sleep upon. Meridian lacked any spells that would serve them in that manner, as he had never foreseen a use before this day to make it a subject of study. Huddled in the small lean-to they had erected in haste, the girls caught up on some much-needed sleep. Difficult as it was to keep from waking every few moments from the wail of the howling wind, the wizard kept watch for any wild beasts that might wander into their camp. Pausing to catch the sliver of the crescent moon above, the old mage caught a brief glimpse of it through the stirring clouds drifting across the night sky.

Though it didn't seem much like summer in this land, the solstice had passed and the time when the influence of the moon would expose the secret path from the mainland to the isle of Tyre was close upon them. It was a navigational hazard only known among the sailing merchants centuries past, whenever the sea withdrew to a low tide. It was a rare phenomena that only happened during this time of the year. Having no love or stomach for sailing vessels, it was an event the dwarves took advantage of long ago to march their armies by foot directly to the island. As fate would later tell, it had been the last journey for thousands of soldiers who had lost their lives, never to return this way again.

Waking to the cold breeze, Ivy rubbed her tired eyes to find Meridian overlooking the shore on the low dune before them. It was a troubled look in his eyes she caught when he turned to her for a moment, not speaking a word. It took a great deal of effort to wake Jinx, who would rather have stayed curled in a ball to dream away this dreary place.

On the last leg of their journey to this remote passage they stumbled upon a strange sight. Among the worn boulders that littered this stretch of shore, Ivy's keen eyes caught something unusual. A strange formation of rocks that seemed to withdraw when a short sprinkle of rain washed over them. She tugged on the cuff of the wizard's robe to get his attention, since he seemed to only be concentrating on his footing. It was clear he was not used to extending this much physical effort, and his tired bones complained with every step.

"What is it?" he responded to the fairy, her almond eyes now weary and red from the biting wind. Pointing, Ivy directed his gaze towards a distant clump of stone, as big as a two story hovel. The old wizard glared at her, having not seen what she was upset about, as Jinx caught up from behind to ask what the commotion was about. "There's nothing there..." he trailed off with a shrug, his words lost in the wind.

An errant flash of lightning lit up the formation for a few brief seconds. It was hard to tell at first glance, but the contrast of black stone stood out from the rough discolored rock that sat wedged within its crevice. His aging eyes weren't as keen as the faeries, so the wizard took a step forward to get a better look. A second flash of lightening caught him in mid-step, as Jinx shrieked in alarm when two large orbs suddenly emerged from the rock face and shifted towards them.

The creatures eyes were horrible to behold. Their elongated iris was encircled by several rings of purple and burnt orange. The beasts' unearthly stare filled them with dread. It was huge, with a thick boney exoskeleton that nearly camouflaged its girth within the surrounding rock. It was like no crustacean that Meridian had ever seen, but something out of a nightmare breeding of a squid and a crab. Instead of pincers, several tentacles lashed forth beneath its shell like writhing serpents. It pulled itself forward out of the crack of rock to assault them; its deathly silence making it even more horrifying.

To their surprise, Jinx was the first to react. Pulling her bow to the ready, an arrow of pure flame materialized and she let loose a volley. Unfortunately, the arrow disintegrated on its thick armor, leaving nothing but a scorch mark. Meridian discovered he wasn't ready for this encounter, as he had heard rumors of deformed beasts roaming the swamps; but nothing had prepared him for this. The sheer size of the creature and its hard shell made it a formidable foe. It seemed to be slow-moving at first glance, which they could use to their advantage; however, that deception was short-lived.

Its eyes were cold and unblinking as the monster lurched forward and snatched Ivy up by the waist as it used its other tentacles to pull itself towards the open beach. Finding herself suddenly upside-down, Ivy had lost hold of her spear when she was jerked off her feet. It fell to the coarse sand as Meridian held forth his staff, but quickly ceased his spell. The thing would likely burn, but he immediately stopped his conjuration when it grabbed the dark-haired fairy, who would also be baked in any fireball he might cast. In this buffeting wind, there would be too wide a space for error to control the mystic blue flame. Fire was not the answer.

Jinx continued to spray arrows onto the beast to no avail; though try as she might to aim for its eyes, her skill was not honed enough to counter the raging winds from the sea. Meridian saw where Ivy's spear had fallen, but their situation became more desperate when the monster scrambled out towards the ocean waves; holding Ivy aloft as its prize. To the woodland sprite, the world was spinning as she was swung about at the end of its squeezing tentacle.

The wizard jumped back out of its way as the giant beast lunged forward, burying the spear beneath the sand as it trampled over it with its bulk. Jinx growled in anger, unable to get in a clear shot past its armor; finding her attacks entirely ineffective. Ivy screamed again, not only from the pain of the barbs of its tentacles coiled around her, but also as she caught a glimpse of the fast approaching sea; realizing she was about to be dragged beneath the waves where she would be beyond any hope of rescue.

Neither Meridian nor Jinx knew of her bestowed enchantment by the water spirits, and presumed she would drown. Needless to say, being torn apart and eaten by the crawling nightmare would just as likely be her fate. Jinx chased after her, firing arrow after arrow that would only snuff out with a small spark upon its thick shell. Frantically looking about, Meridian abandoned his staff and began to dig for the missing spear now buried somewhere beneath the tossed sand.

"Ivy ...Ivy!" Jinx cried out in despair, helpless to stop the giant monster as it carried her companion away towards the cold, churning ocean. She ran after the beast, showing no absence of courage, desperate to try anything to stop her friend from being killed.

With a crack of thunder, Jinx shrieked and was thrown to her side as a blinding streak of white light shot past her from behind. Meridian had found the enchanted weapon buried in the sand, and conjured a lightning bolt using his left hand to direct it onto the short spear in his right; using it to channel the energy at the beast. The shell glowed red hot where it had been struck after a shower of sparks exploded upon its rear.

The creature spun about in agony to see the source of the attack and Meridian standing there with the spear, thin arcs of electricity dripping off of it into the ground at his feet. Turning as it did in haste, it also used the tentacle which still bound Ivy, slamming her less than gently into the sandy beach as it circled. Scrambling, Ivy knew she only had one chance to escape; for if the beast chose to retreat into the waves, there would be no stopping it a second time.

She placed both her feet and a free hand onto the ground, and sprouted her roots as deeply as she could. She had never before attempted this feat instantaneously, and the effort drove her head dizzy to the point she nearly lost consciousness. It was only possible since the wet sand gave little resistance to her spreading roots, and she dug herself in deeply.

The beast lurched forward to ensnare the wizard, who was exhausted from casting such a powerful spell. It was all he could do at the moment, without taking the risk of hurting Ivy. Its tentacles shot forth, only to strain and fall short by mere feet from the staggering mage, who leaned away, wide-eyed with fear. This confused the beast who turned its hideous eyes back towards its one arm left behind that now held it firmly anchored as it tugged furiously.

Though in deep pain, Ivy knew she had no other choice but to fight back; and with her free arm she grasped onto the tentacle that bound her. From her fingers, transformed roots snaked and curled up the taut squid arm, binding it in a cage of wood. Up underneath the hardened armor and into the soft flesh, the roots crept, slithering their way through its organs and the spongy pulp of the mindless beast, goring it with a thousand javelins. Meridian looked on in wonder as dozens of roots erupted from beneath the monsters shell; ripping through its ghastly eyes, which suddenly froze and dimmed into lifelessness.

Ivy passed out from the fatigue, and the roots immediately retracted from the corpse of the beast, back into her body. Jinx got up ever so slowly, still dizzy from the concussion while shaking the sand from her hair. She had entirely missed what had just happened; and was astonished to find Ivy laying curled in the sand with a thick tentacle of the dead monster still wrapped loosely around her. Running over, she pried the arm off of the wood sprite, who lay senseless on the beach. Meridian himself felt drained, and finding it difficult to keep his balance, he struggled to retrieve his crooked staff.

"Oh, Ivy, you can't be dead." Jinx pleaded, trying to wake her friend without success.

"Here, let me help move her," the mage instructed, knowing Jinx had reason to be apprehensive about touching her friend.

Removing his outer robe, he wrapped Ivy within it. With great effort, he picked her up and carried her from the beach to the cover of several large boulders. Still, a bit wary that more of these beasts might be lurking in the rocky shadows, he set her down gently as Jinx followed close behind. It would take some time before Ivy's wounds would heal, her body was cut and bruised from the abuse she had received during the struggle with the nightmare beast.

Jinx watched over her as Meridian marched back to retrieve his staff and the short spear he had dropped in his effort to carry the unconscious fairy. He stared out northward across the windy beach, calculating their time to traverse this hostile landscape.

"I'm afraid we may have to return to the city until your friend has fully recovered." the wizard suggested woefully to the small luck fairy who sat curled beside Ivy. He wasn't exactly sure how he would manage to get her back all the way to Thieves Gate in her current state, or what effect it would have for the two fey to abandon their quest at this stage.

"But, we can't," Jinx appealed, tending to her friend, "if Ivy can't make it, then I'll have to go on alone." she answered, with a pleading look in her eyes.

"You wouldn't survive an instant out there." Meridian shook his head; their most recent encounter served as a sobering testament to that fact. "I was foolish to think that you two could manage with merely a few wizards tricks," he added with a skeptical tone as he pointed to their enchanted weapons that sat leaning against the stone, "and I am far too old to make such a journey, even if I could." he declared to the small sprite.

"But we can't wait, we ...I, at least have to try." Jinx corrected herself, secretly hoping that she would not have to go alone.

Meridian realized that the time of passage to the island was upon them, and it would be another full year before these two emissaries could make another attempt at reaching the island. That is, if Ivy survived her injuries. They weren't entirely severe, but Meridian actually knew nothing of faeries concerning the true frailty of these enchanted beings.

"I believe the High Elves that sent you will understand if you cannot complete your quest this moment, young girl. Your journey is rife with peril, and it would merely be foolish to believe that you..." the wizard began to lecture before Jinx interrupted him.

"Stop talking to me like I'm a child," she scolded him, "I'm probably older than you are!" she shocked him with her tone, but he realized with a raised brow, that her brash statement might be entirely true, "I never told Ivy that the Elves pressed upon me that we have to find a way to stop the Craven before the turning of the first leaf of autumn." she revealed with a hint of humility drifting back into her voice.

This was a predicament. Meridian himself had squandered away so many countless years, hoping the scourge of the Craven would eventually fade away; or that the Elves might someday reappear to set the world straight. He had never dared to suspect that their time was shorter than he or anyone had feared to guess. If the patient Elves in their countless eons were suddenly pressed for time, then certainly something was most terribly wrong.

"There isn't much I can do for your friend, I know little of medicine or even what to do for her." the old mage admitted with saddened eyes. It took a few moments for Jinx, burdened with her heavy heart, to suddenly spring with a light in her eyes as a thought came to mind.

"What do you do when you made those meals for us, the flowers and mushrooms and other greens?" she asked curiously. Meridian didn't know what she was getting at, but it seemed like a frivolous waste of time for her to be thinking about food at this very moment.

"We should really try to figure a way to get Ivy back to the city, you can always eat later." he grumbled with a disapproving tone. Jinx was obviously frustrated by his response, having misread her as he did.

"Don't be silly, I'm not trying to stuff my face!" she chastised him, "I need to know what kind of magic you use to create the plants you fed us." she tried to explain, though Meridian was still lost on the relevance. "Ivy is a wood sprite..." she led on, trying to get the old wizard to realize that fact.

With a quirk and twinge of his brow, the mage worked the problem in his head as he attempted to conceive what Jinx had meant. In short order, it dawned on him the possibilities he had not dared to consider. These faeries were not entirely flesh and bone, but born of nature by the hand of the Elves. What he had seen Ivy do to that monstrous creature was not the result of some petty spell, but an extension of what she was. Recalling her quaint story of being a tree in a forest; her transformation wasn't a mere enchantment conjured by some cheap potion or mumbled incantation, it was her natural element. What the little luck fairy was suggesting was actually quite conceivable; he could effectively heal Ivy by using a creation enchantment to help her body mend.

It was a simple spell he had perfected over the years, a mere parlor trick really. Producing flowers from thin air was taught within every magicians first academic year. Common street vendors could spawn silk flowers by sheer slight of hand, but a true mage could make living bouquets that would blossom before your very eyes. It was a quant testament to the creation of life. With a little work, one could create fields of flowers and green grass, which they used to impress the young maidens from time to time. It was also applied to aid crops of wheat in the fields, or grow ornamental vines across fences and awnings of grand mansions and private chateaus of rich barons who could pay the landscaping fees for such enchantments.

In this case, all he had to do was help Ivy mend herself by applying the basic elements of the spell to nurture her. Plants were very complicated things, but were remarkably self-sustaining given the proper elements.

Meridian wove the spell as Jinx watched in amazement. Between his curling hands emerged a ball of light, tiny speckled strings that glowed so brightly they lost form. He coiled and curled them with whispers as they laced together to take shape. Winding this ribbon of light, he breathed it onto Ivy's wounds where they submerged beneath her delicate skin. Then for a brief moment, her whole body glowed from within, to the tips of her ears and the strand of every hair turning momentarily white. Her true color returned as the glittering sheen covering her skin slowly faded away. Meridian bit his lip in hopes that he had gotten the spell right, and she wouldn't suddenly start sprouting mushrooms or flowers all over her body.

Jinx smiled tenderly as Ivy's eyes opened. Ivy felt quite peculiar, yet didn't know how to describe the sensation. The last thing she remembered was fighting for her life to escape from that armored beast, and using all her strength to defend herself. It was something she had never done before, and the drain from of the exertion had turned everything black. Now the pain was suddenly gone, and she felt herself again ...but not.

"Are you all right?" Jinx pleaded softly, with slight despair at being unable to give her even the simplest of physical comforts like holding her hand.

"Yes," she paused, appearing slightly disoriented, looking around at her present company, "but I feel kinda strange..." she trailed off in thought, unable to provide a more vivid portrayal of how she felt. Jinx looked at Meridian with worry, as he gave a guilty glance back towards the little fey. At least she was lucid enough to speak.

"I would still think it prudent if we returned to the guild, and work out a better means of transport to the island. Perhaps you can attempt to contact the Elves some way to tell them of your delay." the old mage advised, but Jinx knew they had no time to spare, and shook her head.

"No, she's okay, we can still make the passage." Jinx affirmed with a resistive tone. Ivy looked around, abruptly noting that the subject of the controversy revolved around her.

"We made it this far, Meridian, we really need to make it to the tower and find the Drow; they will help us from there." Ivy affirmed to the old mage who looked at her with tender concern.

"Are you certain you are up to this?" he inquired.

"Yes, I feel fine ...it's just that for some reason, you both look like ghosts." she turned to them with her wide eyes that were no longer emerald green, but had turned a faded shade of silver.

*   *   *

Malice

"What did you do to her?" Jinx spat out, grieving for Ivy. The old wizard had not a clue, for he had never used such a spell on a living being.

"There's no way to be certain, but likely it's just a side effect that should fade after time." Meridian offered as an excuse, though hoping his presumption was true. Ivy, however, seemed to be in shock. Everything around her appeared to lack color, the landscape was saturated in deep hues, and opposite in contrast. The dark skies now seemed quite white, the ocean glowed with a sheen of its own, and here two companions appeared like ethereal wisps in her eyes. It was all really quite disturbing.

"Do you think you can stand, Ivy?" Jinx asked with concern, wondering if the wizard's spell had in some way blinded her.

"I'm all right Jinx, it's just that everything looks so strange..." she trailed off, looking around the cold windy beach. The dead grass was now a shining silver, and the light sand of the shore was black as coal. It would take some getting used to, though; it was like awakening to a whole new world.

"What is it you see?" Meridian asked the wood sprite, trying to diagnose her condition.

"Everything is so bright, and you both seem like you're made out of mist." she answered, touching the wizard's smoky hand for a moment, to make sure it was real. Curling his brow in thought, in his studies the wizard had read of similar symptoms. There were certain nocturnal creatures that had an exaggerated form of night vision that allowed them to see in complete darkness as if in full daylight. What bothered him though, was that such creatures were usually associated with vile and accursed beasts of the darkest parts of the underworld.

Ivy looked at her own hands for a moment with interest, as they also seemed ethereal to her altered eyes. Her balance seemed to be fine, and her wounds fully healed; apparently it was only her vision that had changed.   Though Ivy was suffering from some sort of malady, it wasn't serious enough for them to abandon their quest, and Ivy agreed.

Wielding her spear once again, Ivy urged that they continue on, as the turning of the new moon was at hand. The ocean tide began to withdraw more noticeably as they made their way north up the beach; wary of each and every crop of boulders that might well hide one of those monstrous shelled squids. With her new vision, Ivy was the first to notice the emerging sand bar far in the distance.

Long before they were near the pass, they stumbled upon thousands of crab shells that began to litter the beach. It was a strange sight, their small legs curled up, the shells crunching loudly beneath the wizard's feet. The two fey had to hover over them when they could, as their thorny caprices were sharp as jagged stone. Kicking a few about, the wizard noted something of interest.

"Hmm," he murmured.

"What killed them all?" Jinx whispered, staring out at the hundreds upon thousands of dead crabs now littering the beach as far as they could see.

"Well, they're not actually dead, my girl, see?" he dared to pick one up to show her. What appeared as millions of dead crabs were actually just empty shells. "Apparently they have molted," he suggested.

"Molted?" the little luck fairy asked, not being familiar with the word.

"Yes, they shed their shells; much like a snake sheds its skin. They've outgrown them." he informed her.

Ivy also found this interesting, though she was still dazzled enough by the change in her sight to be too astonished over their intriguing discovery. The old wizard, having studied most of his life, wondered if these might be the brood of the species of armored squid they had recently met, momentarily horrified by the sheer number of monstrosities that they might spawn. Though, in perspective, these shells appeared to be of regular crabs; of a variety of different sizes and shapes, and they all had claws unlike the tentacles of the behemoth they had fought.

Struggling against the harsh wind that began to kick up over the strange beach, the wizard was disturbed to find something else he had never seen before. What had seemed like an unusually large clump of boulders at a distance from the exposed sandbar was a colossal sculpture of a nightmarish monster. Half-buried in the sand, it sat facing out towards the ocean; its eyes beheld an evil glare, and its form was not of any beast of nature. The dwarves would never carve such a thing; the question was, who had placed it here?

"What is that?" Ivy asked the mage, noting the strange idol marking the hidden passage to Tyre. Meridian had studied countless scripts and tomes, but there had never been any mention of such a landmark placed here; nor did he recognize what type of wicked creature is was supposed to represent. Not knowing the full purpose of the profane idol, he searched for an answer.

"It appears to be a signpost to mark the submerged passage to the island."

The black glossy stone seemed to fit the creature well; it was the image of a crouching beast either resting or prepared to spring on its prey. Whatever it was, it was clearly a predator. Standing before it, the trio looked out towards the receding ocean as the sandbar road emerged from the cold gray waves. Beached fish flopped in the shallow waters as the shore pulled away. Some were colorful, armored with long spikes and jagged fins. Others were so odd in shape, they were truly unpleasant to look at; their bulbous eyes twitching as they suffocated in the frigid air. Though Ivy would be able to exist under the surface of the waves, unlike her colleagues, these soiled waters were murky and thick with silt.

"This is where I must leave you," the wizard affirmed, feeling an unshakeable twinge of guilt, but knowing he had responsibilities of his own. Havoc would be wreaked if any of the powerful relics in the mages' guild should fall into the wrong hands. He had to resume his duties as the sanctuary's last living guardian. Wards had to be inscribed and spells renewed, it was a never ending task to keep the wizards enchanted treasures and their secrets safe from outsiders.

"Remember to use your wits, and the weapons you now master close at hand." he advised, with a look of worry heavy upon his wrinkled brow.

"Thank you Meridian, perhaps we will meet again." Ivy offered with sincerity, as Jinx nodded silently with her magic bow in hand. Turning toward the sandbar, the path seemed endless as it emptied into the horizon. Somewhere out there was the isle of Tyre, and Ivy began to wonder if she would ever see her green forests again.

Fondling the bracelet on her wrist, she gazed out upon the trail before them with her strange eyes. The sandbar was moist under their tender feet, still saturated with the salty sea lapping at its edge. It was of considerable size, and barely wide enough to allow the passing of a marching army, though not so broad as to be a comfortable reach from the churning seas, where great slithering beasts lurked beneath the surface. Frequently, their scaled coils would skim the surface of the waves, warning of their presence. These sea serpents glared at their prey from beneath the waters, daring them to wander too close to the edge of the path.

Both girls jumped when a serpent of considerable size leapt out of the water with an enormous fish wiggling in its maw, only to plunge beneath the waves with its meal twitching in its long sharp teeth. Either out of prudence or panic, Jinx let out a few volleys into the water with her flaming arrows to ward off the beasts; but the shots only sizzled into harmless vapor as they hit the chilly waters.

Great sculptures of native coral lined the sandbar, with thick branches twisting in agony like a forest of chalky stone. Shells of every shape littered the path, wet and glittering in the fading light. Many were prismatic in color, like rainbows in the sand; a few they passed were immense, so large that Jinx could have crawled snugly inside. The living reef bordered the edge of the sandy trail, lined with branches of delicate coral. Their brittle weave and exotic hue reminded Ivy of her visit to Naru long past, where the mermaids lived in palaces beneath the emerald oceans, however, these waters were hostile and unlivable, a churning pool of dangerous and vicious beasts far removed from the world of the graceful merfolk.

Making their way through the forest of twisted coral that lined their path, more than once Jinx had emptied a few fiery shafts into the looming head of a hungry serpent who dared to wander too close. Ivy wondered what little use her spear was without lightning surging through it. Its short length was clearly designed for close combat, but not quite usable as a ranged weapon when not energized. One toss at a sea creature, and the enchanted weapon would be forever lost beneath the rolling waves.

The two friends made little conversation as they progressed, and it was actually Jinx who was bright enough to ponder on a subject of note that Ivy had failed to consider. After reaching the shore of the island, it would most certainly take them more than a few days to make their way to the Tower of Madness; let alone to find the lady Sorrow. So after the passing of the new moon, how were they to get back? The oceans would submerge this passage for the next year, and secretly, Jinx knew they weren't graced with much time.

Ivy didn't have any answers, nor did she have the energy to squabble about the predicament they were clearly walking into. She only hoped the High Elves had a plan to rescue them from the isle of Tyre once their quest was complete. Unless of course, this was a blind lead finding Sorrow, and just another leg in their journey to find the answers they sought. Ivy didn't like being left in the dark, unsure of what fate they might be weaving for themselves. With an ounce of faith, the Drow would help enlighten them at their journey's end.

The natural sandbar had eroded over time, and frequently dipped dangerously close to the water's edge along its path. It was here that the two girls stumbled upon several sunken ships that had rammed against the barrier reef, their broken hulls scattered along the path. Likely, the crew tried to use this route as a shortcut along the coast, rather than skirting the dreaded isle of Tyre. In mid-winter the route may have been passable, but at any other time, any vessel over laden with cargo would sit much too far below the waterline to safely avoid this ridge. The legendary pass that was known only by a handful of seasoned captains had dissolved into forgotten fables told by drunken sailors in the backrooms of harbor taverns.

Here, many of those ship hands had entered the last chapter of their lives, the curved planks and towering masts of their shattered vessels lay sadly upon the sandbar, covered in parasitic coral like a diseased leper. Stepping into one ship along their path that had been gored straight through, a chaotic mound of broken barrels filled with rancid spices and jarred chests lay strewn about its inner hold. Treasures of shimmering gold and rubies spilled about in plain view, testimony that this passage had not been used for many centuries. Jinx picked up one of these gold doubloons that lay glinting by her foot, and examined its intricate design.

"What are these, Ivy, there are so many of them?" she peered about the shattered hull as they continued on their way, gazing at the piles of thousands of tiny golden discs stamped with their strange images and mysterious runes.

"I haven't a clue," Ivy admitted, remembering the lost temple in a distant jungle she had once visited, and the idol there with mounds of such baubles piled at its feet. After a short moment, Jinx lost interest in the trinket and tossed it back over her shoulder without a second glance. The gold coin came to rest at the edge of the ships bow that lay half buried in the sand. There it twinkled as it lay leaning against a rotted wood bust carved with artistic flair into the stunning image of a mermaid.

Making their way off the higher plateau of the sandbar, the island of Tyre crept into view. It materialized as a foreboding dark mountain rising out of the cold sea, surrounded by a ring of clouds that nearly blanketed its high rocky cliffs; an impossible barrier to any ships attempting to land. The sheer stone walls loomed over them as they approached the edge of the island. The two fey stepped gingerly among giant clams that lay open in this momentary reprieve from the salty sea; exposing enormous pearls the size of their fists resting in the beds of soft white flesh, only to snap shut violently when the fairies ventured a step too near.

The sharp biting wind made it difficult to keep aloft in flight for the two fairies. The cliffs would have been impassable if not for the several stairways etched into the side of the rocky cleft, leading from the sandbar trail and snaking their way up the cleft. They appeared to be roughly made, as if carved in haste with neither care nor form, barely wide enough for the streaming legions of dwarves who had made them eons ago. Now worn by time and the erosion of the seas, they were chiseled from the raw black stone of the island's foundation; the very same ebony rock that formed the strange idol that sat brooding on the distant shore from whence they came.

Climbing the steps was much more exhausting for the two fey than they would have imagined; for the very air here seemed heavy and thick with moisture. Almost imperceptible, a low rumble could be heard by their pointed ears; a hum they could feel from the very rock beneath their feet. Together, puffing for breath as they climbed, Ivy and Jinx were wide-eyed with astonishment as they breached the edge of the cliff. The black stone beneath them faded into a horizon of white, bleached by a blanket of frost and snow. Something was terribly wrong here.

Meridian had warned them that the island had been cursed, but never explained the manner. Here, the very essence of nature had been twisted and crippled. Creeping their way up onto the frost-covered ridge, Jinx brushed the loose sand from her bow as Ivy hefted her spear. The wizard had cautioned them thoroughly about the dangers that lurked on this isolated pedestal above the murky seas. The isle of Tyre had been transformed from the tropical paradise it once was to this desolate sterile wasteland of rock and ice.

Thick mist pooled around the foothills that bordered the outer edge of the rocky shore. Beyond, a vast tundra stretched out over the uneven plain, shattered rifts lay broken across the landscape like open wounds. The absence of foliage made Ivy uneasy. Attuned to the nature of plants, she wondered if the frozen soil itself had been poisoned. Rooting herself might have dire consequences if she became tainted by any toxin that slumbered within and would hamper her ability to transform.

Jinx herself seemed a bit more susceptible to the cold than her companion. A wood sprite was able to bear the coldest of winters, but Jinx was a fairy from the protected groves and not used to such extremes. Here the frigid air bit at her tiny fingers which had turned white as the bitter frost. The vapor of their breath billowed around them at every word they shared.

"What now? If there was a path here once, it has long since been swept away by the snow." Jinx advised as they peered out on the broken plain, streams of sunlight cutting through the drifting clouds above like daggers. Though as barren as this place was, there was a certain beauty in its stillness. What Ivy saw through her enchanted eyes was quite different from that of her companion. A land of black ice, with glowing rifts cutting through the land.

"I would imagine this tower should be easy to spot, and hopefully within we will find the Drow." Ivy added, wondering how any elf would be able to live in these frozen badlands.

Glacial drifts swooped down from the high mountains that snaked through the valley like a white python, the ridges of its peaks marking the backbone of the island itself. Death lurked here, and they could feel it sucking the life out of them by the touch of its frigid breath. The two fey came to a halt whenever an errant howl broke the silence, uncertain whether it was from the wind or the wail of a feral beast stalking these arctic dunes.

As they made their way under a curtain of ice along the edge of a rocky cleft, they came to a stop. Ahead in the distance was a dark object set high atop a jagged peak. It was a spire resting impossibly on the very brink of a massive ledge overhanging a vast emptiness. Below in its shadow, enormous icicles hung, yearning to reach the ground far below. If that was the tower of madness, it had been deformed over time and appeared far different from the impressive image sketched within Meridian's ancient tomes.

It was a long distance to cover, and Jinx kept a fire arrow on the draw of her bow to warm her numb fingers. Ivy's back ached, as did her companion's, who noted cracks at the tips of her delicate wings. Ivy tested her own wings, only to find the pain nearly unbearable as the nerves in their membranes screamed, not wishing to be stretched in the slightest. Jinx, too, was afraid her fragile wings would snap or shatter in the unbearable cold. Unlike Ivy's thin fleshy wings, Jinx could not regenerate hers if they were injured; and she would be crippled for life.

They agreed that it would be safer to make their way along the ridgeline until they reached the shortest span across the plains below. The foreboding tower stood near the middle of the island, shrouded in mist. It was a landmark they had to reach by the end of the day, or they would not have enough time to make it back before the sea once again swallowed the sandbar passage; their only means of escape off this desolate island. Making their way across the icy ridge, they stumbled across remnants of the island's past life of frozen shrubs and fallen trees which lay camouflaged under the blanket of frost that crunched beneath their feet.

The day fell away into dusk as they made headway towards the tower, with nothing but the piercing whistle of the cold wind as their companion. As the shimmer of twilight fell across the plain, Jinx spotted something in the distance moving towards a forest of shattered ice. Ivy, too, could see it, but to her the light appeared as a shimmering ball trailing smoke behind it as the object weaved its way through the frozen boulders of compacted snow. Barely perceptible, almost covered behind the moving orb, Ivy could see another glowing figure; this one ethereal.

The two girls crouched behind the rocks as the strange creature approached, and Jinx readied an arrow which glowed warmly against the deep blue of the snow around them. The crunch of frost became louder at each step it took, as the girls were left wondering what kind of predator was hunting them. When they heard it draw within range, the two girls mustered enough bravado to jump out from behind the broken ring of stones from where they hid; daring to meet this mysterious monster face to face.

With a cry of false rage, they both leapt up, Ivy with spear in hand, poised to launch it at the creature just as Jinx jumped upon a rock to take aim at ...a small, startled girl with braided white hair of Ivy's height, crouched in fear at their sudden attack. Ivy's and her companion's battle cry died away abruptly as they looked at the scared girl, wondering what she was doing here in the middle of this forsaken wasteland.

Her skin was an odd shade of pale, almost indigo in color; while her eyes were large and black as the night sky, though ringed with a vivid tinge of red. She was wearing a strangely laced gown of blue velvet, with her soft, white hair braided into a long tail. The oddest thing about her of all, though, was the large golden lantern at the tip of a short rod she was carrying, which glowed brightly to light her way; but which clearly appeared to be chained to her own wrist. The three girls stood there staring at each other in silence, as the night wind continued to howl around them.

"Oh, I'm sorry, we both thought you were a..." Ivy offered apologetically as she put down her spear, displaying that they meant the girl no harm. Jinx, too, lowered her bow as she gave Ivy an incredible look mixed with astonishment and a measure of guilt. The strange girl stood slowly, looking at the two naked fey, their frozen wings folded behind them.

"You thought I was a what?" the girl seemed to hiss, until it was quite clear that that was the way she actually spoke, "I don't know where you two came from, but if you want to live past this night, I suggest that you follow me ...quickly!" she added in haste as she scanned the valley behind her, then waved the two faeries to follow. The girl was apparently in a hurry as she chose to forego any introductions and tromped off in the direction she had been heading before the two fey girls had nearly pounced on her. The lantern was very bright, but the girl seemed to be holding it as low as possible, stifling its effectiveness. The lamp's ornate golden cage held a glowing orb within its frame, while the opposite end of the shaft it was attached to ended in a short chain bolted to a thick cuff set about the girls right wrist.

Imploring them to hurry along, Jinx and Ivy followed closely behind, wondering what it was the pale girl was continually looking back down towards the dark plain below. It wasn't long until an icy wind began to kick up drifts of snow, which blocked their sight. The arched mouth of a cave suddenly appeared beside their path through the thickening snowfall, lit by the lamp of their escort far ahead. Motioning them to get inside, the small cave was barely big enough for the three of them to fit.

It dipped steeply inward from the lip of the cave, and they huddled down into the bowl of the grotto. The bare stone was cold, but fair relief from the biting wind just a few feet outside the mouth of the entrance, from which thick icicles hung like horrible fangs, making them feel as if they had been swallowed. The strange girl kept her troubled eyes focused on the mouth of the frozen cave.

"Thank you, we almost didn't make it to shelter before that storm hit." Jinx added, shaking the flakes of snow from her short hair. The brightness of the golden lantern cast harsh shadows dancing about the cave, as its radiant light flickered from within; though it shed no heat.

"It's not the storm I'm worried about," the pale girl noted with her strange hissing whisper of words, "Peek outside and tell me if you see anything." But Jinx just looked at her oddly, noting the bizarre request.

"But, you have the lantern." Jinx responded with logic.

"Exactly." she shrugged with a curt reply.

With a slight grumble, Ivy noted that Jinx was up to her old self and rubbing their visitor the wrong way. The wood sprite crawled up to the lip of the doorway herself and peered out into the churning snow. A moment later, Jinx came up to join her at her side.

"I don't see anything." Jinx shrugged, as only the dark blue plain of ice lay outside the slope below them. Ivy, however, observed something quite different. Maybe a half dozen or more white specks were moving across the tundra in their direction. They would infrequently pool together for but a moment, only to spread out across the trail. With her crippled sight, she couldn't make out what they might possibly be.

"Actually," Ivy corrected, "I see something, more than a few of them coming straight this way."

"I was hoping I had lost them," the pale girl whispered with her heavy strained speech, a voice most unnatural. But the two fey had seen many strange things in their journeys, so it was nothing to poke fun at. Slipping back down into the glowing

light of the lantern, the two companions sat beside their new
guest, wondering what trouble they had stumbled into.

"What are they?" Ivy dared to ask.

"Ice ghouls." the girl responded with a tone of dread, as she
rubbed the sore wrist of her shackled arm.

"That might be a good idea to keep from losing your lantern,
but doesn't it hurt?" Jinx blurted in her childish ignorance as she
pointed at the chained cuff. The pale girl gave her a baleful
glare for her stupidity, but realized these two fey were not from
the island nor privy to their customs.

"If I could be rid of it I would," she hissed in her strange tone,
"*this* is what the ghouls are tracking!"

"What is it?" Jinx asked, in all innocence, gently touching the
surface of the bright orb. Ivy, too, turned to observe the strange
lamp.

"Elfire, the flame of life. The ghouls and other beasts that
roam these frozen plains are attracted to its light; which
especially puts the ice ghouls in a frenzy."

"Elf - fire?" Jinx tried to separate the words, though Ivy
remembered hearing stories of such a thing herself long ago,
"What is Elf-fire, and why are you carrying it out in the open
like that if it makes those creatures go berserk?"

"Elfire," Ivy recited, corrected her small companions
mispronunciation, "it is the life essence of the Elves, their
lifeblood in the form of light."

"Exactly," the strange girl agreed, explaining its properties to
Jinx, "...but I was cast out into the plains with this lamp to face
my own fate. Though I know this valley better than my Elders
could have possibly known." she breathed in her whispering
voice. Jinx turned to Ivy, clearly confused.

"You are of the Drow?" Ivy inquired, but already having
guessed her answer.

"Yes," she hissed again, "I am Malice, of the House of Wrath."
the Drow girl answered.

"And ...why were you sent out here alone?" Jinx ventured to
ask, with a concerned look on her face.

"I failed to assassinate a fellow Drow," Malice responded
casually, "I was caught in the act and banished to the surface by

our Queen."

"You were exiled as punishment for attempting to murder someone?" Jinx asked with less than a timid tone while noticeably scooting herself farther away from the pale elf.

"Ha ha, no," the Drow girl's laugh was an unpleasant sound, "I was not exiled for attempting the assassination ...but for *getting caught*. It was an embarrassment to my family house to be so careless in one's duties." Malice hissed her explanation.

It took a few moments for the fey girls to understand the twisted ethics of the Drow, though Malice did manage to clarify in a few, if not quite colorful words. Murder and espionage against rival families or Houses was perfectly acceptable among the dark elves; however, getting caught in the act was an unforgivable strike against the culprit's family honor, who would turn on their own siblings rather than protect them and face shame in the face of the their queen, the Brood Mother.

"Well, can't you just cover up the lamp with the edge of your dress?" Jinx suggested with the stupid logic of such a simple solution. The Drow girl took the edge of her velvet gown and gently laid it over the lamp to block its glare. As Jinx watched, the edge of the dress cracked and sizzled away as the light burst through, and Malice quickly patted out the dying embers.

"You cannot keep Elfire from shining, it is like starlight and cannot be masked by any normal means." Malice explained by example to the luck fairy.

With a strange gargled cry, a hellish creature suddenly appeared at the edge of their small cave as all three girls turned in shock. Its hide was a putrid white, with skin drawn taut over its skull, and a face withered with wild anguish. Its eyes were glazed over so that there was nothing of a pupil to be seen. The ghoul's fangs were long and rotted, as were its viciously sharp claws. It looked down upon the three living beings in the cave, and the glow of the Elfire upon its ghastly skin sent it into a deranged fury.

It cried out once again before pouncing, having found its prey trapped; but before it could lunge, an arrow of fire lanced into its open maw as yellow flames burst out of its eyes. Jinx was quick to the draw, faster than the other two girls could react.

The thing screamed as it clawed at its burning face and fell back into the snow drift just as they heard the tromp of many more approaching ghouls.

Ivy stood as best she could in the cramped cave and drew her spear to the ready, as did Jinx with her fiery bow. One ghoul sniffed at its fallen comrade and peeked its head into the mouth of the cave, as did another. Malice crept back as far as she could, as she was without any weapons and hampered by the heavy lamp chained to her wrist. One ghoul dared to reach in as Ivy gouged it through its hand, far more easily than she would have thought possible. It retracted in pain as the wound sprayed vile black blood upon the virgin snow. The second ghoul took an arrow to the shoulder, the rest of its upper body catching fire nearly instantly. The weapons Meridian had given them were well-tailored for this place and the vile creatures that lurked here.

The beast gave out a howl in a mindless scream of pain, and there was the sound of savage gnashing outside the mouth of the cave.

"Where did they..." Jinx began to ask as Malice put a finger to her lips in a motion of silence. The girls moved to body block the light of the lamp, as their shadows cast over the mouth of the cave. The eerie yelps and horrid gurgles and ripping ceased from outside, and was slowly replaced by the howling wind.

"We might be safe till dawn arrives ...if we're lucky." Malice added, not knowing the nature of Jinx who was crouched beside her. Jinx just gave a doubtful smirk to Ivy, as Malice was lost on the irony of their personal joke. Ivy dared to creep up to the rim of the cleft to get a glimpse outside the cave, where she found a great patch of ice covered in blackened slime and torn pieces of ghoul flesh, along with an array of innards and shredded limbs strewn about.

"Those creatures hunt in packs, and devour their wounded." Malice advised, her voice more hushed than before; not wishing to provoke another attack by of the feral beasts that might still be within earshot.

"That ghoul thing, went up in flames like dry grass," Jinx declared as she, too, made a motion to peer out of the cave mouth, though Ivy shook her head not to do so. Jinx was squeamish, and didn't have the stomach to view something so gruesome, so she reluctantly obeyed.

"They are but filthy scavengers who feed off the dead." the Drow girl spat, "That weapon of yours will come in handy here," Malice reached out to touch the enchanted bow, but Jinx pulled it away, not quite trusting who this 'malicious' little girl was, "And pray tell, what is the purpose of your journey here?" Malice sought to inquire.

"We are here to meet the Drow, and ask them for their assistance in a ...a confidential matter." Ivy added, siding with Jinx as to whether they could trust this would-be murderer.

A wry grin filled the Drow girl's face as she brushed off her velvet gown; her dark eyes flashing at the two fey in the dancing light.

"Perfect, then I will take you to them." Malice smiled.

*   *   *

Woven Lies

"You will take us to them, personally? But I thought you said you were exiled ...banished?" Jinx exclaimed.

"With a little help I can sneak my way back into the temple," Malice answered with her breathy voice, "and you can make your way to the High Council of the Drow to seek audience with the Queen Mother." she shrugged at the logic of it. "For now, we should rest until the morning, and make our way across the valley tomorrow once daybreak arrives."

Ivy gave her companion a disconcerted look, however, they were in a strange land and any help from the locals would be a great service; even from a murderous elf. It seemed like they had just closed their eyes before the breaking of dawn began to scatter away the misty shadows. Outside their tiny cave lay a pool of frozen blood; brittle bones with scraps of flesh were littered about the snow bank. Making their way down the frigid slope and across the broken tundra, the three companions kept their heading onwards towards the tower standing like a beacon across the valley of ice.

"What if those ghouls attack us again? They appeared to move a lot faster than we can run." Ivy inquired to the Drow girl. Malice advised her new companions that ghouls only hunt at night and in large packs, feral scavengers who would only attack their prey in overwhelming numbers. Their bodies were soft and brittle, and were accustomed to feeding off the dead or the wounded. Though the ghouls slept during the day, there were still far worse creatures lurking here that they needed to be wary of.

"Yeti's roam the foothills and ice forests near the southern edge of Tyre," Malice warned, "but it is the shiver worms that you need to look out for."

"We have never heard of those creatures, what should we look for?" Ivy asked, quite curious as she always was to learn about dangerous beasts and other nasties that roamed the far reaches of the Faerylands.

"Well, a Yeti is a big and hairy brute twice as tall as the largest ogre, and can track its prey through the fiercest of blizzards. If you ever do cross one, however, it will likely be the last thing you do." Malice cautioned, "Worm pupae on the other hand, are a delicacy worth collecting if you stumble across a nest, but adult shiver worms are white as snow and hard to spot, and can grow to immense sizes. They burrow through the thin ice and leave pitfalls for their victims, only to slink in to devour their trapped prey."

The pale girl continued to inform them about the dangers of the area, and what they should expect from the Drow Council. She wasn't so blind as not to notice the bracelet that Ivy wore was designed in the same unique style as the dark elves. Whenever one of her people was banished to the ice, there was little hope of survival. The heavy lantern she bore would quickly become a burden, and the Elfire would serve to attract unwanted attention from predators. Life above ground here had long since become inhospitable, that's why the Drow buried their temple and became cave dwellers. Their society was divided into seven houses representing the seven sins, and revolved around ritualistic killings and struggle for dominance in the name of their queen who they would try to impress for her favor.

The Drow were the opposite of everything Ivy had ever known about the High Elves of the forest. Instead of light, they preferred darkness; instead of the preservation of life and the innocent, they chose to hasten death and exploit the weak at every opportunity. It was hard for her to believe the Drow were a sister race to the Elves, and Ivy began to wonder how she would be received. As the doctrine explained in the tome Meridian had shown her back in his guild, everything within sight of the tower was sacred ground, and they did not tolerate trespassers.

Ivy touched her bracelet, hoping it would still be honored as a token of friendship after all these centuries. She realized that people changed over time, and it wasn't always for the better. Considering their circumstances, Jinx thought it fit to fiddle with the lantern to see if there was a way to remove it. Malice wasn't too fond of the fact that the fairy girl was standing so close to her while she examined the golden chain bolted to her gilded cuff.

To Malice, even in this stifling cold air, Jinx smelled rich with perfumes of nectar and honey; a scent so delicate and sweet it nearly made her puke. And fairly enough, to little Jinx, the Drow girl had an unpleasant musk of damp earth and mildew with the lingering tinge of copper, much like the odor of dried blood. Honestly, she couldn't stand it. Almost in unison, they gave one another a disgusted look and stepped away.

"I can't seem to find a weakness in the chain, so there's not much I can do, I'm afraid." Jinx rushed for an excuse.

"Yes, well, there's really little anyone can; the chain is usually not meant to be removed." Malice agreed as she tried to cover her nose without seeming too obvious, and faked a sniffle so she could turn away from the fairy girl.

In her early years, Malice had been taught stories of the race of Faerie, created by the woodland Elves. A marriage of Elf and nature spawned the fey in all their flaws; divided and deformed by their elemental essence. The wings on their backside made them look like insects in her eyes, which was an insult to any fey when such comments were uttered aloud. She had been taught the Faerie were all childish and irresponsible scamps, created by the High Elves in all their pompous vanity, simply so they could have submissive servants to impress their authority upon.

Truthfully, this was the first time she had ever met a true blooded fairy, but these two girls bore weapons of death and destruction, and had used them skillfully; which were traits highly valued by the dark elves. Every Drow child was reared from a young age to not only be obedient to their house, but to fend for themselves and were thoroughly instructed in the arts of war. A handful of the dark elves found their calling in the arcane arts instead, weaving spells and warping magic to their own vile intent, instead of resorting to the crude hacking and slashing of blades like their warrior kin.

Though frowned upon, Malice had taught herself to use darts

with deadly efficiency. Rather than risk harm to herself in direct melee with an opponent, she could strike at a distance with her bladed spikes. As of late, she had been harvesting specific types of toxic moss and corrosive sap from mire roots that grew among the moist caverns. Concocting poisons was disfavored among the warrior classes who believed the sting of a blade was the only honorable way to slay a foe; face to face with their opponent, be it beast or fellow Drow.

Malice, however, did not share their views and found it much more challenging to sneak about the shadows in silence and strike down a foe who was unaware that the time to meet their end had come. There was a certain satisfaction she found in practicing such skills, though her recent failures that had left her abandoned to this icy waste proved she required far more practice in her craft.

One of the sons from the house of Envy, who was trying to gain favor in the eyes of their queen mother, chose to insult Malice personally and did so more than once in her presence. What better way to teach the brethren an ounce of respect than to silence his wagging tongue, which she had planned to sever from his corpse as a token. Many times she had waited, hidden within the shadows upon a darkened balcony which overlooked a path the insolent boy took often. Many times he had passed beneath her, never knowing her baleful eyes were watching his every step, until one day she found him on the path alone. So eager she was not let the opportunity pass, Malice seized the chance to strike him down.

With the slightest hesitation of experiencing her first kill, she let spin her poisoned darts at him. As fate would have it, he knelt at that moment to tighten a loose strap. Wearing light armor which the male warriors were accustomed to, she had aimed for his exposed neck, and the deadly spikes missed by a breath. They clattered on the cobblestone path only to come to rest on the edge of the dress of his elder house mother; the vile poison from the darts seeping its telltale stain into the delicate white weave of her trailing gown.

Malice had not done her homework, having failed to discovered why the boy had been waiting there, as he was to escort his sisters to a banquet that evening. The sisters from the house of Envy, too, were educated in the warrior arts, and far more nimble than their brothers burdened in their heavy gilded armor. There were several witnesses who saw Malice standing there on the ledge, shocked at what twist of fate her moment of revenge had crumbled into. A grand chase ensued throughout the weaving halls of the temple, and though she gave a good run in her heated attempt to escape, they eventually caught her in the end.

It wasn't the attempt of murder she had planned for the arrogant lad, but her capture that was the unforgivable blemish of shame that scarred the dignity of the house of Wrath. Her freedom could have been bought with blood rubies, or worse, to serve her time as a slave to the house of Envy for a century to her own disgrace. The Queen herself decided that those options would not suffice, however, as Malice chose to dishonor the way of the Drow by using poisons, and thus, foregoing the honor of a clean kill.

For this she was bound with the purity of the Elfire, and cast into the frozen desolation above as an example to the others. The house of Envy had their revenge, and her own family was forbidden to mourn the loss of their child. So was the way of the Drow, for compassion was not a word taught in their language.

Stumbling upon these two fey who now accompanied her was another twist of fate in pale elf's eyes, for she had taught herself to exploit every chance that presented itself. Malice wasn't as conniving as most Drow she knew, but she certainly had the spirit to learn. Over the past few years she had already spent several nights upon the icy tundra, having snuck out by way of the hidden chambers in the abandoned section of the great temple to explore the world above. The passages had been damaged by quakes and shifting of stone and were considered far too unsafe to breach. Malice though, was adventurous; and braved the collapsed chambers for the sake of curiosity.

She had come to the surface during the moonless nights, having learned its cycles; for the Drow had spent so many countless eons underground, the full light of day nearly blinded them. She had spotted the small cave they spent the night in many times before, but was unable to safely venture such a distance until the day came that she had been forced to seek shelter after her expulsion from their sanctuary.

By chance she had crossed paths with these two emissaries of the forest Elves, and had survived a certain death at the hands of the ghouls that hunted her. Malice knew she could not knock at the gates to the underworld and stroll back in to the Great Temple of the Drow, so a little scheming was in order.

She would take them back through the hidden route through the collapsed passages. If she could be rid of her shackles of the Elfire, and complete her task of extinguishing the life of her target from the rival house; she would regain her honor and be once again accepted back into the house of Wrath.

"Do we have to climb all the way up to that tower?" Jinx huffed as they hiked along through the ice field, making it clear to Ivy what she thought of such a foreboding task. Yet again, Malice saw her chance to take the initiative.

"The tower is controlled by the Obsidian Order, those that belong to the Sisterhood of Blood who reside there would kill any trespassers on sight," the pale girl butted in, cautioning them of that approach, "The Drow never leave the caverns, so you will find no doorway to the great temple within," she advised, "They have all been long since sealed from the time of change after the fall of the great battle of Tyre." she added, hoping the two fey would swallow such an elaborate tale.

"But, how did they banish you to the surface then?" Ivy asked as she stepped gingerly along. Malice cursed the logic of the little fairy's question under her breath.

"I'm not quite sure. I was beaten unconscious," she lied again, but pointed to bruises she had received during her botched escape from the sisters of the rival house, "...and awoke abandoned on the ice with this chained to my wrist." she added for flair as she rattled the golden links.

"Well, that's great, what now?" Jinx blurted with a tone of exasperation.

"Well," Malice trailed on, making sure she had both their pointed ears, "I do know of a way in, long forgotten by most," she added with a hint of truth, "and hopefully the passage is not blocked.

This news was sufficient to intrigue the two fey girls to let Malice lead the way, for they had been through a great deal of grief thus far on their quest. It was then that Malice began to twist and weave the wildest lie she had ever composed. She led them on in silence as she began to concoct a grand tale too fantastic for them *not* to believe. So deeply concentrated in thought was the little Drow girl, that her keen senses failed to notice the silhouette of a Yeti on a distant ridge; who stood glaring at what it considered three hot-blooded meals trailing in the snow bank below. Its wild long hair fluttering in the howling wind, though, entirely oblivious to the fact that something even bigger was trailing silently in its wake.

Malice led her two companions towards the field of shattered ice below the overhang of the tower far above. Here, enormous icicles had fallen over time to leave a vast cauldron of splintered ice that glittered like crystals in the morning sun. Prisms flitted at their every step as colorful rays caressed their skin. It truly was a magical sight, if not for the freezing conditions and flurries of snow that reminded the trio of the bleak landscape that engulfed them. It was here at the far edge of the ice field that the Drow girl had discovered where a collapsed tunnel from the abandoned section of the temple had led outside to the surface.

With a little effort, she had cleared the way many moons ago so that she could make use of it. Malice would sneak out whenever the opportunity would arise, as the main entrance near the foot of the tower high above them was under constant guard. She had kept this hidden escape route secret for a reason, suspecting she may have great use of it; and that day had come. Though instead of escape, she was breaking her way back in, having never fathomed that she would one day be exiled from her own people.

Stalking their trail, the Yeti found the scent of its prey easy to follow, its keen senses able to track through the thickest of blizzards. The monster had been hibernating for the past several months, and it awoke with a pressing hunger. Its lair was several leagues to the west, where if anyone was to venture inside, they would find it filled with the bones of many a dwarf. Trinkets of gold and silver, of armor and shields, and the finest of battle swords and war hammers were scattered about; all objects of curiosity to the Yeti. It held but an inkling of intelligence, though it was safe to say its animal side had dominance and far more persuasion over its instincts; especially in matters where an empty belly was concerned.

Since the battle of Tyre a great many centuries ago, the bodies of the dwarven army slaughtered here had laid unburied. This in itself was an insult to the Dwarven race, and a scar upon their pride. Many wild and feral beasts scattered the remains of their corpses over time, gnawing away at the gristle and stringy flesh left clinging to their stocky bones. To this day, many a fine sword and shield still lay hidden under the thick snow that now blankets the island, never again to see the light of day. Stumbling across these weapons as it scoured for food, the Yeti collected these curious remnants.

It knew not the value of such treasures, and did not care. It would chew and gnaw on the tasteless marrow of bones of the dead, though it did not have a taste for ghouls, but they, too, were on the menu if his stomach felt pangs. Most beasts of these icy plains learned to avoid a Yeti if given the fleeting chance, for they were horrible beasts that could snap most anyone and anything in two. They were known to hoard the corpses of their prey to feed on at leisure, or dismember creatures they caught alive, so as to preserve a warm meal at a later time; though not grasping the fundamentals as to why their unfortunate victims would bleed out and die.

There were many other beasts wandering these icy dunes, but Yeti's were extremely territorial, and kept to their individual sections of the isle. Though with all its intellectual downfalls, there was one thing a Yeti could plan well; and that was surprising its prey! To the hungry Yeti, these two-legged meals wandering through the snow drift far ahead seemed easy enough to catch. He kept just out of sight, and froze as still as stone whenever they would turn his way; blending into the landscape around him as if invisible.

He knew every trail, every glacier and chasm; and when he saw them enter the ice field below the spiked mountain, it was an opportunity he could not resist.   Within the soft blue shadows of the towering cliff above, his bone white fur would be indistinguishable from the snow around him.   The cauldron was a maze of sharpened ice crystals shattered across the small plain.   Occasionally, a goliath icicle would crack under its own weight and fall, adding its remains into the maze below, gracing the ice field with a design of its own.   The boom of its collapse would echo across the valley, breaking the tense silence possessed by the howling winds.

The wild yeti had chosen to intercept them at the center of the maze against the far wall where the embankment would be too steep for them to escape.   His massive bulging hands were strong enough to crush the life out of them with one squeeze, and in no time his groaning stomach would be the happier for it.   As the three girls began to weave their way into the first layer of the broken ice, the Yeti made his move.   Tromping across the snow bank out of their direct sight, he raced for the edge of the glacial rift.   Though the Yeti were great hunters in their own right, there were yet others even more devious that stalked this tundra.   Upon other side of the rift, the three girls pressed on.

"I know of a collapsed tunnel that will help us get inside," Malice assured the two faeries as she peppered truth into her lies, "it's just up ahead here."

Ivy and Jinx were trusting their new companion to get them off the frozen ice and into the temple, though she was a bit sketchy as to how she would be joining them; considering her status as an outcast and all.   She had been saving that story until they were in the caverns and out of the frigid cold.

Ivy was startled and wholly unprepared, as was Jinx who gave out a loud shriek and fell to her side.   Malice, too, was just as startled as the two fey, but recognized the beast that now stood before them.   It had been still as stone, undetectable to their keen ears or seen out of the corner of their eyes.   Even Ivy's sensitive night vision had not seen the giant creature that had jumped from a stack of ice that overhung their path.   The ground shook around them as it dropped down in front of the group, its clawed feet squarely set in the icy path as all three girls fell on their rumps from the impact.

The Yeti was a horrible sight, much larger than any troll Ivy had ever seen, and twice as ugly. To her the thing looked like a beast of thick black fur, with eyes that glowed like pinholes of fire. That perception was closely shared by Jinx and Malice, who saw the creature as a towering monster of fur and snow, and its eyes ...its ghastly eyes were horrible to behold. They were white as bleached ivory, and its blank stare filled them with fright. Only Ivy was immune to its paralyzing gaze, and stumbled to her feet as she reached for her fallen spear.

She wondered for a split second why Jinx had not drawn her bow, and Malice too sat there glaring wide eyed at the monster, both motionless. The Yeti, being both a hunter and a scavenger of these frozen wastes, was a little perturbed that one of its meals was scampering away so soon, as he usually got a sense of pride when terrorizing his living prey with his presence. Nonetheless, he was used to throwing boulders at those trying to escape his reach, but there were none in this ice field to speak of. So he reached out to pluck up Malice and use her body as a deadweight to take Ivy down if she tried to flee. The impact alone would kill them both, breaking their frail bodies on the hardened ice floe beneath their feet.

The Yeti's senses were keen, only overridden by the grumbling hunger echoing from his empty belly. Merely feet away from his hairy claws grasping onto Malice who sat stunned before him, a heavy shadow fell directly over him, strangely enough, noticing the shadow itself kept growing ever thicker. For the first time in his wretched life, a look of worry washed over the Yeti's crooked face.

Ivy yanked Malice to her feet by the collar of her dress as she grabbed Jinx by the scruff of her wings, pulling them both up the embankment and behind a thick icicle stem as a violent spray of ice and snow suddenly showered over them. A loud boom of thunder cracked the air, as something large and heavy crashed to the floor where the Yeti had once stood; smashing it to pulp. Bits of fur with flesh still attached splattered the embankment behind them as they cowered from the blast of ice.

As the shadow had fallen over him, the first thought the Yeti had was that a chunk of ice had separated from the ceiling above, but he was still confused as to why he had not heard the tell-tale crack of the break that always preceded a collapse. That would have given him several seconds to find cover or seek higher ground and relative safety.   It was always dangerous being down in the cauldron of shards, and reason why every beast of the island avoided it.   As his eyes had shifted upward to behold his doom eclipsing all else, the Yeti died still boggled, even dumfounded as to the cause of his unpleasant departure from this world, for it wasn't a falling shard of ice after all that had crushed him into nothingness.

Mere hours ago outside of his cave, a great stone embankment sat, not exactly where he remembered one being before. The Yeti's eyes had been blurry from recently awaking from his long hibernation.   His churning stomach ached and growled, a constant reminder of his immediate needs. Many moons ago he had happened upon a shallow cavern behind a frozen waterfall. Within he found a dwarven war hammer of exquisite detail laying upon a bed of gravel, and promptly pilfered the weapon for his collection. Little did the Yeti know, this enchanted item had already been claimed by another.

The sands of time run slower for some creatures than others, so it took many agonizing moments for the stone giant that dwelt under the waterfall to know he had been robbed of his prize. Entirely undetectable from the rock around him, the Yeti had nary a clue of the danger he was in. Making his way back to his lair, the sounds of distant thunder the Yeti thought he heard were actually the footsteps of the disgruntled giant following him in pursuit. Once back in his own lair, the Yeti tossed the weapon into his trove and promptly faded into a deep slumber.   For many moons the stone giant waited patiently outside the mouth of the cave, to exact his revenge on the thief that lay protected deep inside the small lair where he could not reach. As months passed, storms and blizzards came and went, until the day the Yeti ventured out once again; never realizing that he was being stalked.

The girls peeked out from their refuge to marvel at what they

saw before them. Nothing but a great crater lay where the Yeti
once stood, surrounded by a blast of ice and snow and thin
streams of vivid red. Over the lip of the frozen caldera, a giant
made of shifting stones covered in snow and ice had turned and
tromped away towards the glacier on the horizon; the group
noting something wet and stringy clinging to the underside of
the leviathans enormous granite club, still matted with bloody
clumps of hair.

Still shaken by their encounter with the two goliaths, they
slowly stood to take account of what had just happened. Malice
conceded that they had been attacked by a Yeti, yet she had
never seen a stone giant in her lifetime. Few tales were told of
them, most of which they had considered mere fable until this
hour. Jinx had managed to hold onto her bow, and Ivy retained
her spear; so other than having to shake off the shock and
trauma, they were otherwise unscathed. As much could not be
said for the unfortunate Yeti, whose empty stomach that had led
its owner to this place was now but a mere stain splattered upon
the snow.

Had they been a few minutes earlier, they could have avoided
the encounter altogether. The trio had been much closer to the
hidden entrance than the two faeries knew. With prudent haste,
Malice led them up to the side of the cliff where the small inlet
into the broken passages lay hidden and well-concealed by the
wall of ice surrounding it. Wiggling their way through the
opening, the passage widened, and to the drow girl's surprise,
both Ivy and Jinx began to give off a slight glow. In the
darkness of the caves, Ivy had to explain to her that the
illumination of their skin was natural for a faerie.

Even the abandoned part of the great temple was a spectacular
sight to see. There were intricate carvings upon every pillar,
few were merely decorations, but many depicted strange and
exotic creatures entwined in a freakish dance; forever frozen
upon the stone monuments. Alters and doorways and alcoves
lay scattered about the ruins. The collapsed sections were
obvious, and the sifting grit and soil from between the groaning
cracks made it clear as to why no one dared loiter here.

It was a long and tiresome route through the maze of bridges and broken stairways to reach the lower sections; and it occurred to the faeries that what they had seen was only a mere fraction of how truly monumental the grand temple was. Stepping out of an upper balcony they came into view of the grand cavern that housed the ruins. Neither of them would have believed just how large in scale it was constructed, hidden beneath the surface as it was. The floating castle of the Dwarves could have easily fit within its girth. Figures could be seen far below walking banner-lined trails and twisting stone bridges, as flocks of bats soared through the enormous grotto.

"Sadly, I must leave you here to find your way to the council of the Drow," Malice began with a pout, "The tyrannical prince I attacked for killing my parents, will do the same to me if I am seen here again." she offered with a pitiful look and a fake frown as she wove her lies to snare their sympathy.

"What will you do?" Ivy asked, not really comfortable leaving this dark elf to her fate out here alone.

"The question is what will you do?" Malice led on, "It is known the prince is not fond of the High Elves or the Faerie for that matter. You may meet a fate far worse than mine," the pale girl embellished. The two fey gave each other a look of worry at her comment.

"I have a token from the wizards' guild," Ivy answered, showing the drow girl her bracelet, "so hopefully that will give us audience with your queen."

"The prince is an audacious and insolent child who was given too much free reign. He killed his own sisters one day in a fit of rage, and everyone is too afraid to face him ...even our own queen." Malice lied, hoping her fib hadn't tripped too far over the edge. Though Jinx, however, seemed to have fallen for it.

"So why does the queen let him live? Can't she have the guards banish him as well?" Jinx inquired.

"It's not that simple," Malice elaborated with a hint of cunning, "you see, the Drow honor strength, and many of the royal guards follow the prince, who is the next royal heir. Though their loyalty is divided, the Queen herself cannot bring herself to send her only son to his doom. Only one of her daughters yet survives, and I fear her time, too, is short," Malice tried to persuade them.

"So what will happen to you?" Jinx asked with a hint of concern, feeling her predicament.

"I must survive alone in hiding here until that wicked and spiteful lord is overthrown." Malice turned away, trying to hide her evil smile from their view. Oh, how these naive faeries were so easily tricked. Turning back in full character, she continued with her sob story once again, "If he murders his last sibling, or worse, the queen herself, there will be nothing but chaos among the Drow; and little hope of the aid you seek." she added to catch them in her web.

"Are you saying this prince is the same person you tried to murder, out of revenge for your parents' death?" Ivy asked, as she pieced the girl's story together, which started to make some bit of sense, as broken as it was.

"Yes, yes it is..." Malice turned, smiling inside as to how gullible a fairy could be. She was molding them like clay, "and for their honor, I must complete my task to vindicate not only myself, but also for my people."

Together, Ivy and Jinx pondered her words, while Malice stood overlooking the temple below; not wishing to over-embellish her story so flagrantly and sour the sweet retribution she was now plotting. After many long moments of whispering among themselves, Jinx came over to offer a solution.

"Truly, it is of dire import that we speak to the Drow council," Jinx started to say.

"...But we can't take the chance of any power struggle or rebellion on the part of the Drow." Ivy finished for her, "We must find a lady named Sorrow, everything depends on it." she pleaded with sincere desperation.

"The Queen Mother would know where to find this person you seek," Malice offered, not knowing if that was true or not, having no idea who Ivy spoke of, "but I have to at least try to save her and her daughter, even if it's the last thing I do." she stated with a hint of false chivalry.

"...Then we will help you." both Ivy and Jinx finally agreed.

Malice struggled to hide a smile of glee, so she turned away as if in deliberation as to what they were offering. Pinching herself, she worked up a fake tear and turned back to her companions.

"Thank you so much, I truly couldn't ask for better friends." Malice replied softly, knowing she now had these two faeries right were she wanted them.

*   *   *

Sorrow

Jinx was truly boggled as to why the hex of her touch had no apparent affect on the golden chains sealed around the pale girl's wrist. They had to find a way to remove the Elfire bound to Malice, or they would have little chance of succeeding in their plan. For one, the lantern acted like a beacon to every creature within sight, preventing her from sneaking about the shadows unseen; and Malice could certainly not wield any weapons with such a handicap. Ivy figured the lantern was likely covered with a type of counter enchantment to prevent such tampering, much along the line of what Meridian had done to protect her fey companion's flaming bow.

Though Malice had friends among the Drow, there were none so loyal as to risk their own lives or banishment for her sake as it was their core philosophy to be selfish in such matters. Another problem was that the Brood Mother of the Drow was reputed to have powers of clairvoyance not fully understood by the lower cast of dark elves. Malice continued to feed the two faeries with bait as to the spiteful intent of her target whom she titled as an evil prince. He was not, in truth, but a mere lord of many other sons from a rival house, who had scorned and wounded her fragile pride.

Her capture and banishment was embarrassment enough to drive Malice to make a second attempt. Her fury was fed by a long history of conspiracy and murder so very common among the brood, which would gain them a reputation of being ruthless and daring, and the notoriety of someone not to be trifled with. It was exactly the type of status Malice desired so desperately for herself. Her peers had gained their positions through centuries of devious scheming, but Malice did not possess that kind of patience. She was impetuous and arrogant, and cared little about the consequences that might stack against her. The young elf girl believed it was her fate to rule her House, if not the entire brood of Drow themselves. The drow girl's unbalanced ego and her delusions of grandeur knew few bounds.

"I have to be rid of this accursed Elfire," Malice demanded, nearly dragging the weight of the lantern along, her arms having long since grown weary from its burden. Few that have been banished had ever survived this long. There was only one place she knew of to have the enchanted lantern and its chains removed from her; the very place where it was bound to her at the Hall of Odium.

"What a strange name." Jinx noted softly as they made their way from the abandoned chambers of the temple to the lower sections where they had to proceed with a notable degree of caution.

"It is a march of shame, where the families of the seven houses witness those exiled as they are expelled from the temple." She snarled, but caught herself and instead gave a saddened whimper when she turned back to face the two faeries. "There is a chamber where the chains of the Elfire are crafted and attached to those condemned," she stated as she rubbed her sore wrist and bleeding skin where the golden cuff bound her.

The problem was, it would be very difficult to reach the chamber undetected. Not only did the enchanted lantern shine like a beacon, the two faeries themselves were glowing and would catch the attention of anyone within sight. As a solution, Malice suggested that they rub themselves with mud and ash. Considering the circumstances, they agreed; though they found doing so to be highly unpleasant. Finding the ingredients for their camouflage, they gathered enough soot from a burned out fire pit and smeared it over their bodies, effectively hiding their fairy glow.

Malice, however, was still handicapped by the golden lantern chained to her; as there was no means to cover it. Within a layer of loose ash she drew a map for the two faeries to follow down into the Odium chamber to look for a key. Malice was a little sketchy on what they should be looking for, since there was in fact no keyhole in her shackles to speak of. With a little goading, however, she convinced them to sneak their way in to the chamber to find a means to be free of her chains. Since the hall was rarely used, they expected to find few guards.

Leaving Malice behind in the upper halls, both Ivy and Jinx were able to flit their way down the side of the great temple within the shadows of the cavern. Their delicate wings had since thawed, and it was nice to have recovered their sense of freedom. Behind a pair of armed guards they came to rest, and snuck down the steep steps of the Odium in silence.

A great skull with pointed ears graced the outer entrance, as the warming glow of a strange flickering light danced in slow motion upon the inner walls. As quiet as they had to be, Jinx still gave out a gasp as they saw the chamber beneath. Gilded lockets and chains of every size were hanging from hooks upon the walls. The ceiling itself was domed over a central block of glazed crystal which glowed from within; for it was here that rested the very source of the Elfire. Luckily for them there was no one else present within the chamber.

This place was no stranger to pain, as they also discovered a blood stained alter with more than its share of binding clamps and barbed chains. The fey noticed that everything here, even the simplest tools were etched and decorated with great skill, as if they somehow shared a common talent with the Dwarven smiths. Searching the room under the glow of the central crystal, they found several items of interest.

While rummaging through the room, Ivy stumbled across a shackle much like the one Malice had bound to her wrist. Strangely though, there was no clasp or locking mechanism within it; it simple closed upon itself along its embossed design on the cufflink. This bracelet was also chained to a large lantern crafted with exquisite skill; but this one was empty, devoid of the living flame of the Elfire. It was a mere globe of milky white glass awaiting to be filled with the mystic energy.

There was also a table filled with an assortment of weapons the two girls had never seen before. Though there were daggers and swords, there also included an array of strange and exotic tools of violence that glimmered in the light. Wickedly curved sickles and spiked gauntlets of steel, giant blades that looked too large to be wielded by a common Drow, and hatchets made of glowing jade. Among them they found a collection of darts, sharp bladed spikes cut with hooked grooves to hold the paste of deadly poisons. Recognizing them from the stories Malice had told, Ivy gathered these, suspecting they were the property of their accomplice. They were still desperate to find anything that resembled a key, but were at a loss to find one.

"I don't know what we're looking for." Jinx whispered as quietly as possible so the guards up the stairwell could not hear.

"You're right," Ivy answered, exasperated with their search, "there's nothing here but that glowing orb.

There were a pair of insanely tall double doors at the far end of the room, but they were sealed shut by a means the two faeries could not fathom. Motioning to her companion, Ivy suggested that they return the way they came; cautiously sneaking out behind the backs of the armored sentries that stood guard outside just beyond the lip of the entrance. The faeries flew up above them through the shadows of the cave, the two guards below, oblivious to their presence.

Malice was astonished that they had rescued her personal weapons from the vault. With a whiff, she could tell the poison paste had nearly dried, but would still be fairly potent.

"There was nothing like a key, nor wand or device that resembled anything we could possibly use to remove your shackles." Ivy advised her, though Malice seemed clearly upset by the news, "There was only the glowing orb in the center of the room; perhaps that central crystal..." she began to suggest before Malice interrupted.

"You're right," she looked off in deep thought, "maybe the Elfire itself is the key!"

"I would say it might be worth a try, for I saw chains similar to yours in the Odium, but there was no physical lock nor clasp within it that I could tell, and it was attached to an empty lantern. It may very well be that the living Elfire is the source of the binding enchantment." Ivy agreed.

There was one problem though; it would take both of them to carry Malice down by hand. They could try to set her down slowly, but faeries weren't built to carry much weight other than their own; let alone someone who was anchored with heavy gold chains. Since they couldn't cover the lantern, their descent outside the temple in the shadows would be as obvious as a shooting star. There was no way to go that route without drawing a great deal of unwanted attention to themselves.

"Then what we need is a diversion," Malice suggested, willing to risk that gamble if it meant getting her free of these chains. Besides, it wouldn't be much of a personal risk if she used the two faeries as decoys. If they did happen to get caught, it was of no consequence to her; and if they ratted her out, then she would take her petty revenge out on them when the time came.

They slipped through the shadows of the inner sanctum while trying to hide the light of the Elfire from view, they finally made their way down to a bridge that spanned the platform outside the upper rim of the temple. Tiptoeing inside, Jinx came upon a wondrous sight as she peered over the highest ledge of the central auditorium. Glowing from below, ethereal chandeliers bathed the decorated walls, heavy with massive carvings. Layered with black marble and the onyx stone from the heart of the island, sat a grand court inlaid with a seven pointed star. At its points were bold symbols, each representing the seven Drow houses.

The central symbol was dark and sinister, and the emblem sharply creased into the image of a spider. The echoes of distant conversations rose up to meet them as an incoherent jumble of noise. Ivy and Malice finally found Jinx, and came to her side to gaze over the edge at the bustle of dark elves below.

"Ah, the Drow council," Malice whispered in her strange voice, "and there, the Brood Mother." she pointed with her free hand. Jinx saw her now, a tall woman with a lavishly cut gown and hair woven into a headdress of silver. Her skin had a strange hue to it, almost metallic, "This is perfect," Malice smiled, "you two can create a commotion just outside the council chamber, and that should draw the guards away from the Odium." she insisted.

"Create a commotion ...us?" Ivy looked confused.

"How are we supposed to do that,?" Jinx followed Ivy's dumbfounded look, "We're not going to run off attacking elves willy-nilly." she declared.

"You don't have to hurt anyone, there are several banners

outside the main entry, you can use your bow to ignite them; the resulting fire should attract enough guards to get them away from the chamber." Malice offered with a look of desperation on her face. When both of the faeries gave a disagreeing look she pressed them on, "You can easily fly out of harm's way once you create the distraction, just head back to the upper ledge and wait for me there after I get this thing off." Malice noted the lantern shackled to her. Ivy was the first to speak up.

"Sure, we'll get those guards away from the entrance for you, Malice, and wait for you back at the ledge ...just be careful." she added with a look of concern.

"You, too." Malice gave a grin, though she held no real concern for their personal safety.

The drow girl went back out and waited at the outer ledge to see when the guards were drawn away. She watched as Ivy and Jinx fluttered down into the shadows and around the edge of the great columns beyond her sight. She mumbled to herself in anticipation that this her plan would work, and she'd be rid of her shackles once and for all, and she could then proceed to enact her revenge.

As the minutes drained away, it seemed to take forever for the two faeries to do the dirty work Malice had assigned them, until her patience had grown thin. She was just about to make her way to the inner ledge above the council chambers to see if there was any change when she noticed an royal sentry had approached the two guards stationed in front of the Odium and all three elves hurried away, which left the entrance open.

There were a series of columns mounted at the inner temple that brought her to the bottom ledge. In her climb down, Malice cut and bruised herself in her haste to reach the level of the entrance, her descent being far less graceful than she had anticipated, but the weight of the lantern threw off her balance considerably.

Sneaking down the steps, she remembered her last visit to this room where she had been stripped of both her weapons and family crest, and shackled with the Elfire. The thick golden bracelet she now wore had been closed tightly around her wrist, and the orb of the lamp touched to the heart of the Elfire crystal.

Once filled, the bindings glowed and sealed shut upon her arm.

To her humiliation, she was then dragged down the hall of the Odium, where all the other elves of the seven houses could witness her shame. As she glared at them in hatred, she was prodded into a caged lift that left her upon the barren plains of Tyre. It was difficult enough to see in the brightness of daylight, but nightfall had come too soon, along with a pack of ice ghouls on her tail, whereupon she had stumbled upon the two forest fey.

Besides her own poison darts, she found other weapons that had been confiscated from previous convicts; but before picking through them, she would have to deal with her own chains. Malice scrambled through the room, looking for any kind of scroll or wand that might release her from her bindings, but found nothing. Her last chance at escape would be to try to reverse the enchantment by draining the Elfire from the lamp back into the heart of the crystal.

Holding the golden lantern with her weary arms, she pressed it to the glowing stone the same way she had seen the Drow priestess do. Again and again she tried till she let out a shriek of aggravation. Nothing was happening, the Elfire would not siphon from the bound lamp. With a hushed curse of annoyance she threw the golden lantern to the ground in a vain attempt to shatter it, but it lay undamaged. Her mind now swam with fury, realizing she would be unable to fulfill her intricate plans for reprisal if she could not free herself. Her hair tousled and her eyes full of anger; but not so much as not to widen with fearful surprise when she turned towards the door upon hearing a familiar voice that sent a chill up her spine.

"Once the clasp is closed and the torch is lit by the living Elfire, it becomes one with its host, and will only extinguish along with the life of the one to whom it is mated." the Brood Mother declared, in the same strange wisp of a voice all the dark elves seemed to share. Beside her stood several armed guards who spread about the room; in their company Ivy and Jinx stepped out of the shadows behind them, though they were not restrained. It took a moment for Malice to realize the two girls had not been captured, but were accomplices to the Drow queen standing before her.

"You ...you sneaky, little backstabbing freaks," Malice hissed, showing her true colors, "I will get you two for this, you fairy filth!" she spat. The brood mother raised a hand and the guards seized Malice by her arms as the queen approached the insolent girl; another priestess entered the room behind her. The queen plucked the poisoned spikes from the girl's belt, then with a second thought in contemplation, held a single dart aloft in her hand. Malice looked on in fear as the priestess attached a second cuff to her left wrist and touched its chained lantern to the crystal globe. Now both her arms were shackled with the heavy gold chains. The guards then dragged her as she fought each step down the narrow hall of the Odium, to the shuttered cage at the end of the corridor. Above this walkway lay a series of stone balconies for attendees to view the procession. Though now, the terrace sat empty. Just before Malice was thrown into the cage, the drow queen approached her once again.

"For your cleverness in making it this far back into the temple, I will offer you this one dignity, young girl," the queen added with pomp, tucking the single poison dart into the girl's tight girdle, almost grazing her skin with its toxic blade while Malice looked on with fright. "Fate is cruel, Malice; I suggest you use this wisely ...before you freeze to death." then waved her hand casually as if to shoo the brat from her sight. With the gesture, the guards slammed the cage door and it was cranked by pulley up a narrow shaft to the surface. Malice could be heard screaming curses at them all until her voice faded away into nothingness.

The brood mother made her way back down the hall to the two fey girls, her slender features accentuating the vermilion silk dress she wore. The queen carried herself well, her frame was long and slender and the entire orb of her eyes were stained a blood red. She was different from the other Drow, very different. Her skin had a copper sheen to it, and it almost seemed like it was faintly tinted with stripes much like those of a jungle cat. She was taller and noticeably thinner than any of the other dark elves around her, almost as if she was something more than pure elf.

"You need not worry for your safety; if she manages to make her way back to the collapsed route outside, she will be disappointed to find the way sealed." the queen offered to the two fey who hadn't asked, but merely wondered of that outcome. With a snap of her fingers, she set off several guards to see to the task. The fact was Ivy and Jinx had not betrayed Malice, so much as did not trust the multiple holes in the stories she used to cloud the truth whenever she tried to manipulate them. The faeries were trusting, but not complete dolts to the point of putting themselves in harm's way without question.

Since they were there to meet the Drow Council, Ivy had thought it best that they introduce themselves before making enemies among them. The royal bracelet that Meridian had given her was a token of good will, and gained them immediate audience with the Brood Mother herself. It was highly unorthodox how they had made their way into the Drow sanctuary completely bypassing the front gates that were well-guarded; but with a few direct questions, the queen revealed the spiraling lies Malice had told the two fey in order to gain their trust; and that there in fact was no murdering prince and enlightened them to the true scale of the drow girls deceit. Needless to say, they were both shocked and offended at the level of her conniving that would have put them in harm's way. Malice had certainly earned her name.

They accompanied the elf queen back to the council chamber to get to the business at hand. There Ivy discussed the quest placed upon them by the woodland elves, and respectfully requesting the whereabouts of the lady Sorrow, who had crafted the jeweled memento for the Dwarves.

"I believe she still lives," the queen advised as she unfolded the top half of her dress, exposing a second set of arms, much to the shock of the two fairy girls present before her, "the individual you seek is a member of the Obsidian Order who reside in the Tower on the cliff above the temple." she advised.

"The Tower of Madness?" Jinx inquired, with a quizzical look on her face. The queen flashed her a curt smile devoid of any hint at mirth.

"I can see by the curious gleam in your eyes that you wonder

as to the purpose of its name, young fey," the queen asked as
the split in the sides of her dress unfolded even further, and yet
a third pair of thin arms emerged as her hands flowed with her
speech; one taking up a scroll, while another a wine goblet
rimmed with rubies and several other items from trays set about
her black throne. With her question, Jinx gave a slight nod. Ivy
stood beside her, leaning on her spear.

"We believe Sorrow may have knowledge to aid us in
awakening the Undying spirits of our world. Though the race
of huskmen has long since passed, the spirits still slumber as the
Craven threatens the world above." Ivy announced.

They were a strange lot, seven representatives of the seven
houses of Drow surrounded her as she stood near the queen's
central throne. Among them, Ivy noted a dark elf who stood
covered in sparkling jewels, lavishing herself in robes with
threads of fine gold and rare gemstones in excess to the point of
appearing so gaudy it was almost ludicrous. Unlike the other
elves, another head of house was lounging in a veiled carriage
held aloft by several slaves who fed her and did her bidding by
the lazy snap of her fingers. Ivy thought it very unorthodox for
elves to have bound servants, but they were Goblings so she
was told, lesser creations of true Goblins. Goblings were
another breed, though smaller and less loathsome, they were
still ugly little beasts who held a vicious glint in their eyes.

Another of the house representatives was a brooding lady with
raven black hair, whose shifty eyes and whispered remarks of
disgust could be overheard by the others, but were strangely
ignored. Another lady was dressed in revealing attire, her eyes
were sultry and seductive as she licked her fingers in a
suggestive manner while caressing her soft milky skin. Yet
another dark elf of the house beside her wore burnished armor
of distinct design and stood at attention as if all eyes were on
her. Plumes of feathers fluttered out from her great cape as she
presented an air of arrogance and conceit.

Ivy recognized the mother of the house of Wrath, whose white
hair and dress was similar to what Malice had worn, and she
glared at the two fey with a silent rage burning in them
whenever their eyes met. The last house was of a type of elf

that Ivy had never seen before. She was disgustingly obese, nearly as fat as two oxen, and constantly feeding her face with bits of greasy meat and delicacies spread on a pedestal beside her. The slop of her feeding dribbled down her dress, staining her gown. She would lick the grease from her short, stubby fingers before mindlessly grasping for another morsel to devour from the tray of food piled adjacent to the wide padded lounge that supported her girth. Ivy wasn't ignorant to the fact that only women were present in the council, and found that a profound point of interest.

"Ah, you speak of the race of men," the Brood Mother noted to Ivy's comment, "once a notable species in their own right, though quite foolish in the end." she folded one pair of arms beneath her dress to be hidden while the other two pairs held her gently as she leaned upon the edge of her elaborate throne. "What they lacked in magic, they made up for in ingenuity; though eventually it was the source of their own downfall."

"Excuse me, but you seem very different from the forest elves; do you not care that the Craven are consuming the Faerylands?" Jinx announced, only to be sprung upon verbally by the queen.

"Of course, we care!" she snapped at the small fairy, in a tone that was undeniably condescending, "Take note, little fey, that the Drow do not hide from the world above, we are as much a part of this land as any woodland elf." she glared for a moment with her scarlet eyes, then caught her temper and drifted casually back to her former self, "Think of it this way, Faerie spawn; any tree or flower left in complete darkness would wither and die, yet if left forever in the burning light of day its dry leaves would scorch and smolder away ...it is the twilight between dusk and dawn, the shadows between the void of darkness and the burning light in which we exist. This thing we call life has a very precarious balance." she noted to Jinx especially.

Leaning forward, one of her thin arms reached out and caressed Ivy's long raven hair, as her blood red eyes met hers.

"If we all existed in the shadows, however, life would be stale indeed," the queen mother grinned unpleasantly, as Jinx noted her tiny sharp fangs within that smile. "Some beings drift

closer to the light, as the woodland elves and the children of the
fey," she gestured to the far right with one hand, "...and some
lean closer to the darkness, as do the Drow," she illustrated with
another hand spread to the far left. "We are all of shadows,
existing in the shade. The danger comes from those that cross
that brink, that blurred line between darkness or light; either of
which is all-consuming."

Ivy could see what she meant, as the Brood Mother conveyed
the wisdom the High Elves chose to keep to themselves. There
was no good nor evil in the world, only how we perceived it.
Too close to the light and one can become no worse than those
who dwell in the darkness, blinding themselves to the woes of
others and self righteousness as the Elven Lords once did. The
Evermore that breathed life into the world was now dwindling,
as the marker between darkness and light was being erased. Ivy
understood it now. It was all the beings that lived within this
shade struggling between right and wrong that kept the balance.
For what were the two ends of a scale without the central stem
by which to measure them?

It was as if in that stare from the queen's terrible eyes, she
could read Ivy's mind as their gaze locked. With a wink and a
nod, the queen withdrew her hand from the girl's cheek, and
leaned back into her tall throne, "You understand now, little
one," the Brood Mother whispered with her strange voice.

Feeling lightheaded, Ivy took a deep breath, wobbling slightly
as the sensation washed over her. It was as if the queen had
spoken directly to her mind in a way she had never before
experienced, and it was draining, having sapped her of her
strength. A servant priestess approached the throne and
whispered into the queen's ear, whereupon she turned back to
the two girls.

"My guards will escort you to the forge of the tower, where
you must prove your worthiness to the Obsidian Order." the
queen mother hissed, motioning to the guards, "The person
whom you seek is a priestess of the order known as Medusa
Sorrowblade, and I do not envy your encounter with her."

*   *   *

The Hunger

Jinx and Ivy were attended to by female servants and allowed to bathe the ash and grime away that screened their fairy glow. It was in the lavish chambers of the bathhouse where the two young girls saw the story of the Drow. Most of the carvings within the temple were in dreary bas relief, but here colorful ceramic tiles were pieced together to create intricate and highly detailed murals that depicted their long history. Unfortunately, Ivy's weirding eyes were unable to appreciate the subtle hues and vivid colors spread throughout the chamber.

Attendants scrubbed them clean with sponges and fine oils, though Jinx seemed not to care for the scent of them. Ivy enjoyed the warm soak, but poor Jinx accidentally broke a few tiles and ornate spigots that she touched out of innocent curiosity, and quickly hid the damaged pieces below the soapy water when she thought no one was looking. Jinx was truly tickled, unused to the attention they were given and she seemed to be thoroughly enjoying the flagrant luxury.

They were given soft gowns woven of fine spider silk to cover their nakedness. The two fey girls grumbled at the need for clothing, though they reluctantly, but politely agreed to suffer the discomfort until they met with the priestess Sorrow in the tower above. The low cut backs were hemmed to allow freedom for their wings, and their weapons were also returned to them buffed and polished.

Many of the younger Drow elves came to watch as the two fey girls were led up to the outer gate, as they had never before seen a true woodland fairy. The main gate was high atop a grand stair that wove up the inner wall of the chasm by way of several switchbacks, making it a formidable barrier against any foe breaching the outer gates. Much like the underworld where Ivy spent her time growing up, there were tunnels that led beyond the great temple into the depths of the earth. It tugged at her emotions as she thought of the friends she had left behind in the

Undergrove so very long ago. Ivy had many questions for the Drow queen, who all but kept herself unavailable for the two emissaries.

When they reached the top of the stairway, there was nothing but a blank wall leaning before them. A drow sorceress stood forward, and with a wave of her hands a glowing glyph formed in the air, commanding the portal to open. The stone slowly began to melt away in bits, then in torrents as the strata sheared apart with a grinding roar. From the exterior, the doorway was well-hidden; appearing to all else to be nothing more than a rocky mountainside, marked only by a single stone cairn.

The Drow covered their eyes as bright sunrays pierced the shadows of the cavern, eclipsed by the great tower that stood before them. The path that led to the tower was marked by several great stones, similar to the ones Ivy had seen lining the green gardens on her short visit to the world tree where she had first met the Elven maiden, Dawn, the very elf who had sent her on this quest.

These henge stones, however, were black as the pitch, carved from the very heart of the island. As the rest of the Drow remained behind in the cavern, several guards ventured out to lead the two fey girls near the base of the tower; though they dared not take a step past the first henge stones that stood lined along the solitary path.

"Present them with your token from the Mages Guild you possess, and it will grant you entry." the male guard instructed as he pointed to Ivy's wrist, his eyes both stern, yet worried.

"And where might we find this Priestess Sorrowblade inside?" Ivy inquired to the sentry, as she noted there was nobody from the tower there to greet them.

"I know nothing about the interior workings of the Tower, nor the Obsidian Order, young fey," the guard offered, "Even the Brood Mother is not privy to their secrets."

"Oh," Ivy found that fact discomfiting, "but I thought the Order were of the Drow?"

"They are," the guard admitted with an uneasy tone, "...or were. The Obsidian Order are a congregation of Drow who devote themselves to the balance. Once beyond these walls, they never leave," Then he lowered his voice with a glance over his shoulder, "I've heard stories they lose their sanity locked up in there; but then again, they may just be stories." the head guard suggested as a minor condolence, "Sorrowblade is a warrior priestess of the Order; request her audience."

"But, if she's a warrior, how does she do battle locked away in a tower?" Jinx butted into the conversation.

"That, young fey, is something you will need to answer for yourself within." The sentry cited to Jinx, who promptly turned on his heel and returned to the front entrance at the stairwell where the other guards awaited. As the sun shifted and the glare of light brushed over the entrance, the rocks and boulders shifted to conceal the entrance once again. Ivy and Jinx were now alone on the ledge high above the snowy plains left to gaze up to the dark sinister tower looming before them.

They had come a long way to get to this point, but their unceremonious reception seemed extremely troubling, even disappointing. Directly in front of the entrance to the high tower sat a great fire pit, surrounded by a low ledge around its circumference. The charred sides of the forge were evidence that it had been used to great length in the past, but it now sat cold, partially filled with chunks of scorched coal and deep piles of ash. Its actual purpose was lost on the two faeries. As they neared the central door at the opposite end of the open hearth; with silent footsteps, several maidens with bleached skin stepped out from the shadows of the doorway, each dressed in vivid red veils.

They neither approached nor addressed the two girls, but stood as still as statues except for their thin silken veils that fluttered softly in the evening breeze. Ivy approached cautiously, her right hand stretched outwards so as to display the bracelet as the token of passage to these hooded sentinels.

"We are sent from the Council of the High Elves. I am Ivy Elvenborn, humbly requesting an audience with the lady Medusa Sorrowblade." she offered to their responding silence. The veiled elves turned away and made their way into the darkened doorway, all except one. The last guardian held forth a hand and motioned with the crook of her finger for them to follow. The girls noticed her overgrown cracked nails filled with grit at the tips of her bloodstained hands. As unsettling as it was, the two faeries had no choice but to comply as they stepped into the stone doorway that swallowed them in darkness.

The moment they stepped foot in the tower, Ivy began to miss the daylight. There was an overwhelming feeling of oppression hanging in the air, drumming through the walls of the narrow corridors. They followed the veiled priestess who kept ahead of them just at the edge of view. Jinx was following in the dark corridors by the sparse candlelight of flickering flames set in tiny alcoves in the walls. For Ivy, whose eyesight was devoid of all color, the darkness of the walls seemed to glow. The ethereal guardian priestess that led their way moved like a mist as she threaded them through the twisting maze of the tower.

Both girls never recalled taking one step up or down, but were shocked when they passed an open balcony that revealed they were now half way up the tower itself. With no time to stand gawking in wonder, they had to keep close pursuit of their elusive escort for fear if they lost sight of her they might sacrifice any chance of ever finding their way out again.

The roar of torches passed overhead as they chased after their guide until they reached an antechamber bolted by a thick wooden door that was blackened with age. The veiled guardian stood silently beside it as she opened the portal and motioned them inside. Her youthful milky white skin was offset by the wrinkled blood-splattered hands she withdrew from beneath her gown. Without a word, she turned and disappeared into the shadows of the corridor.

The windowless room before them was oval, the air thick and stifling. Dozens of trinkets of silver and raw gems were scattered throughout the chamber. There were also blades of every shape and tiny trays that held unfinished brooches and charms. Candles hidden in corners throughout the room seemed to burn coldly, as if their flames were somehow subdued from their natural flicker. Before a small glowing forge stood a woman in a aged grey veil who turned to face them as they entered.

Unlike her fellow sisters, she wore a headdress wrapped tightly about her that entirely covered her eyes. Though beads and trinkets hung from the wrapping, there were no eye holes to speak of, and the fairy girls wondered if she was blind. A pair of wicked looking short swords encrusted with ruby gems lay on the work table beside her, mated by a single chain linked to either end. With a tilt of her head, the priestess seemed to look directly at both girls, though her eyes were hidden.

"What is it you seek..." her strange voice trailed off, revealing her Drow heritage, though she was something other than true elvish now, which Ivy could not quite decipher.

"Are ...are you Sorrowblade?" Ivy asked, "The same jewel smith who created the amulet known as the Tears of Sorrow for the Dwarven kingdom?" Turning to face her, the strange woman gave a hiss of agreement.

"Ssss, the Tears of Tyre." Sorrowblade acknowledged, "And why would you travel so far to seek such knowledge of what you already know?" she breathed in the freakish voice unique to the Drow.

"We were sent by the High Elves to seek the Heart of Flames in the forges of the Dwarves, but our journey has only led us on to this place to find the creator of the amulet it referred to in hopes that you can answer a riddle for the Elves." Ivy answered as best she could.

"The High Elves...?" Sorrowblade hissed once again, as if their mention agitated her. "And why would I answer to the *most High Elves*?" she added with a crack of disdain seeping into her voice.

Ivy shoved her hand forth to show the priestess her token bracelet, though feeling a bit odd not knowing if she was showing it to someone who could not see.

"This was given to me as a token of good will from the Mages Guild beyond Thieves Gate." Ivy disclosed trying to gain her trust, "The Guild of Wizards recognize the dire need to aid the Elves in fighting the Craven, which is now suffocating the Evermore. We cannot seem to awaken the Undying who still slumber, leaving us to a dark fate. Without them, the Craven will surely destroy us all," Ivy pleaded to the warrior priestess.

Medusa stroked the sharp blade of her jeweled knives, as her thoughts lingered in the past. Uncounted centuries had passed since she had made these chained daggers, back when the High Elves and the Drow were one. There was a time when the Elves were but a single race, of the forest green and the moonlit nights; when life itself was a dream. A time long before the race of men, or the plague known as the Craven existed.

She was a young elf from the eternal city, where forests grew as great cathedrals. Her skin was pure, her head draped with the purest snow white hair that braided down to her supple thighs, and her eyes of clear aqua blue could charm any songbird. But change had come to the Faerylands, one that threw their world into chaos. The sins of mankind disrupted the balance, and over the eons their influence displaced the race of elves. The earth mother withdrew the Evermore to protect itself, forcing the Elves to follow. Their perfect existence was forever torn, casting them to the four winds and the depths of the seven seas; dividing the elves into separate tribes who had all but forgotten their true heritage.

These tribes were left isolated over time, having lost what they once were and degenerating into something the race of Elves weren't meant to be. Some tribes reveled in the art of magic and creation, while others found the craft of war a more prudent and tactical calling to pursue. Some clans of Elves idolized loyalty and compassion as beneficial, while others discovered that skills in evasiveness and subterfuge were an easier path to survive upon. Whatever talent they found most effective in their given circumstance, it was only natural for the race of Elves to excelled in its practice.

This wasn't their true calling, of course, but survival was in their blood. When the curse of mankind came into the world, the Elves found an enemy in them they could not fight because of their surmounting numbers. Once before the Elves had combined forces to fend off the scourge known as the Craven. Even the other enchanted races joined together to aid in their struggle. The great battle of Tyre repelled the darkness of the Craven, but in the loss of this decisive war it managed but a small victory.

The isle of Tyre was once a green and vibrant paradise, lush with life, surrounded by blue skies and tranquil seas. The plague known as the Craven materialized as a dark cloud that first appeared as nothing but a tropical storm, but the Elves soon realized something was amiss.

As mankind had destroyed themselves their poison had spread across the lands and seas and between all the realms; nothing was safe from their venom. As the cloud enveloped the island, the plants and animals withered and died, bringing sickness and contagion. The raw magic the clan of the Drow relied upon seemed to ebb away, until it was but a fraction of what it once was. What little was left they kept safe, the essence of the dying elves they collected in the Elfire crystal rather than let it sap away into the Evermore which began to slip so very beyond their reach.

Reborn from these dead lands came strange and unnatural beasts, afflicted by the presence of the Craven. The dwarves were first to call to arms, seeing the danger that was about to befall them. They sent a great army to Tyre to help the tribes of the Drow battle their dark enemy and stop it in its tracks; but as the battle ensued, a great sickness overcame them. Unable to tap the Evermore or aid their falling comrades, the High Elves from the great woods who were skilled in such magical cures, were called upon and swore an oath to provide their support.

But as the conflict dragged on, the woodland elves never arrived, as the dwarves staggered sick and dying; their bodies littering the island like discarded chaff. The Drow used what little magic they had left to sink their Great Temple beneath the land, where the curse of the Craven could not reach them to inflict its strange malady. The passing of the moons turned into years, and the years to centuries; and yet the wood elves never came to check on the brethren they had left abandoned to their dark fate. A hatred grew between them as it did with the races of the dwarves, and here the Craven triumphed.

All was not forgiven, though Sorrowblade had suffered through these events that scarred her for life. She mourned the loss of her sapphire blue eyes that were now glazed and dead. She mourned the loss of the tranquil isle she had called home, that had now become her prison. But more than anything, she mourned the loss of who she once was, forever stripped of the joy she once knew.

Long ago the Drow split again, creating the Obsidian Order, assembled of only the most powerful of female Drow who were attuned to the darkness and could draw upon the fleeting essence of the Evermore. They remained on the surface to keep the Craven at bay. The price they paid was to be forever isolated from their fellow Drow, for in their struggles they became tainted, forever stained by the touch of the Craven. In the memory of the lives lost and the sacrifice of the Dwarves, Sorrowblade created the jewel known as the Tears of Tyre. Over time its title had been bastardized to honor its creator, but even that meaning was lost to those uneducated as to its past. The Tears of Sorrow became a symbol of the dwarven race to remind the woodland Elves of their dishonor.

"What you seek is impossible..." Sorrowblade's voice trailed off, knowing the fairy asked too much.

"We need to find a way to awaken the spirits of the earth, or..." Ivy began, but was cut short by the blind priestess.

"Or the Craven will choke out the Evermore, and you, I, and all of the living creatures of this realm will be the last of our kind." she admitted with her cold words.

"If you cannot help us, then we need to find the Eye ...the Eye of Omens." Jinx blurted out, desperate for an answer. Turning towards her, Sorrowblade let out a foreboding that surprised the young girl.

"You have the mark of death upon you, small one, and will not see this endeavor to its end." she stated with the hiss of her voice. Ivy was a bit shocked, not knowing if it was a threat. Jinx herself seemed rattled, but looked away as if avoiding her blind gaze.

"What did she mean by that?" Jinx asked, a bit puzzled at the sudden twist of the conversation, though Ivy never got the chance to answer.

"The Craven is known by many names, but you need to understand your foe before you can defeat them." Sorrowblade proclaimed, "Long ago, this dark scourge was once known as *the Craving*, though its name has been twisted and distorted by time and the telling of tales. It is a dire hunger that consumes life, and then twists it into something is shouldn't be." the blind priestess testified, "We hold the Eye of Omens, but forbid its use as it is a relic of magic created by the wood Elves; and we do not trust their kind." she proclaimed.

"But, don't you realize what will happen to us all if we fail to awaken the Undying?" Ivy protested, ignoring her concern over the dire prediction the priestess had laid upon her companion.

"I do," she answered bluntly, "...but perhaps the age of the Elves has come to an end." Sorrowblade answered with bleak disdain.

"Why would you allow everyone and everything to die?" Jinx demanded with a measure of sincerity Ivy found moving. Apparently, Sorrowblade was also touched by her spark of emotion and was reminded of those countless ages ago when she was once a beautiful elf maiden herself, living in the green maw of the forest under the leaves and glittering sunlight. It all seemed like a dream now, and the blind priestess felt her heart drop with despair. How did she end up like this?

"Sorrowblade, I understand the anger you and the dwarves must harbor against the forest elves," Ivy began, "but little do you realize they are a dying race." she announced, much to the surprise of her companion, who had no knowledge of this. "The High Elves are but a fraction of the Drow. A mage of the Wizards Guild told me what occurred here on this island, and I assure you that the woodland elves would not have forsaken the Drow or their comrades during the battle that scarred this land, unless they were truly powerless to do so."

"They broke their promise to help us!" the priestess shot back.

"And broken promises can be forgiven." Ivy debated with equal passion. "The High Elves need your help now," she pleaded, "We are but two fey emissaries. Do you really think they would dishonor the Drow by not coming themselves to ask for your aid in person unless they were *truly* unable to do so?" Ivy offered.

The blind priestess pondered for a moment, stroking the razors edge of her knives with the shattered nails of her wrinkled blood stained hands. Finally, after a long aching moment of silence, she answered.

"The Eye of Omens is here, brought by the magi ages ago. I will confer with the sisters of the order, and request that you be allowed to use it. But be warned that it cannot be activated here, for its magic is not of our own, nor can we handle it lest it become tainted by our touch." the priestess proclaimed as she displayed her stained hands to accentuate the point of the matter. "The question is, young fey, what will you do if you look into the Eye and cannot find a way to awaken the Undying?" she asked.

"Then all will be lost unless we find a way," the woodland sprite replied, trying to conceive what that really meant.

The faeries were left waiting in the antechamber as Sorrowblade consulted with her fellow sisters. Here there were no Brood Mothers nor queen, nor head priestess to seek permission from; for all the sisters of the order were equal in their duties.   Disturbing hisses filled the maze of narrow hallways as they deliberated Sorrowblade's request. They too warred against the Craven, but knew not if the messengers of the wood elves were to be trusted.

With head bowed, Sorrowblade returned to her guests, bearing tidings of woe.

"The Order will not allow you to take the relic." she informed them solemnly. This decision worried the two faeries who had come to the end of their wits.

"But ...why?" Jinx blurted back in defense, "Don't they realize the danger we are in?"

"We, the sisters of the Order have been keeping the Craven at bay for centuries, channeling the Elfire and our living essence to stem it from spreading." the blind priestess affirmed, "Though we have been losing ground year after year, there are many of us who tire from the suffering we endure; and there are those of us who believe it is a losing battle we fight."

"So, you're saying that everything that you've suffered through so far was just a waste, and they just want to give up?" the luck fairy chastised the blind elf, "What gives you the right to speak for all the other beings in our world?"

"Without the Obsidian Order, YOU and every being in this world would have faded long ago!" The old drow responded with a hissing shout back at the small girl, surprising her with the level of contempt in her voice. Speechless, Jinx stepped away to let the elf's hostility drain, as it took many moments for Sorrowblade to regain her composure, "However ...you have a valid point to be made, little fairy." the priestess admitted.

"Lady Sorrow," Ivy interrupted the two, trying to be the voice of sensibility, "this battle is shared by others at every corner of the Faerylands. Please understand, we cannot give up on them; there are so many that rely on us; we at least owe it to them to try." Ivy pleaded. Though Sorrowblade's response was not what she expected, having changed her tone from vicious anger to mirth in a heartbeat.

"Hah," she chuckled with the hiss of her voice, an unpleasant sound to say the least, "you *owe* them do you?" the priestess laughed again, "You have been to Thieves gate and met the walking filth that stalks those streets, you owe them a chance too, do you?"

Ivy thought of the thugs that had abducted her and Jinx, but at once she also realized they were merely victims of their environment tainted as it was by the Craven. Most any person or beast would act out of desperation, but the choices they made in doing so showed their true character ...but did it show their true nature? Wouldn't the afflicted people of that city now be living better lives if the Dwarves had come to their aid with welcoming arms, instead of trying to contain them?   The dwarven folk consider themselves a noble race, but lay in drunken stupor in the halls of their kingdom while others suffer for their choices. It didn't seem fair.

"Yes," Ivy finally answered, "yes, we do owe them an opportunity to change." Ivy replied to the drow elf, "Your own Brood Mother showed me that there are those that choose to do right or wrong, and must live with those decisions every day. Today, I choose to do what is right." she exclaimed, and Jinx stood beside her with her arms crossed, giving a supportive nod.

"You Faeries could instead choose to go back to your forests, and live your lives peacefully in your gardens until you fade away, long before the plague ever reaches you." Sorrowblade offered, but Ivy only shook her head.

"That wouldn't be a choice, that would be cowardice."

Sorrowblade only responded with a bow, but neither approved nor disagreed with her poignant answer. Turning as if to lead them back outside the tower, the priestess paused.

"In light of the fact you two have shown such heart and journeyed so far only to face disappointment, I will at least offer the courtesy to allow you to look upon the Eye of Omens so that the tale of your quest to the High Elves will not end so fruitlessly." the blind Drow offered as a condolence.

Both Faeries were clearly in a sour mood as they followed the priestess through the narrow halls to an alcove that seemed nothing more than a dead end. Though apparently blind, the priestess appeared neither handicapped nor slowed in her actions; affirming to Ivy that appearances can be deceiving.

She touched a single stone in the wall, which depressed slightly and then began to grow, pushing the other set of stones around it with a grinding rumbling as they were forced to reorder. That single stone enlarged until it became a stone doorway itself, as embossed etchings of archaic runes burned upon its surface before opening to the secret room beyond. In front of them stood a portcullis heavy with the stale reek of iron. The faeries stood away, knowing what was before them.

The priestess placed both hands on the walls to either side of the gate and the embedded stones began to glow a dull red as if made of burning coal. With a screech the grate lifted both up into the ceiling and down into the floor; the spikes of the gate being crafted into the likeness of jagged fangs of some primordial beast. There sitting in the middle of the room was something that appeared to be a square stone, spinning slowly on its edge. In its center was set a large gemstone, shining a dull amber. It floated above a short pedestal under a beam of soft white light from a source hidden within the low ceiling above; the relic itself seemed quite unimpressive otherwise.

"You may stand at the entrance, but do not enter the vault; as it has protections." the priestess advised.

"And uh, how does it work?" Jinx inquired with her hand to

her chin, trying to see within the dim room, where there appeared to be several dozen tight alcoves set inside the cloister surrounding the relic.

"It is ancient magic wrought by the hands of the first Elves to give one sight beyond sight, of prediction and foreboding. The Drow cannot use it, though it was said the one who uses it can be granted foresight of a single query ...though it comes at a price." Sorrowblade answered as she stepped away.

To Ivy's shock, Jinx jumped into the room with a fluttering beat of her wings before the blind priestess could react. Ivy stalled for but a brief moment as Jinx grabbed for the relic poised above the pedestal. The wood sprite lurched towards the girl to pull her back, not quite believing the degree of her impetuous behavior. Jinx could be unruly and even bratty at times, but this impulsive conduct was beyond excusable.

Clawed bloodstained hands gripped Ivy like a vice, and pulled her back from the gate which slammed shut on the girl. The jagged spikes of the iron gate screeched as they interlocked. Unable to move, Ivy struggled in Sorrowblade's grip as she tried to stop her companion.

"Jinx! What are you doing?" Ivy screamed back into the cell as she fought to free herself from the blind drow, but was unable to move.

"There is no time, we have to find a way..." Jinx shouted back in defense of her actions as she dropped her bow to the floor and reached for the relic floating above. As she grasped it by its frame, she was astounded that it would not budge from its levitation. A familiar hiss erupted as her hands broke the beam of light that held it in place, which created an aura of protection within its diffused glow. From the deep shadows of the narrow alcoves stepped several dozen creatures. Their tainted skin was deathly pale and corrupted with stains and unnatural growths. Their eyes were identical to those of the ice ghouls they had fought before; dead and glazed, and what else she saw was unnerving. Their hands were stained with blood, they were wearing the tattered remnants of red silk gowns clinging in strips around them. These monstrosities were the remains of the afflicted Drow sisters who were now beyond salvation, who devolved into the hideous creatures that roamed the frozen wastes.

Many sisters of the Obsidian Order who were tainted by the Craven eventually lost their sanity, their minds warped and rotted by its poison. Here they lingered awaiting death, clawing at their own putrefied flesh. Those elves that were driven mad by their infection were imprisoned here to capture their essence to be drained into the Elfire which the Drow used in place of the fading magic of the Evermore.

Like a creeping death, they lurched towards the tiny invader of their sanctuary. Jinx glanced at her bow lying on the floor, but realized there were far too many of the ghouls for her to defend herself for long. She had but moments to spare, and chose to grip the relic tightly.

"Show me how to awaken the Undying so we may save our world!" the small luck fairy breathed with haste into the Eye of Omens. What Ivy could see from beyond the tight bars was little, but the gemstone mounted within its frame flashed briefly with images she could not make out. Jinx stood mesmerized as her eyes widened, transfixed by what she witnessed. In mere heartbeats, the amber stone dimmed, and Jinx released the ancient relic. With a few fearful steps back, she cowered from the hideous afflicted drow who began to swarm upon her. With nowhere left to run, she backed towards the gate and turned to Ivy, tears streaming down her eyes as the mindless ghouls at her back began to rip and tear at her wings and tender flesh.

"I ...I saw it Ivy, I know how to save the Faerylands!" She cried through the pain as she gripped the iron bars in her last desperate attempt to tell her companion through the gate. Upon touching the bane of iron, a black stain seeped through her hands, and up her arms to cover her body. A look of fear crept into her eyes, one of disbelief that her natural hex had not protected her somehow. A short scream of pain escaped her lips, only to be suddenly silenced. The clawed blood-stained hands of the sickened and enraged sisters shredding her wings and hair were muffled as Jinx fell apart into a blackened pile of ash to the floor around them.

Ivy looked on in horror and anguish at the fate of her friend as she tugged at the binding arms of her captor; the black soot settling into powder at her feet. With a tear of sap welling in her silvery eyes, Ivy couldn't believe it; Jinx was gone.

*   *   *

Condemned

Ivy wept, the first time she had ever done so from feeling such a loss. Jinx was only trying to save them, and had put herself in peril; but the knowledge she had gained was lost when her tiny life was snuffed out. Her sacrifice had been in vain.

"Mourn not your friend," Sorrowblade callously hissed into Ivy's ear, "for she has condemned you." the priestess threatened her with an unmistakable tone of finality. The growls and hisses of the sickened elves behind the bars faded away as shreds of the luck fairy's wings drifted to the cobblestone like dry parchment among the pile of black soot. Slowly, they crept back into the darkness to endure their eternal suffering.

Sorrowblade's grip was like steel and the sisters of the order appeared to chastise her for exposing the relic to the two faeries. Their strange breathy speech erupted into bickering that swelled as Ivy was bound in heavy manacles. Surrounded by these heartless Drow, Ivy realized her long and arduous quest had come to a sudden and unpleasant end.

All the candles that burned strangely out of phase flared brightly for a long moment as the sisters of the Obsidian order glanced at one another, as if startled by what it implied. Ivy looked up and strained at her chains as the vibration of a gong from a huge bell rumbled through the strange stairless tower. Without another word, the sisters scampered off in different directions into the maze of corridors beyond the central chamber where Ivy was held captive.

"What was that sound?" Ivy asked the blind priestess who was now her warden, which was an ironic turn of fate considering what she had gone through to find her.

"It is the calling..." Sorrowblade finally answered after a long pause as she waited for the ring of the bell to fade so she could speak above its dying tone that resounded through the endless labyrinth of corridors. "You must be brought to face the wrath of the Brood Mother."

It was an unprecedented turn of events, considering the sisters of the order did not answer to the queen. Yet, she was being expelled from the tower back into the hands of the Drow who dwell below. Ivy didn't understand what was happening.

"What is this calling?" the wood sprite began to get nervous as to what was going to happen to her as the priestess roughly bound her wings with a long strip of red silk cloth.

"Enough talk!" Sorrowblade hissed as she pulled a small dagger from her side and struck Ivy unconscious with the butt of its jeweled pommel, "You have caused us enough grief already that I should also have to suffer your constant yapping."

৪০০৪

Ivy's head throbbed where the blind elf had struck her. She awoke on her knees, both her wings and hands bound behind her back. The sisters of the order had left her leaning against the edge of the burning forge in front of the tower, its heat giving little comfort against the chill of the air. Nightfall had come, and she watched through bleary eyes as the mountain cliff beyond the stone path dissolved away to be replaced by a hollow darkness. A number of figures approached, rattling of armor and swords; and dragged her away into the black hole of the mountain.

Down, down the long stairs they went, Ivy still unaware of her surroundings until she was doused with cold water. The Drow queen sat before her, glaring at her with those horrible bloody eyes. All six of her hands were grasping the multiple arms of her bizarrely shaped throne. Thankfully, it wasn't the floor of the council chamber she was sprawled across, as Ivy sat up to see where she was. It was a large room lined with looming statues that were sculpted so as to appear as if they held up the ceiling on their backs. There were several armed guards, including many Drow acolytes who stood about the room, exchanging hushed words of concern.

"Do you realize what you have done?" the queen finally spoke when she saw Ivy was cognizant. Her raven hair tousled, the wood sprite gazed upon the queen with her silvery eyes as she stirred. Ivy gave a soft groan, but for lack of an answer, the Drow Mother responded for her, "Your companion used magic that is polar to our own, and you have awakened the Dwellers." she spat. In truth, the Brood Mother was angry, for she had hoped this day would not be for a great time to come. She had soldiers and warrior priests, but the Sisters of the Obsidian Order, who were the Drows greatest weapon, were confined to their tower to battle on a different front.

A pair of acolytes helped Ivy stand, brushed her hair out of her eyes, and straightened her silken gown which helped her regain a minor sense of dignity before the queen.

"This is not of my doing, I had no idea that my companion was going to do what she did." Ivy tried to defend herself.

"Oh, I think you most certainly did," the queen accused, "It is my understanding that she also paid the price for her disrespect," the Drow queen stated bluntly; a tone which Ivy found offensive. Ivy opened her mouth to curse at the queen for being so cold, but quickly realized that might attract immediate reprisal by one of the guards with another blow to shut her up.

"...And what are these Dwellers you speak of?" Ivy finally responded after forcing herself to quell her temper.

"The magic of the Woodland Elves is contrary to our own, and you should have realized that we Drow exist here upon a very precarious balance." she spoke with her gliding hands, which nearly took on a guise of some strange exotic dance, "by using that relic of the High Elves, it accentuated the arcane enchantments of the tower; manifesting itself like the beacon of a lighthouse across a black and stormy sea. The foolish actions of your accomplice has awakened creatures afflicted by the Craven, ones that hold a seething hatred for anything but the corrupt darkness in which they dwell." the queen chimed, clarifying the direness of the situation at hand.

"Are ...are you going to kill me?" Ivy feared to ask, but was at a loss to inquire otherwise. She had been through so much, just to witness how life could be snuffed out so carelessly, and without purpose. The queen seemed to ignore her question for the moment as she conferred privately with a priest on matters at hand, then turned her attention back to the shackled fairy.

"Oh, no, my dear, that would be too kind," she gleamed with a malicious smile upon her thin lips, "Besides, your presence holds a unique opportunity for our defense."

"Your defense?"

"The Dwellers are moving towards the tower of the Obsidian Order, and their path of destruction leads directly past the front steps of our sacred temple; endangering us all. Beyond this sanctuary lie many deep and mysterious caverns even the Drow have not fully explored. Many of the most tainted creatures of the Craven have clustered there, and were content in their existence until the ripple of Elven magic snapped our precarious measure of peace. We have fought them back over the eons since the day the Craven tarnished this land," the queen stood to pace around the Elvenborn, "and they have learned to tolerate the Drow and our resilience. This temple is the last haven of the Drow, and it must not fall!"

"So, what will you have of me, why not let the sisters of the Order deal with them?" Ivy responded in confusion, wondering what kind of trouble this spidery queen was leading up to.

"Few have ever entered the Tower of Madness and returned, and the sisters of the Obsidian Order cannot leave its walls, for they are wed to every rock, every stone built upon it. Needless to say, you have seen the strangeness of it, for they are the living conduit of the Elfire, the spirit of the Drow. Within their walls, however, our essence remains neither touched nor revitalized by the Evermore; it germinates and rots, bending, twisting into something we can use as a shield to ward off the uncleanliness of the Craven." the queen enlightened the fairy who was still confused at the purpose of her quant education into this matter.

"If you give me the Eye of Omens to take back to the High Elves, I promise to return with their support," Ivy pleaded in vain, "There are more encompassing issues at hand here."

In response to her brash plea, the queen gave a loud cackle at her implied ignorance.

"You think me the fool?" she cried, waving her six arms, "The woodland elves have deserted us before and left us to rot, trapped upon this accursed island; and you would actually have us turn a blind eye to that insult and grant you our trust? On the weak promise by a fey who has already broken her word?" the Brood Mother snapped back, "You ask too much! Besides, it is far too late; the Dwellers have already begun to flood the outer caverns and will be upon us before the first moon."

Her comment reminded Ivy that after the passing of the 3rd evening of the new moon, she too, would be trapped here until the next summer solstice. Needless to say, she wasn't going anywhere at the moment as it was.

"Then what do you propose?" Ivy finally offered, noting that she clearly had no leverage in the matter. With a smile of consideration, the queen folded all three pairs of her arms across her chest, mindful that she had this fairy to bend to her will as she pleased.

"You have shadows within you, young fey," the queen admitted softly, surprising Ivy with her strange choice of words, "though you are an Elvenborn, you have a streak of darkness running through you unlike other fey. I can see it, I can feel it, I can smell its fragrance upon you." she stated, using dramatic gestures upon each point as she looked into her eyes, caressed her cheek, and lightly sniffed the nape of her delicate neck.

Unfortunately, Ivy had understood what she meant. She had always had an unexplainable attraction to dark magic. The life of a forest fey was lacking; boring in comparison to the stories she had been told of the powerful beasts of shadows. She didn't crave such powers over others, but for something far more personal ...something she could not quite explain. Ivy Elvenborn did not quite know her true self, but was about to have it revealed to her. With one powerful hand, the Brood Mother ripped the delicate silk robe from Ivy, leaving her naked before her.

"This will not do," the queen dropped the torn gown to the floor, which a servant quickly extracted from her feet. "I have something more fitting in mind for your transformation." The acolytes brought forth a jeweled chain embedded with hundreds of scarlet gems, flattened rubies cut into discs. They unshackled the fairy and wrapped the jeweled chain around her in a way that resembled an exotic form of armor. Unbinding her wings, the tall queen approached Ivy, taking her hands into her own.   Her second pair grabbed her waist, and her third cradled her head so that their eyes were locked.

"You are strong, so I will give you the opportunity to discover what you were meant to be." the queen's voice lost its breathy tone as Ivy looked into her mind once again.   From behind her, two more servants approached; one bearing Ivy's enchanted spear, the other held a circlet of spikes, embedded with a single jewel.   Holding Ivy's head still, locked in trance, the Drow queen passed a small token of her essence to the girl, bleeding through her touch as a glowing darkness.   It seeped into her delicate skin only to quickly fade away.   Unnoticed by the fairy, the gem on the token bracelet upon her wrist turned from its evergreen hue to a deep scarlet.

Troubling images swam through her mind, enhancing her sense of confusion as her excited nerves began to tingle.   Along her back, her forest green wings darkened to a midnight shade of black, as dark as her raven hair.   Somehow, Ivy felt more confident, more grounded and at ease as the sense of benevolence and self-sacrifice she had worn for so long evaporated away; and an all too familiar feeling of selfishness she had once known as a child had returned, and she welcomed it.   Unconsciously, for a moment, a twisted smile flashed across her face which the Brood Mother did not fail to notice.

"Good, you feel it, don't you?   The easing of needless burdens from your shoulders when you set your conscience free." the queen whispered into her mind.   Releasing her grip on the girl, she touched a single finger to Ivy's blush lips as a sign to silence her.

Ivy felt something inside her growing, deep within the center of her being.   A seething temper, like a slowly churning rage that began to swell.   It felt so primal, yet strangely calming with the sense of ease and relief it brought at its climax.   Her skin began to crack ever so slightly, with tiny runs that scored her delicate flesh that imitated the intricate lines and patterns of tree bark.   It was the core magic of her essence that she had stumbled upon as a child, and she understood now the true powers she possessed.   Ivy wondered for a moment with passing scorn, why the High Elves had kept this knowledge hidden from her for so long, forcing Ivy to discover her powers on her own time.

If it be known, a wood spirit is truly a terrible being to behold and one to be rightfully feared. Ivy was born of the untamed forests, she could sing with the wind, speak with the trees and every moss or fern or blade of grass. She could pull strength from the very soil, crack stone with the might of her roots, and rend flesh with the cuts of a thousand leaves. She now felt the full potency of her powers and they were deadly indeed.

Folding several arms beneath her gown once again, the Drow queen turned back to her throne, releasing Ivy to her own recognizance.

"I give you this gift, but beware that I can just as easily strip it away." she warned the young fey who had transformed before their eyes.

Ivy stood erect with her shoulders firm, with a sense of pride washing over her that she was something to be feared, truly realizing she could quickly end any common Drow who slighted her. Upon the queen's command, an acolyte stepped forward from across the room to offer the wood sprite her spear, but Ivy casually turned a wrist as woody branches shot forth from her fingers to snatch the weapon from the servant's hands, who was still a dozen steps away, and retracted to their former shape. As Ivy tapped the gilded butt of the spear to the ground beside her, every elven guards in the room took a nervous step back.

The queen herself, though, was a power to contend with, bound with the strength, stealth and cunning of a predatory arachnidan, a widow spider; the dark symbol of the Drow.

As the Woodland elves had created the Faerie, the Drow had borne the lineage of Goblins. They were fey in their own rights, spawned by the hand of elves, but birthed within the shadows and of the putrefied mire of the earth. As opposite to the Faerie as anything could be, the High Elves of the forest looked over their children with love and protection; but the Drow cared not for their own twisted and bastardized offspring. Filled with hatred and selfish greed, it was no wonder the races of goblins became estranged from the dark elves when their kind was so callously disposed of into the dark pits and caves of the earth eons ago.

Being their nature, the Drow had cared not for the well-being of their own creations. Even the lesser Goblings were used as mere slaves. Like the numerous types of fey in the forests, Goblins branched out into several clans and tribes of fey of the darker realms. They preferred the essence of the defiled mud, and bore no inherent sense of compassion as the race of Faerie felt for one another and all living things.

Gifted with a new understanding of her powers, Ivy presumed the Drow queen wished to christen the wood fairy as her champion against the Dwellers. In that assumption she was sadly mistaken.

"My sister fey is dead, by the hands of your corrupted priests who cower within their obsidian tower," Ivy responded, "and you would expect that I should now risk myself as a warrior of the Drow to face these creatures, these *Dwellers* that come calling at your door?" At her audacious claim, the Brood Mother gave a loud cackle that resounded throughout the hall.

"Such arrogance mere moments after releasing your true essence? Don't be such a fool little girl!" The queen spat back in her face, "You will lead my warriors to defend against the onslaught that approaches, not as my champion ...but as bait!"

Another drow priestess entered the chamber and presented the queen with a sealed box carved of ebony black stone. Upon her nod of approval after examining the contents within, the maiden approached Ivy and withdrew a large amber gemstone which she set within the empty centerpiece of the girl's armor. Using a set of silver tongs so as not to touch it with her own pale flesh, the jeweled chain Ivy had been draped with clasped to the jewel the moment they touched. Unsure of what the object was, Ivy took a half step back, wondering what the queen had placed upon her.

"What you see there is the gemstone plucked from the Eye of Omens, and the very object that the Dwellers are now drawn too like a beacon," The queen announced, as Ivy looked down to her chest at the sparkling amber jewel. Realizing what the queen had in mind, the faerie tried to remove it, only to realize that the enchanted chain armor itself was bound to her flesh. Though her fingers twisted into roots around lengths of the chain she was still unable to gain a secure hold or pull it from her bark patterned skin. The gemstone contained an eerie light that danced within, as she recognized it was the relic that Jinx had used.

"What did you..." Ivy began to form her question before the queen interrupted her.

"A proper question would be why not just give the entire relic to the Dwellers and dissuade them from their march upon us, hmm?" She gave a wry grin, "The Eye of Omens is far too powerful a device to relinquish, most especially into the hands of our enemies, foolish child." The queen got up and casually examined the markings of the black box that had contained it, which had been recently delivered to her by the sisterhood, "Although we cannot use its magic, the sisters of the Order realized that the relic disperses its bewitchment into the oracle stone embedded within it. True, it can not be used again until a new seeing stone is replaced within its frame, but only the High Elves possess the knowledge to do so. Thus, I've decided to make an acceptable sacrifice considering the circumstances. Both you and that accursed gemstone are replaceable, the relic itself is not." The queen taunted her with an evil grin.

Ivy was fuming, and sharp thorny roots began to stretch from her fingers, but when the Drow Mother's glare met her eyes, she quickly realized attacking the queen would be a grave mistake. Whatever she had done to release her powers, the queen had reminded the woodland fey that they could just as easily be stripped away.   The Brood Mother of the Drow possessed powers beyond her comprehension, and was a foe not to be trifled with lightly or on mere impulse. Ivy realized she would have to bide her time and seek an escape from this situation at a later point. At least under the present circumstance, she was unbound from chains and armed once again; and she would use this to her advantage rather than waste it in some foolish attempt to defend her pride.

"So then, what now?" Ivy demanded with a smoldering glare in her eyes.

"I have rallied my warriors to defend Phantom Pass, the sole gateway to our lower realm. There you will be placed beyond its breach where you may choose either to drive them back, or succumb to their onslaught." the queen announced her fate, believing that the girl had no real chance of defending herself against the horde.

"So why bother with the soldiers, and not just sacrifice me to them and be done with it?" Ivy contested the Drow queen's logic. Sitting back in her throne, the queen unfolded two set of arms to rest upon her chin regarding the course of action she had already set into motion.

"We have dealt with the Dwellers before. With their kind there is no real guarantee that relinquishing the source of their agitation will sate them, thus it would be prudent that we dispatch a garrison to hold the pass. The sacrifice of a true Elvenborn and forfeiting the seeing stone that unhinged them, quite frankly, will greatly improve the chance of appeasing them and halt their advance. They are very fierce and aggressive creatures, so a show of force would do well to dissuade them from continuing their surge against our sanctuary." The queen finally shrugged with the logic of her tactics, though her callousness did nothing to comfort Ivy from her own impending execution.

As the queen consulted with a number of her priests, an order was put out to call warriors from each of the seven houses of the Drow as representatives of their family crests. Female oracles who were also skilled in the mastery of spell craft readied staffs and wands and other instruments of sorcery empowered by the living Elfire. Ivy was ushered out before the Drow council as a formality before her punishment was dealt, and was ushered away by several guards brandishing smoldering fireblades. The queen had one last word of spite for the fairy as she was driven from her site at the mouth of the temple.

"Heed that this fate was brought upon you by the hands of High Elves, young fey. Yet remember it was the Drow who gave you the gift of insight to your true powers, Elvenborn, so that you may meet your end with honor." she breathed with a hint of distaste as she turned her back on the condemned girl.

Ivy realized there was a measure of honesty in her words, wondering why the High Elves would hide so much of her true talents for so long, and send her on this perilous and now pointless quest which they should have fulfilled themselves. She had never felt so betrayed; where were the elven lords now in her hour of need?

It was the grievance of the Drow who had suffered much since the High Elves left them to their fate. They only saw the arrogant forest elves as living in their flowered gardens without a care for their elvin kin who had been scattered to the four winds. Trapped on this accursed island, the Drow were forced to fend for themselves, severed from the living strings of the Evermore and unable to weave the vital essence of creation from the empty darkness that had suffocated the world around them. They were left with only the bare means to staunch the plague that engulfed the isle of Tyre by the sacrifice of the sisters of the Obsidian Order who shielded the seven houses of the Drow at the cost of their own lives.

It was drawn to Ivy's attention that whatever the Drow did, they did with great ceremony and flair. Hundreds of the Drow's greatest warriors marched forth over the suspended bridges and causeways, wearing exotic armor that interlocked like scales. The strange weapons they bore were vicious in their designs. Cruel blades curved like claws, and spiked clubs wrought in silver. Wands of the sorcerers gleamed with tips of the Elfire leaving wisps of glowing smoke in their wake, followed by scores of female warriors bearing double chained blades. The Drow spent their lives training for battle, for they reveled in the glory of it.

The bridges converged into a central path that wound deep into the caverns and Ivy was escorted by a legion of dark elves bearing long pikes streaming with colorful banners. She had expected a long journey to their outer gates, hopefully giving her time enough to devise some sort of plan to escape. Though her wings were unbound, the dozen guards surrounding her were armed with curved fiery swords, their enchanted flames licking their long sharp blades; an effective deterrent for the wood sprite to consider. She would have to wait until she was safely out of their range before taking any action; for to do otherwise would be not only reckless, but likely fatal.

She was surprised that the garrison came to a halt before approaching the third hour of their march. Before them stood two great cliffs straddling their path, nearly identical in height. Hidden within the rock walls were a collection of sharply cut pathways that led to their plateaus. The flag bearers mounted their pikes at the top of these cliffs, their colors wavering in stark contrast against the dark rocky sediment of the grotto. From this vantage point, it appeared as if the path entered a narrow canyon of stone that stretched into oblivion. It was here the Drow prepared to make their stand, yet Ivy was boggled by the fact that there was nothing blocking the narrow fissure. No gate, no stone fortress or walls to act as a barrier spanned the cliffs as she would have expected.

The lead guard directed Ivy to an empty clearing just beyond the brink of the cliffs where hundreds of Drow stood at bay, readied with shining silver weapons in hand, as were the sorcerers armed with their wands and staves. Ivy was confused as she turned to see them all staring into the dark chasm of nothingness beyond, as if transfixed. Why had the powerful Drow not built a defensive wall against these Dwellers? It made no sense to her in the slightest.

With practiced discipline the Drow stood patiently though Ivy clearly had lost her own. There was nothing but the silence of the shadows, occasionally broken by the clatter of a falling pebble or stone from the gloomy canyon beyond. Safely out of range of the fire-wielding warriors, Ivy considered taking flight down the dark path to disappear into the rift before the sorcerers could react. While contemplating that course of action, she came to find why Phantoms Pass had earned its name.

From the edge of the cliff walls an eerie mist began to form, weeping from the very stone. Rippling swirls came together to form ghostly images, though far too blurred to truly take shape. She thought her mind was hearing things when faded whispers echoed through the cliffs; turning behind her she thought they were the Drow, but their lips were sealed shut. The incoherent voices came from the darkness beyond, and for a moment, Ivy trembled.

A drumming could be heard far away, becoming louder as the dark canyon started to glow by the embers of what appeared at first to be torchlight. As the small pinholes of light began to dot the cavern walls and ceiling high above, she was trying to understand what she was seeing. The Drow elves had evolved with a measure of night vision living beneath the ground for so long, but nothing as close to what Ivy had with her glazed weirding eyes. For the first time since she had been changed by the wizard's faulty healing spell, Ivy saw colors other than the dull grey of reverse light that had afflicted her vision.

Vivid stabbing hues of red and yellow pierced her eyes, as she saw the walls themselves come alive with the moss and lichen that covered the cavern walls. A majority of the disfigured creatures marching on the path towards her still appeared ethereal, but there was one that stood out among all others, shining with an opaque glare that Ivy could not mistake. She faltered for a moment not knowing if all the legends she had heard were entirely true. She was seeing a dragon.

Ivy turned, considering taking her chances by darting back over the heads of the Drow to escape, for she had no wish to test the strength of her new found powers against such a legendary beast. To the Drow, the walls had come alive with the color of the moss and fungi growing upon the stone, burning their energy at the presence of those afflicted by the Craven. Some would say it was eerily beautiful, in the most destructive of ways. Their proximity seemed to suck the very life out of everything around them. Moss and mushrooms of every size grew at an accelerated rate as if time itself was on fire.

Ivy's cockiness suddenly withered, for she had no defense against such accursed magic. There she stood, alone between two armies bent on her demise. In growing desperation, she again tried to pry off the amber jewel from its central clasp bound to her armor. The light within the gemstone danced strangely, as if antagonized by the presence of so many minions of the Craven. Distraught, Ivy turned to face the Drow, estimating the gamble she was about to take. To face the

Craven like this was certain death; she had no other choice but to escape over the battle lines of the Drow and find her way back to the surface.

Ivy fluttered her black wings, testing their strength as to what side of the cliff she was to shoot for. Truly, there were far too many Drow, wands and bows in hand for her to escape the next few moments entirely unscathed. The moments tensed to the point she realized she had to make a move before the two armies clashed, and she arched to the tip of her toes to take flight when a heavy gale suddenly heaved down upon her. Turning her head over her shoulder back towards the canyon, it had all been blotted out by the dragon looming over her. The flash of its enormous wings kicked up the dust of cavern floor.

Its head so large it could swallow her whole, its scales rippling with a prismatic sheen to her flawed eyes, seeing what others could not. The Drow warriors faltered a step as the beast reared its head and gave a deafening roar. The ground beneath her was solid stone under the layer of dust; and even if she could root herself, this eternal creature could snap her like a twig. She would have rather faced a hundred stone giants than this beast that glimmered with the very fabric of the Evermore. She could see its energy, weaving and moving across its scales, shimmering within the taut fabric of its wings. The beast had advanced before its troops, drawn to the very gemstone that was the cause of their rage.

For a fading moment Ivy thought about going out with a fight, but there was no purpose to it. The woodland sprite braced herself and stared the dragon in the eye with bold defiance. She was about to die, and would do so with dignity.

*   *   *

Stormrage

From behind the girth of the great dragon poured the multitudes of afflicted who were bent and twisted into something far more obscene than any goblin. A rattle of armor came from the Drow warriors stationed on the cliffs above, the tension in the air so thick it could be cut with a dwarven blade. Through her eyes and seeing the ghostly images of the minions surging around her, Ivy wondered for a brief moment how it was that a dragon could be party to their kind. From all the stories she had heard they were all but extinct, and true dragons were one with the elements that kept equilibrium within their world; yet this one was ablaze with the threads of the Evermore. Why had the presence of the Craven not destroyed it as well?

Through her weirding eyes, Ivy could not see this creature as the surrounding Drow did; for they did not see it as a dragon at all. Even to the corrupted goblins and beasts that surrounded it, the creature appeared as a great horned demon of mist and smoke; a guise well-fitting for the likes of those afflicted by the Craven. The monster glared at the surrounding cliffs peppered with the warrior Drow, and its gaze drifted back to the small fairy who stood alone before it. The gem inset in her chest gleamed once, enraging the goblins; and with one curl of the beasts wings around her, Ivy Elvenborn vanished. The great demon roared once again in defiance of the Drow, shaking the very bedrock of the cavern. With resignation, the giant beast slowly turned and made its way back to the dark shadows from whence it came.

In a psychotic rage, the twisted goblins screamed threats at the Drow, as both a show of force and sign of their displeasure; but eventually turned to follow the retreat of the great demon back into the depths. The Drow stood shaken, but held firm as they watched the Dwellers slink back into the rift, followed by the dimming glow that surrounded their presence. The strange mist that bled from the rocks eventually faded away, and the Drow were satisfied that the Dwellers had accepted their sacrifice.

ଞ୍ଚେଷ

Ivy awoke, much to her own surprise.   The last thing she remembered was the dragon folding its great wings around her and snatching her up. She had struggled briefly, but passed out cold when every ounce of strength drain from her body. Sitting up, she found herself in a perch above an enormous cavern, lush with strangely colorful and exotic plants ...had she died ...was this the Evermore?

When she stepped out towards a grand balcony that overlooked the realm below her, a tender but powerful voice reached out to her from behind.

"I would ask that you do not linger by the landing, as it would not bode well that you be seen at this time." the voice advised, as Ivy turned to see the great dragon poised behind her, laying at rest with only its head reared to address her. Ivy looked around for her spear, only to find it laying far out of reach; however, this unusual change of events gave her pause. Speechless at first, Ivy struggled to find the words while she saw that she was unhurt; but noticing that the jeweled armor bound to her by the Drow queen was now gone.

"What ...what is this place" the fairy stuttered, "...and how do you come to be here, for I had thought the race of dragons had vanished?" Wide-eyed, Ivy felt weak as she tried to find her bearings, while also noticing that not only was the Drow chain gone, but her skin was no longer shaded with the tile of bark. In its stead, layers of scales lined her body.

"Most interesting..." the large dragon replied with great thought, "how is it now that you see my true form?"

"I, I don't understand." Ivy stumbled in reply yet again.

"Forgive my rudeness, young fey, I am known by many names, but among the race of Elvish folk I was once remembered as the mighty *Stormrage*. I have been hiding among the creatures the dark elves call the Dwellers for eons, long since the time of the battle with the Craven that has forever scarred this land," the great beast answered, "In their perception I no longer appear as a Dracos, but as a horrible beast of shadow and smoke, this is nothing more than an illusion, a required mirage to hide amongst them."

"But, why the deception." Ivy blurted.   At her childish ignorance, the dragon gave the slightest hint of a grin.

"It is my knowledge that such illusions are no stranger to the race of fey, which I believe your kind practice as faerie glamour. A cloak to protect yourselves from those whom you wish to conceal your true nature," Stormrage breathed with his powerful voice, yet it was strangely soothing to her sensitive pointed ears."

"I thought you were going to kill me," Ivy took her surroundings in, trying to make sense of it all, "why is it that you fight the dark elves and not join them against their common foe?" she asked with an expression of confusion.   Here was a living dragon among the twisted followers of the Craven, what would be the purpose of such a ruse?

"You misunderstand fey," the dragon replied, "posing as a vile and powerful champion of these demented creatures, I am in a unique position to be able to help keep the peace between them."

"But why would you want to live like that?" Ivy inquired, realizing the dragon had suffered this situation for eons within the very heart of their enemy.

"Ah, a wise question indeed," the dragon breathed, "...in truth, it began as a matter of circumstance, rather than choice, I will admit," Stormrage answered in his defense, "During the great battle of Tyre, when the legions of Dwarves began to perish, even the spirits of the land and sea started to wane. I watched as the war between the Craven and the Drow began to falter, though I failed to takes sides as do the Undying. In the end, I, too, was affected by the outcome of that struggle." the dragon confessed, "As their presence suffocated the skies, even I was forced to concede to the strange forces at hand. I truly had no wish to enter this trial between the realms, but the mindless minions of the Craven also sought to label the Dracos as their foes," the dragon then sighed, as if in regret, "The dragons sought neutrality by turning a blind eye to the struggle of lesser beings, and as a result, many of us perished because of the senseless arrogance of that mistake."

The words of the dragon resounded in Ivy's head, as did the very same admission by the High Elves who had also suffered by the hand of their own vain and cavalier misconceptions.

By seeking neutrality, the race of dragons were just as guilty as the Undying who sought to slumber while the rest of the world suffered, which many creatures of the Faerylands viewed as an act of cowardice. In their infinite wisdom of refusing to take sides, they eventually condemned themselves to the same fate they had sought to escape. Truly, such lofty detachments were rarely productive on any scale, even for the great dragons. It was what Stormrage revealed to her in the following moments, however, that compounded that viewpoint.

"My companion and I were sent here by the High Elves to seek a way to awaken the Undying, for only they can help turn the tide in our struggle against the Craven which is now smothering the Evermore itself out of existence." Ivy explained to the dragon who tilted his large pointed head in deep thought, stricken by her words.

"Oh dear, oh dear..." he replied, his mournful eyes drifting off at the revelation of what Ivy had just revealed.

"...But, my companion is now gone, lost forever when we were captured." Ivy added on a sad note. The dragon dropped his great head to rest beside her, with a slight look of guilt; in as much a way that a scaly dragon can appear as such.

"I realize that there has been a level of animosity growing between the woodland and the dark elves, but I wasn't aware of its extent," the dragon admitted, "But I have to ask; didn't either of them educate you about the Undying?" he gave the fairy a quizzical glance.

"Um, well, no ...not really," Ivy confessed, "Though I have heard many stories from other faeries, and even met a water spirit by the name of Tempest." she related, while holding up her hand where she was touched by the spirit under the waterfall. The contact with the elemental spirit had enchanted her with the ability to exist in the underwater realms. With a mild look of surprise, the dragon reared up his head slightly and gently breathed upon her exposed hand, whereupon the usually invisible stain of the enchantment began to glow ever so slightly, then again faded back to its former state.

"Hmm, well, I wondered where she had gone." he mentioned blandly. The statement took Ivy off guard.

"You knew her, the water spirit?"

"Well, yes, I did, but that was a long time ago, when she was... I mean, *before* she had transformed." Stormrage quickly corrected himself, further boggling the wood sprite who stood there with a wrinkled brow. "My apologies, young fey, you seem confused and have a right to be."

"Yes, I am," Ivy replied, "The elemental spirits of the earth we call the Undying, transformed from *what*?

"Well ...from dragons, of course." Stormrage stumbled across his words with the obvious answer. Ivy was transfixed as her eyes widened. Why had nobody told her? It was maddening the games that the Elves played with the lesser fey! She stood there gawking, not knowing what to say in response. The dragon addressed the fairy to help put her at ease, "I'm assuming from the look on your face the Elves failed to tell you this fact, perchance?"

"It sure would have saved a lot of time and aggravation if they would have just come out and told me that!" Ivy fumed, "I mean, why is it that the Elves always find it necessary to befuddle everyone with riddles and hidden agendas? Grrrrr!" Ivy growled, her face momentarily turning a notable tint of red.

"Well, I can't rightly help you there, little fey," the dragon replied, "but I'm sure they had their reasons ...whatever they might be." He looked off into the shadows without a real clue.

Ivy was flustered at what she had been put through just to find out certain facts that could have made life a whole lot easier had they just been forthright from the start. What would be the purpose of such lack of candor, which pretty much tipped on the brink of outright deception. She would have to address Dawn if and when she next saw her, about these insulting games the Elves were so determined to play on the lesser fey.

"So then, *you're* a dragon," Ivy accused with a demanding tone, "how do we awaken the Undying?"

"Well, young one, that is a tricky question." the dragon answered, searching for a way to begin explaining himself. Ivy sat down and crossed her arms, giving him a stern look; making it clear he was on the spot and would have little chance of being able to weasel out of giving her a clear explanation.

Stormrage had the powers of illusion, and used his magic to manipulate several stone shards lying about into elaborate forms to help illustrate the story in the air before her. Dragons were among one of the very first living creatures created by nature, and because of this, their powers were vast and left them with an abundance of raw magic at their control. There were dragons of the seas, the mountains, the winds, the rain, of the fires of the earth, and every combination in between. They helped keep the world in balance from the perpetual struggle of order against the utter devastation of chaos.

Though as wise and powerful as they were, they were still mortal, but were gifted with a unique ability in the cycle of life. Just as the fey returned to their own individual essence when they passed from the living, so did the great race of Dracos when their time had come. Though still a part of the Evermore, they kept their individuality and thus became what was known as the Kami ...the spirits of the earth; spread out amongst the very corners of the world. They also watched as the Elves came into existence, and by communing with the spirits of the land and sea, they, too, learned to coexist with nature.

There was once a time when every part of the world was in great harmony with the elements and all living things; thus, the Gaia, our world, created new life to share this joy. Stormrage had to illuminate for Ivy, that by the very nature of life, order and chaos have equal reign; and so, some creatures were swayed towards one extreme, and some towards the other. The more life there was, the more colors and hues of the palate. Being one of the first respectful races who learned to exist with nature, the Elves were given the knowledge of how to recreate new life of their own.

"And this was how the Elvenborn and all the fey came into existence," Ivy exclaimed, "born of nature..."

"...And of the elements both pure and tainted." the dragon added.

"So, then, how did everything turn so terribly wrong?" Ivy

inquired with a worried look on her face.

"It is that presumption where you fail, young fairy," the dragon corrected her, "for there is no right or wrong assigned to order or chaos." Stormrage attempted to enlighten her with a wider perspective, which she found truly enthralling. The truth was that in their world, the Dracos, and even the race of the Elves were far, far older than she could have ever dreamed. Many times the swing of balance between order and chaos had come to pass over the earth, as the pendulum arched from one side to the other. As it was with day and night, love and hate, war and peace; each had their time to exist. The most recent of events was the tipping of the scales by the pitiful race known as mankind.

"So the *Kami*, the spirits of our world will reawaken after their passing, young fey." the dragon advised. as if it were a simple answer to all the toil and grief she had endured.

"But, you don't understand," Ivy shot back, "The race of men has already long since faded, but the Undying still slumber as the Craven is suffocating our world!" she pressed on as her voice hit a high pitch, "How long have you been down here *not* to notice that?"

Stormrage scratched his scaly chin with a great claw in thought. True, he had been down here ever since the great battle of Tyre, eons past; having lost track of time or events on the surface world. But then, if the human race had passed into infinity, why had the dragon spirits not yet reawakened? This was certainly disconcerting.

"If what you say is true, then we must prove that mankind is dead so the elemental spirits may stir to bring balance once again." he counseled.

It was indeed a great deal for the little woodland fey to take in. She was a little choked up at the thought that the dire chaotic darkness drowning her world was nothing but a mere natural event in the eyes of the dragon. It wasn't that they were entirely blind to the turmoil and grief suffered by others, but such stretches between passion and misery was the natural flow of learning they had experienced since time began. Each creature would return to the Gaia to be remade, much as the race of

Faerie would rejoin once again with the Evermore. This time, however, the pendulum had swung much too far out of balance; putting the existence of their entire realm at risk.

It began to make sense to her now; the Craven, known by its multiple names over many millennia that had come and gone, was the very essence of chaos in their world as it tilted into disorder; which gave the delicate and precious times of peace and harmony their very meaning. Somehow, though, the great cycle of life had fallen out of rhythm and it now threatened everything.

It all seemed like far too much of a task for one little fairy. She would have to bring these tidings to the attention of the High Elves. Without Jinx, Ivy almost felt lost. She had no clue as to how she would escape the cavernous realms of the Drow and her way back to the mage's guild beyond Thieves Gate. It might be possible that the wizard Meridian could help her find her way back to the world tree or even the edge of the grey forest, but even he admitted that the magi had lost all touch with the woodland elves long ago. What was she to do?

Against the dragon's advice, Ivy strolled over to the stone ledge looking out over the vibrant swarming of life below. She was stuck here, a guest of the dragon, and yet still a prisoner of the Craven and christened a condemned exile of the Drow from whom she had sought help. As much of a pain as her little companion had been, she realized if Jinx was here, she would know what to do and take the initiative as she always did. With a sigh of guilt, Ivy felt an ache as she missed her friend. The great dragon rose and came to Ivy's side, the smoky illusion that masked him to the other creatures was but barely visible to her.

"I need to get back to tell the Elves what we must do, though I'm still confused as to how we can awaken them and prove to the Undying that the world of men has passed on?" Ivy whimpered to herself as she searched her thoughts for the words. She had a shaky feeling that the Elven race, which the Faerie had looked up to for guidance, was just as helpless as all other fey were in this circumstance. At least Dawn had taught her one thing, and that was to listen to her feelings. Stormrage had overheard her yearnings, and offered a solution, though it was a risky one at that.

"The goblins you see toiling below chose to side with chaos, for which I do not blame them because they were discarded by the dark elves," the dragon noted, "I neither fear nor hate them, but simply understand their desire to find meaning. Had the Drow displayed a measure of compassion for their creations, these creatures would have had a chance at a better life than what they know now. It is merely a series of unfortunate circumstance that sets them against you." Stormrage recounted to her with such a measure of care and consideration in his voice that it moved her.

In a way, Ivy could relate. Those born of the Faerie were themselves known for being playful pranksters and horribly childish in many ways. Though through the guidance of the woodland Elves, they had learned to have an inherent care for the world around them, for every plant and animal and to spread happiness and joy.

The Faerie were once inquisitive dreamers in their own simple way, seeking such brightness in life where others might not, so much so they could even find beauty in a puddle of water. But that was all long ago. Naive to the ways of the world, now the Faerie were a dying race as were the great and wise Elves themselves who lived in hiding, grasping for a way to save the world they once knew. Had the Elves brought this fate onto the world by giving up so completely on mankind and leaving them to their fate? It was a grave possibility that nibbled at Ivy's conscience.

"Have you ever tried to reconcile with them, to teach them to be more than what they are?" Ivy fought to express what she was feeling.

"Well now, you surprise me, those are very wise words coming from a fey." Stormrage related to her level of insightfulness, "Perhaps, just perhaps there is hope for the Faerie after all." the dragon smiled back at her, "But your question lacks the true understanding of the nature of chaos. They revel in their own vile and brutish nature, and any form of order or civility is viewed with disdain, even as a form of weakness. This is what happened to the race of men, as they turned on one another without care nor concern for their own kind, and even less for other creatures who had never done them an ounce of harm. They took and took until there was nothing left to take, all to fill the emptiness they felt inside. Mankind ...such blind creatures they were." the dragon gave a loud sigh, shaking his head in dismay.

"Do you blame the Elves for what has happened?" Ivy dared to ask, wishing to know how the dragon really felt.

"If I did that, then we Dracos would also have to blame ourselves," he answered with a shrug of his muscular wings, "for it was we who shared our views with the Elven kind since they, too, were children." Stormrage closed his eyes in deep thought, considering the eons that had passed and what they could have done differently. "When we choose to shed our physical form and become one with the elemental plane, we then become eternal ...undying." the dragon explained the meaning of the title well known to the Elves and fey, "There was even a time when we tried to teach mankind as did the sympathetic Elves who once reached out to them; but Men feared us as but wicked beasts, and rejected the wisdom we shared when the true magic and purpose of life was revealed to them. They even went so far as to murder many of the Dracos, ending them before their time." he added with a sour tone.

"But, was there a chance if the Dragons and the Elves together might have tried a little harder to correct their ways?" Ivy tried to grasp for the good in them, apart from all the evil stories she had heard about humankind.

"There again you miss the proper perspective, my little fairy," the dragon answered as he swung his head to meet her eyes and glanced down to the bustle of goblins and twisted beasts in the cavern floor far below, "The race of men made a conscious decision to turn out the way they did. Though, yes, there were quite a few among them who desperately tried to press a voice of sanity throughout the ages of their existence ...but their shallow cries were all but lost amongst the majority who drowned them out. They were oblivious to everything but their own desires, even while they murdered one another. They were unreachable ...flawed."

"Aren't these creatures also flawed? What will become of them?" Ivy asked, gesturing to the twisted creatures milling about in the confusion of the vast cavern below their perch.

"Learn this, young fey, to put it simply, it is not your place to judge. The goblins and other beasts here who serve the Craven may or may not follow in the footsteps of mankind to meet their own oblivion; but that is the way of things. There are many creatures who have flown the skies and swam the oceans and walked this earth which are now gone and will never be again. Some beings were so delicate and unspeakably beautiful that the Dracos themselves shed tears at their loss, some were so vile and corrupt that their very presence was a scourge to all living things. But all in all, they were alive, and life itself is a mystery we have no right to scorn."

Ivy stood there overlooking the panorama before her, a strange and hostile world living deep within her own; and she understood the dragon's words. The Faerie coexist with other creatures of the forests and streams. The poison oak with the daffodils, or the thorn bush with the lotus, or the hemlock to the honeysuckle; they did not seek to weed out what may harm, but knew each had its place and purpose upon this earth.

The situation at present, though, was anything but natural. Ivy explained to the dragon how the surface world had been poisoned by the race of men in a way never before seen. The Faerie had sacrificed themselves to cleanse the land so that life could once again flourish, but they were fighting a losing battle without the aid of the elementals. Even the scourge known as the Craven would eventually sicken and die. The pendulum was broken, and there would be nothing left but a dead world if the Kami could not restore the balance.

Stormrage could only think of one solution to the impending problem. He would have to help Ivy escape the lair of the Dwellers to the surface realm above, and assist her to awaken the spirits who slumbered even as their world died around them.

*   *   *

The Keep

Beyond these caverns where the discarded creations of the dark elves dwelled, there was a broken rift in the tall sable cliff that led out to the open ocean. Though the crackling thunder and churning skies above the island were far too dangerous a place for a lone fairy to survive, they were of equal match for the wings of a dragon. The buffeting whirlwinds and barrage of hail and thick clouds that blanketed the skies were home to Stormrage. The flash of lightning and rumble of thunder were the elements that were a part of him, earning him his name. Ivy was justifiably concerned about making such a trek through the heart of the Dwellers' lair, and Stormrage had considerations of his own to attend to.

"What I propose is that you allow me to mask you from the creatures here so that we can make our way safely out of this domain until we are beyond their reach. It's a very tricky illusion, as you will have to ride on my back, and keep very still as not to dispel the enchantment and expose us both." the dragon explained.

"I can certainly try," Ivy contended, "but I would like to ask exactly what it was that you did to me?" the fairy inquired as she curiously touched the reptilian scales now embossed upon her skin. The dragons' response what not what she had expected.

"There is a heavy stench of Drow magic upon you, of the kind that I have rarely seen." Stormrage responded, glaring closely through the narrow slits of his eyes as he examined her, "You didn't let that arrogant dark elf that calls herself the Brood Mother touch you, did you?"

"Well actually..." Ivy started to reply before the dragon interrupted her, after which she admitted that the Drow queen had in fact placed a bewitchment upon her.

"You should be more cautious, there is venom in her touch. That spider witch has a way of weaving lies, and it would be best to avoid her web entirely if you can." he barked back at the girl, "Apparently the effect of her spell allowed you to absorb her own malevolence, and evoked the suppressed dark desires that lie within you. Clearly the enchantment was still active when I snatched you up to protect you from the Dwellers before they got too close, and my touch allowed you to absorb a part of me in some way. That Drow magic; nasty business it is!" the dragon spat.

Ivy remembered what the Drow queen had excited in her mind, a part of herself that had been lingering within the depths of her spirit. It was the raw power she was capable of ...and it felt good! Now though, that air of superiority and selfish lack of caring for others was suppressed yet again. If she had absorbed a small shred of the essence of the dragon in its place, she certainly didn't feel any different other than just being her old self once again; though Ivy did find the large scales that tinted her skin and the change in her wings a bit interesting, if not outright disturbing.

"It took some doing to remove that peculiar chain that was bound to your flesh, which seemed to be powering the Drow enchantment." Stormrage admitted, then took a moment to uncover something from the dark shadows of his lair and handed it to her, "I believe this is yours," he said as he offered her the large amber gemstone from the relic he had removed from its setting on the jeweled chain, "This powerful item is clearly not of the Drow and belongs to the Elven lords of the forest realms. I would implore you to return it to them." the dragon stated to the fairy girl.

The gem still sparkled with a dim light that danced inside. Ivy's heart leapt, for if she could get this into the hands of the High Elves, they might be able to view what Jinx had witnessed in the seeing stone. By his instruction, Ivy affixed the gem to her spear and flitted up onto the dragon's back. Setting herself snugly between the powerful wings, he warned her again not to move or it could breach the delicate weave of the illusion set upon them both. He had already applied a masking spell upon the gemstone to neutralize the aura that attracted the reprisal of the goblins within this domain.

The woodland fairy was a little dismayed at the dragon, who chose to wait till that moment to mention that their escape from this realm would be postponed until they first took a detour to the very heart of the deep caverns for a visit with their oracle. Ivy had dealings with oracles before, and knew they were nothing but trouble.

"I have lived among the Dwellers for a great deal of time, and need to confer with one of their priests as to the location of a certain place only spoken of in legend," Stormrage advised, "And remember, young one, do not move nor speak no matter what you may see!" Simple enough instructions to abide by, though Ivy truly had no idea how hard that order would be to follow. She would be taken into the heart of the Craven, to gaze upon sights no Faerie had ever seen.

Ivy nearly swallowed her tongue as the dragon launched himself from the high precipice, diving into the cavern below. To the goblins, the great smoky demon that resided above their domain was their champion; a creature of power and might to be feared. They had learned to avert their eyes in his presence to keep from being victims of his reprisal. Stormrage had created an illusion of a beast of dread and terror, a perfect guise where chaos reigned. Over the eons in this place, the dragon had established a reputation for himself based on fear; one that Ivy was about to witness first hand.

The goblins here had been busy at work creating grand scaffoldings and rickety bridges that spanned between the chasms of this underworld. Timbers and rock that had been scavenged from the lands above were rebuilt into precarious platforms that intersected with others. Within the grotto, gargantuan plants had grown wild, their roots snaking their way across the cavern walls. Within them the goblins had created intricate and confused tree houses in which to dwell.

Without cause or warning, Stormrage swooped down and snatched several of the poor creatures with his great claws and tossed them like refuse to their deaths far below. Ivy gasped to keep silent as she watched their faces twist in terror as they fell screaming into the shrouding mists that choked the bottom of the narrow rift. The dragon had a character to portray, and did so with viscous acts of violence that earned him a quota of respect and foreboding from the goblin horde. These wretched creatures only respected strength measured by force and trepidation; and the dragon did as he willed to keep them on their toes. He knew that if he showed any weakness or pity that they would likely turn on him in a moment, and the dragon knew there were far too many of them for him to fend off. It was best to keep in his role as a fear-mongering beast of darkness as they expected him to be. If his material body was destroyed before his time of transformation to the elements, then everything he was and had learned would be lost forever.

Stormrage approached several groups of goblins and put on a scene, gifting them with a horrendous deafening roar that earned him their cowering. Every once in a great moon a particularly smug ogre or brute seeking position or fame among his brood would raise its head in defiance to challenge what they thought was a mere demon, and the dragon would make short work of any upstart, leaving them not more than a bloody stain upon the rocks. He would cheat, of course, using his powers of illusion to daze the offender and cause them to falter in combat; only to meet a messy end.

Through the twisted rifts and chasms he flew, between the web-work of rope bridges and shanty hovels lining the walls. As shoddily made as they were, Ivy found them to be a marvel of construction. The method of their formation was a complete mystery except for the obscenely thin steps and long ladders that led to each abode. Danger was a part of daily life for the horde of goblins and other twisted beasts who made this place their home.

Past the straining flap of his wings, Ivy saw one structure that stood out among the jumbled mess of the others. Several massive stone slabs had been erected to create a citadel, each gashed with jagged images and runes in a language she did not understand. Ghostly fires hemmed the perimeter of the building that rose high above the thick foliage and alien jungle plants that lined the ledges peppered throughout the rift.

Centered within the tiered courtyard before the grand entry, Ivy could see a talisman of eight arrows spiraling outward

etched within the solid rock. It was here the dragon landed with
a great roar. She noticed that his powers of illusion also
allowed him to mask his voice, which was now deep and
horrible. From out of the shadows of the citadel strolled a
wretched creature that appeared goblin-like in only the most
lurid of ways. Ivy bit her lip to keep from making a peep in
disgust. It had several sharpened bones and rings pierced
through its lips and cheeks, and its earlobes had been disfigured
to stretch far below its shoulders; weighted down with thick
beads of pitted gold. Its face and arms were heavily tattooed,
and he walked with a gait as if injured; and measured his stride
with a curled staff that was also braided with trinkets to match
his own apparel which clattered as he moved.

In a guttural tongue, the dragon demanded something of the
occult priest, who gave a glare at him with his one good eye and
snapped a leathery sack off from around his thin neck; shaking
out its contents to the ground at his feet. Small bones, rocks
and bits of shells scattered across the floor, and the priest stood
there staring, waving his hand across them while humming to
himself. In the same repulsive language of the goblins, he
answered back to the dragon in very short words, as if
suspicious as to the reason of his summons. but Stormrage
made a show of power; with a loathsome roar and the beating of
his wings, the decrepit priest retreated and hurried back into the
safety of his temple. Whatever he had revealed to the dragon,
Stormrage seemed satisfied and leapt once again into the air as
Ivy clung on for dear life.

The lesser beasts scurried out of the way when Stormrage
reared his head, making Ivy truly wonder what his fearsome
mirage actually appeared as that would scare them so. The odd
side effect of Meridian's spell to heal her had affected her vision
so that she could not only see in darkness, but allowed her to
view things as they were, even through the most strongest of
enchantments. Ivy gripped onto the dragon's scales with all her
strength as he weaved and soared through the cavern rifts.
Slowly the remnants of the goblin's constructions faded away
until they were far from the heart of the Dwellers abode. Near
the end of the fissure, Stormrage came to rest on a thin ledge

where he clawed at the brittle stone to keep his balance, so he could turn to speak with the girl.

"Take a moment to get a grip as best you can, for we have a long journey ahead." he breathed deeply. Ivy could see high above them a great opening where the salty wind and the crashing of the seas could be heard buffeting the cliffs outside.

"What did that strange priest tell you back there?" Ivy inquired, a bit more than skeptical about the terse conversation they had shared.

"You must understand that we are very far from the woodland realm from whence you came, little fey, and unfortunately, I cannot return you there." he uttered to her surprise, "If I should leave this realm for long, these creatures I watch over may war against the Drow in my absence; and I fear the dark Elves don't truly comprehend the size of their numbers." he offered her in a sad tone, "It would be a massacre; and though they are but Drow, they are Elves, nonetheless."

Ivy realized that the dragon was acting as a warden to keep the two sides from dissolving into a final conflict that would end with the extermination of the dark elves. Though the tribes of the Drow had split apart from the High Elves, their presence was still a vital part of creation and balance, even if it was unseen by most.

"There is a place far from here where we can still attempt to awaken the Undying and complete the task you were assigned, if you are willing?" The dragon offered as Ivy pondered her options ...which were few to nil as she saw them; so she nodded in agreement.

"It is legendary sacred temple known as the last stronghold of the Ancients, in a land once lost among the blur of antiquity," the dragon answered while shifting his balance on the ledge, as loose stones tumbled in the rift below, "...a secret and forbidden place now known as Soulstorm Keep."

The name itself was an insult to the Faerie. Ivy had learned from the Elves that the spirits of all living things were one with the Earth as were the fey to the Evermore. Yet it was the race of men that separated themselves from creation to such a distance that they turned up a smug chin to both the Elementals and the Elves, claiming no more to be a part of the spirits of the earth, but they were instead made of individual 'souls' to prove their superiority over nature. Dawn had once touched on the subject with her on how Man had worshiped false gods, fabricated deities they created as an excuse to place the guilt of their misdeeds upon; a ploy they frequently abused to absolve them from facing any responsibility for their own actions. The race of mankind was truly cowardly in every sense.

"And what are we to do once we reach this fortress?" Ivy finally blurted, noticing the dragon was beginning to lose his grip on the shallow ledge. Stormrage released his grasp on the loose stones and leapt upward with a sharp beat of his mighty wings towards the opening high above, and out to the roaring sea beyond; answering her curtly with strained breath as he did so, "...I assume we will find out when we get there."

*   *   *

Balance

Beyond the breach of the cliffs the great sea stretched out into the gloomy horizon. Dense storm clouds rolled and flashed with thunder, scaring Ivy enough to make her recoil. These skies, however, were a second home to the dragon. To Ivy, it was a terrible experience being whipped around like a rag doll, as she was pelted by hail and high winds. Though the dragon was well-armored, the poor girl wasn't, and had been taking the brunt of whatever foul weather escaped past the heavy beating of his massive wings. The little fairy clung to the dragon, hugging onto his neck as close as could be; holding her own wings tightly against her to keep them from being ripped apart by the powerful gale.

Grafting her feet in-between the dragon's scales, tiny roots crept from her fingers and toes, allowing her to keep a firm hold on her mount. If this caused Stormrage any discomfort, the dragon failed to make a note of complaint. She closed her eyes tightly, trying to drown out the howling winds and the splash of the angry seas below; weary and exhausted, somehow she found a way to drift off to sleep.

Unsettling dreams they were that climbed through her head; of spiders with disturbing faces and screaming tattooed goblins falling to their deaths. The sound of drums and marching hordes haunted her mind, and red-robed elves with hollow eyes. The vision of her friend Jinx crumble into dust was the last thing Ivy experienced that caused her to snap awake from her nightmare. Looking out over the ocean past the slowly beating wings of the dragon, she was surprised to see how calm the waters were. Stormrage now soared out over the open sea towards an endless cloudscape slashed apart by streams of sunlight. With a smile, she caught a glimpse of the trailing edge of a rainbow moments before it faded away.

The sunbeams cutting through clouds, sprinkled out over the glittering ocean, were inspiring. Even in this vast emptiness, the little fairy found the view breathtaking.   Here there was nothing but the realm of two elements, locked in a dance for dominance over the other that neither could truly win.   The ethereal beauty of the clouds playing in the wind was a result of their marriage, the lofty offspring of their coupling.

Ivy wanted to ask the dragon where they were, but was unable to fight the wind; and even then, realized her query would be pointless. All around as far as she could see there was nothing but the dark ocean waters stretching beyond the horizon.

She felt an ache, realizing just how hungry, how tired and completely exhausted she was. As weak as she felt, Ivy was shocked as they passed under a stream of sunlight that glinted off the dragon's wings. Strangely enough, she felt a burst of relief as the sunlight caressed her skin and dozens of tiny leaves sprouted to life that were whisked away by the wind as quickly as they had formed. The curious reaction faded when they escaped the ray of light, only to have it repeat itself once they passed under yet another. Though astonished, Ivy couldn't help but giggle as she raised her arms, spreading a trail of tiny leaves in her wake. Upon her hand, the image of the leaf from the world tree began to glow brightly.

Straining to look back, the dragon gave a brief smile as he spoke over the howling wind that whipped past them.

"The essence of magic is different here, I can feel it. The presence of chaos has upset the order of things, so mind yourself, little fey." he advised, though Ivy found no cause for alarm. The sunlight tickled, and for a brief moment she felt a wave of happiness once again; not truly realizing how long it had been since she had laughed, and how the weight of all the hardships she had endured had stripped from her the most simplest of joys.

Stormrage lifted his glide up towards the clouds, giving Ivy a startle. It had been a millennia since the dragon had soared the open skies, and there was a place he wished to revisit once again. Thick haze enveloped them as a wet mist obscured even the tips of the dragons wing's. Little Ivy held on for dear life, wondering what the dragon was doing. It was like being lost in a fog, a misty soup so thick that she could barely see.

Suddenly, without warning, they breached the top, and Ivy gasped in awe.

The dragon skimmed over the ocean of billowing clouds beneath them, soaring over a vast mystical landscape. The blue of the sky settled like a haze near the horizon that merged with a tranquil darkness speckled by stars. Ivy laughed in glee, there were so many of them; trillions of tiny specks twinkling in vast rivers that enveloped the entire sky. As the sun began to set, the blue hue turned a warm fiery red as the entire cloudscape simmered with burning yellows against rich violets and indigo blues.

The dragon dove once again through a short break in the clouds towards the ocean's surface far below. Ivy felt her stomach sink in a queer way as she watched the water's surface rush towards them with the shrieking wind. Pulling up, Stormrage leveled out as they neared a massive mountain range that loomed into view. Ivy could only guess that this dark and brooding landscape was their final destination.

"What is this place?" Ivy shouted towards the dragon's head in front of her, as the beats of his wings began to slow at their approach.

"It is an old and ancient place, a land once known simply as the Vy." The dragon answered, not having the breath to answer her further as he tilted into his dive. Stormrage soared like the wind itself, gliding through tight valleys and over crags and peaks of mountaintops the tiny fairy thought they would surely hit as they swooped past. The fading darkness of the sunset enveloped them as the shadows of the vale seemed to swallow them up. Stormrage now knew where he was going. It was a place imprinted upon his being as it was to his kin before him. Without notice, the dragon flared his wings as they came to settle at the tip of an unassuming glen at the foot of two towering mountains.

The first thing Ivy noticed was, it was quiet here ...too quiet. She could hear the deep panting of the dragon and even her own heartbeat, and she found it strange that there was no song of the wind nor sign of life; only the still silence.

"So this is Vy? What a strange name." she whispered.

"It is a simple name for simpler times, when the world was young," the dragon replied, "Once steeped in magic so pure, you would drown in it."

"Doesn't look like much now..." Ivy glanced around in the fading light, seeing only broken shale mottled with faint scars of lichen, but not a tree or bush in sight; she then noticed a structure carved from the very mountainside before them. A great mound of oblong rocks that reminded her of the Stonehenge circles the elves used as a doorway to the lower world of the Faerylands; except these were monumental, many times larger in dimension. The great stones formed an outlandishly tall and narrow doorway that led into the heart of the mountain.

"Looks can be deceiving, young one," the large dragon replied, and Ivy bit her lip, knowing full well he was right. "This was once the land of giants, and beings which birthed the Elves. When I say this place is *old* little fey, I mean that in every way." Stormrage nearly scolded. Ivy bent down to grasp a loose stone near her feet, and it glistened in her hand as something indescribable touched her mind.

"And the dragons, they were born here also..." Ivy seemed to say in words not of her own, as she looked towards the dark mountain peaks gleaming with the last slivers of the setting sun. Stormrage gave a toothy smile for her insight.

"Yes, you feel it too. A presence here of something more that you cannot see nor touch, but you know exists as it speaks to your heart." the dragon answered with a soft wink of his eyes.

It was true, Ivy experienced something; it was similar to what she felt when she became a tree and could feel the living forest around her. It was a sensation both strange, and yet, strangely familiar.

"Long ago when the world was nothing but a thought, an emotion that ebbed and flowed, the pure and primitive creatures sprouted from the elements," Stormrage whispered in words that sunk deep, "among the beasts of horns and wings and tails, and those that slither and crawl came ones on two legs called the Seekers. They were of the same seed from which sprouted the savages of the jungles, the dwarves of the deep, and even the race you call the huskmen."

Ivy turned to the dragon in surprise, astonished that mankind was once their distant kin. She had thought the human race was a single entity, ruthless monsters that murdered their own kind. The Elves had told the fey many dark fairytales about humans and the evil they had delivered upon the world.

"You called them the seekers?" Ivy inquired.

"Yes, they were very curious creatures who rose above other mere beasts, who sought to find the magic in their world; to grasp it and understand it." Stormrage explained, "They were simple, but had a great passion burning within them. At first they were quite solitary, few in numbers. Honor and strength became a custom among their kind, each one a great warrior, each one a king of his domain," the dragon enlightened the small woodland sprite as they stepped towards the great temple hidden within the earth, "These Vy Kings soon began to take their contests of prowess beyond their territorial and mating rituals. Although they had as great a reverence for the spirits of the land and sea as other creatures, they tried to weave magic of their own through the elements." Stormrage sighed heavily as they passed within the shadow of the towering doorway to the dark hall beyond, "There eventually came a time when the Seekers became so obsessed with property and possession that they began to kill for soil and sand, for tree and stream and shore ...as if it was something they could own."

"The Elves taught me as much," Ivy realized her eyes were seeing perfectly in the darkness of the tunnel ahead as it opened up into a grand cathedral with a roof so high it was beyond sight, surrounding a cupped caldera of worn stone within its center. There were no markings, no glyphs, no statues to ancient hero's ...just the enormous circular basin. "They said Man once had a great civilization, but were addicted to suffering and bloodshed." she noted with a tone of detest.

"The Elves were half right, little fey," the dragon answered while he circled the room, raising his head up to the thick suffocating shadows high above the cold stone floor, "but, don't be so harsh on mankind when you speak their name. They were beings who merely wished to love and learn as all those who breathe with life do. They simply fell from the path that was meant for them." Stormrage said sadly as he looked into the deep bowl within the floor, and in his eyes Ivy saw a hint of emotion, as if he knew something he wasn't telling her.

"...How can you assume that?" Ivy finally dared to press, wondering how the dragon could make such a presumption. The dragon circled back around to her as Ivy took a seat on the lip of the empty stone cauldron.

"It is the essence of the Dracos to see, to know what mankind could have been," he answered lightly in her pointed ear and laying down his bulk beside her with a fold of his wings, "Do you remember when we soared above the clouds, and what you saw there?"

"Oh, yes!" Ivy recalled as she looked up with a grin stretched upon her face, as if she was reliving the moment again, "It was beautiful, there were so many stars." she responded with a gleeful sigh.

"And have you ever stopped to wonder why you feel so happy when you see them?" the dragon asked with a curious tone.

Ivy was stumped for a moment, as there was a true sense of longing when she thought about it. On the surface she had presumed because the Faerie had been forced to live so long underground that they missed the open skies, the warm caress of the sun upon their skin, or the gentle cascade of moonlight and the twinkling laughter of the stars. There was a sense of openness and freedom that they had lost being imprisoned as they had been in the underworld for so long. That, however, did not answer the dragon's question, and she knew it. There was something more to the equation.

"Actually ...I'm not quite sure." she admitted with a lightly confused look washing upon her. The dragon nudged her gently with his snout to break her from her puzzled gaze.

"The Faerie, too, are primal creatures as were the Seekers, and you share a level of fascination for life," Stormrage began, "But the Elves, in their wisdom, have chosen to keep the Faerie in a child-like state, safe from the sins that could cause them to follow in the footsteps of Mankind. The one advantage you have is that you understand your essence and connection to the world and have a deep respect and reverence for nature. Magic still lives within you through this connection. Mankind killed themselves through their insane pursuit of acquiring magic that was not theirs to possess; and ultimately it was their undoing," tilting his head until her eyes locked with his, "They were too blind, however, to see that they already possessed a form of magic stronger than any other ...the power to dream."

"I, I don't understand..." Ivy began, trying to grasp what the dragon was telling her.

"The stars above, those countless millions upon millions of candles sprinkled across the night sky ...each one is a realm of its own, just like ours. Many are inhabited by people and beings who you will never meet, some not yet born, some already long passed. Each one locked in a cycle of life and death, of order and chaos." Stormrage enlightened her, "The Elves may have not revealed this to protect you, to keep the curious fey from attempting to reach beyond their grasp. Just as you recall that brief moment in time we spent under the vast emptiness of stars, and its memory that brought you such joy?" he asked as Ivy nodded solemnly, "Then I will conclude your education with these words of ancient wisdom I hope you will find worthy to treasure." the dragon paused, "Be happy with what you have, for life is not a fairytale, little fey, there is no happily ever after ...only the few cherished moments experienced in our lives that we are left to grasp onto."

The dragon's words sent tears welling in her eyes, though she wasn't quite sure why they affected her so. She remembered feeling the same way whenever she had thought about the tree of life, and the long journey she had endured to find the world tree in the garden of the Elves. There was truth to his words, deeper than she had ever felt. It wasn't the long and arduous struggles or hardships she cared to remember, though there are people whose lives are whittled away, haunted by the misery they endured. On the opposite page, it was the few happy moments Faeries clung to and tried to share with the world ...to do so was at the very core of their being, to exist as they were meant to be.

"Why are you telling me this?" Ivy protested, wiping a

flustered tear away from her cheek. It was all so much to take in, sending her emotions spinning. Stormrage looked away for a moment into the basin beside them, and answered after an awkward moment of silence.

"Because of what I'm about to ask of you."

The finality of his words struck Ivy, as she gasped to stifle her tears. The dragon got up and gingerly stepped within the great basin, folding his wings up within its circumference. His strange actions confused the little girl who hopped up and walked along its edge.

"What do you mean?" she finally asked him, "What is this place, exactly?" Ivy inquired as she peered around, noting nothing terribly exceptional that would lead the dragon to bring her here.

"This," the dragon raised a talon to the round walls, "is our destination, a place of myth and lore known as Soulstorm Keep." Though looking around, the little fairy saw nothing of interest that would earn it such a grand name.

"This place? It is nothing but a hole in a mountain ...though a large one at that." Ivy admitted as she glanced up into the emptiness above them. "Didn't you say this was the last refuge of the Ancients? ...But, there's nobody here."

"During their short reign upon this earth, the race of men became ever more consumed with madness in their pursuit of power; becoming entirely oblivious to their relationship with the Gaia, attempting instead to master our mother of all nature. They tampered with dangerous magics far beyond their comprehension, and used them to find buried places in the earth that were never meant to be found," the dragon recalled, "This was once such a place. In their foolish curiosity, with great golems of iron and steel they unearthed this holy shrine, not knowing they were violating a sacred and forbidden place from a distant time."

"And what happened?" the little woodland sprite sat transfixed by the dragon's words.

"These sons of the Seekers uncovered a source of powerful magic, an essence they could not possibly understand nor fathom; and in their blind ignorance they could not truly believe what they had found." Stormrage said with sad eyes. This little fairy before him could not understand the grief and turmoil the world had truly suffered, nor the misery the Undying had endured as they felt the spirits of billions of beings dying in violent agony as mankind destroyed the world around them. So thus, one by one, they chose to close their minds and sleep until the passing of all humankind, and the beast known as Man had been washed from the face of the Earth.

Ivy awaited long minutes for the dragon to elaborate on his confusing words, but he never did. Though curious, she knew some things were better not asked, and could now just see the tip of wisdom shown by the Elves. Sometimes curiosity was a very dangerous thing. There was, however, the most obvious question.

"So, what did you want to ask of me?" she finally dared to inquire.

"The world is out of balance, and the spirits of the earth and sea and sky must be awakened once again," he stated as Ivy nodded her head in agreement, "and there is only one way to do that ...you must kill me."

Ivy jerked her head back in shock, her pale eyes wide.

"But, for what purpose?" Ivy protested, rejecting the thought of being party to his death.

"To awaken the sleeping spirits, my body must die so that I can become one with them," the dragon declared, "and though it is not my time for transformation, this place will preserve my essence from being lost to the void." Stormrage tried to calm her with his gentle tone; knowing he asked much of a faerie who herself was a creature of life and creation, not of its destruction. "Once I have ascended into the primal elements, I will be able to stir the spirits from their slumber and bring a measure of equilibrium back into our world."

"But, there has to be another way," Ivy argued, now realizing the dragon had been settling into his death bed.

"Before we arrived, I had hoped there might be, but I had felt the emptiness inside, and know now that I am the last Dracos, the last of the true dragons; there is no other way," he sighed, "This is not so simple a choice, nor will you likely survive this task either, little fey; but realize there comes a time in our lives when we must make personal sacrifices for others, for this is the measure of who we really are."

The dragon's words cut deep into the little fairy, for Ivy knew she had a responsibility as an Elvenborn. She had been a belligerent and selfish little girl for so long, until she learned to see beyond herself. As a Faerie, she loved life; as an Elvenborn, she had learned to protect it.

Stormrage could see in the sudden slump in her shoulders and heavy sigh, that Ivy had understood the shared wisdom and sense in his message.

"What must I do?" was all she finally replied with a look of defeat washing over her.

"Bare that enchanted weapon you hold, which can channel my essence, for you are about to learn why I am called the mighty Stormrage!"

There was a mark of pride, yet sadness, in the dragon's voice as he raised his horned head erect with a grave stare in his enormous blue eyes. His scales began to crackle as tiny arcs of light pinched between them. Ivy stood transfixed, grasping her short spear with both hands as she watched the dragon heave its body as a great force welled up inside him. From his chest and up his throat an inner glow seared through his thick scaly armor until it burst forth from the dragon's mouth.

With a thunderous crack that echoed endlessly up the great chasm above them, white hot lightning struck forth at Ivy as she braced her javelin upwards in defense. The bolts cut through the air with a sizzle, searing the stone around her as their trails slapped against the walls and shot up the entire chimney of polished stone above. Ivy's wings began to glow with the sheer force of power from the dragon that was conducted through the enchanted spear. It was truly frightening to be in the center of the blinding storm that had been unleashed upon her. Ivy gripped tightly as she felt the spear hum with energy, as the amber seeing stone tied there still dangling from its haft began to glow with a life of its own.

The last fingers of electricity escaped from the dragon who stared at her, and then gently closed his eyes in the split second that it took for the enchanted lance to spit forth its feedback. Blue lightning shot forth, fanning out around her, back upon the dragon. Stormrage screamed with a roar that filled the roofless room, resounding with a tone that seemed to shake the very foundation. Deafened and nearly blinded, Ivy watched as the dragon's painful writhing seemed to transmute into a look of serene gratitude.

Once again the crack of lightning filled the Keep, now ablaze with javelins of sapphire blue energy and the shattering boom of thunder. Ivy began to feel a burning ache as the stabbing fingers of electricity began to shock her with every touch, increasing until she fell to her knees in pain; daring not to drop the spear until the dragon completed his metamorphosis. As the air buzzed around her, the strange scales on her own skin too began to crackle and peel, as showers of sparks bounced around her. She couldn't feel her hands anymore, and everything around her diffused into a blinding white until she could no longer make out the form of the dragon; then quite suddenly, everything went black.

ଽଠଢ଼

"Ivy ...it's time to wake up," a soft voice drifted within her dreams as flitting images from her toilsome journey fell away like the receding waves of a storm that had crashed upon a rocky shore. There was a colorless memory of the hardships she had endured, and the friends that had been sacrificed along the way. It took many, many long moments for the feeling of anguish and heartache to dissolve away. Ivy lifted her head to look around her, searching for the familiar voice that had released her from her nightmare.

Beside her sat the cauldron, glowing with a bright blue pool of electricity dancing upon itself; but it wasn't the source of the voice that had been whispering in her ear. With blurry eyes she glanced across from her to see a small fairy girl sitting beside her. As her vision adjusted to the light, Ivy was surprised to see that it was Jinx! But, how could that be?

She sat up looking at her with astonishment, just noticing that her friend was softly caressing her cheek with tenderness; so happy to see her that she forgot to fear her touch. The subtle color of the world around her returned to Ivy as her almond-shaped eyes once again turned to their former emerald green. Looking at her arms as they tingled, she also noticed the embossed scales upon her skin had entirely faded away.

"Jinx, is that you?" Ivy implored, "How did you...?"

"I'm not quite sure myself," Jinx answered as she caressed the cracked amber gemstone laying beside her feet.

When she had been destroyed by the poisonous touch of the iron cage within the tower, her body had turned to dust. Not long after Sorrowblade had taken Ivy as her prisoner, no one was there to notice the tiny wisp of light that escaped from the small pile of blackened ash that was once Jinx, and was absorbed into the seeing stone within the Eye of Omens. It was the ancient and powerful relic of the High Elves that had sustained her; though her body had been destroyed, Jinx was not dead.

The little luck fairy was not of any particular element, thus she didn't revert to sand, or dew, or mist or smoke, but into a spark to be reborn as all faeries of fortune and chance are. Lucky for her, there was a source of powerful elvish magic present to preserve her tiny flame of life.

Strapped to the enchanted spear, the gemstone was at the center of the shower of raw magic that transformed Stormrage back into the elements from whence he came. The magical leaf from the tree of life embedded into Ivy's hand, had protected her yet again; its living energy had also seeped into a glowing jewel which hung a mere breath from where Ivy gripped her spear. As luck would have it, the power and primal essence of the dragon which Ivy had absorbed, was the very catalyst that gave Jinx her rebirth to become a fairy of good fortune as she was meant to be. The two little faeries turned to the glowing pool of energy as a voice spoke from within.

"It will take time, but balance will be restored." Stormrage whispered as the pool of light pulsed gently, "The Undying have been awakened, and thank you for your sacrifices little fey. We have informed the High Elves of your presence here so that they may return you to your forest home." the voice of his spirit echoed.

Ivy stood beside her friend who had cured her by her touch, and had also disenchanted the powerful hex of the Drow that had been placed upon her.

"It is we who owe gratitude for your sacrifice, my friend," Ivy responded to the pool of light dancing before them, realizing how much the dragon had given of himself to right a world that cared so little about him, "but what about the Craven ...what will become of them?"

In the hours before as Ivy had lain unconscious at the foot of the blazing pool, far beyond the shores of Vy, chaos had met its match. The elementals spirits of the waters had swelled the turbulent seas, sending forth towering waves to crash upon the high cliffs of Tyre. The pounding ocean breached the weakened gap in the blackened stone, pouring as a torrent through the fissures into the deep caverns below. There, a decrepit one-eyed goblin priest stood before his foul temple as a colossal wave swept over him, knowing he had been betrayed by the loathsome beast that had once ruled their corrupted realm.

The cold dark waters that writhed with the dead and twisted bodies of the afflicted came to rest at the edge of Phantom Pass, where they were met by the startled Drow guards left stationed there high above on the edge of the plateau. Yet, unknown to the rest of the Obsidian Order imprisoned within the Tower of Madness high above the temple of the Drow, a blind priestess turned a crooked smile. For though the Sisterhood of Blood denied the fey their heartfelt request, she had secretly used her guile to achieve her own ends. Showing the two fey girls the Elven relic and allowing access to it was no clumsy mistake, but a way to test the two Faerie emissaries of their true spirit and resolve.

"Young fairy, the Craven will always be among us. For now, their hand has been swayed; but they will again have their time ...as you have yours. Live your life with honor, Elvenborn, and know that you have done well." Stormrage answered as the pool of light began to fade, and Ivy knew his words would always live in her heart. Jinx looked around the chamber and down at the pool of dancing light with wonder in her soft eyes.

"I saw all of this when I looked into the seeing stone!" she proclaimed suddenly as she remembered what she had witnessed when she had used the elven relic, "How did we get here," Jinx babbled with excitement, "oh, what did I miss?"

Ivy hugged her friend, having missed her so. It was the first time Jinx had ever experienced being so close to anyone, and as small a thing as a hug was, it gave her a feeling of warmth and joy that had been missing in her life for so very, very long. Silent tears of happiness came to her eyes as she realized she was no longer jinxed.

As the wood sprite held her fairy friend, it slowly dawned on Ivy that she couldn't fully reveal all of what had happened and what she had learned, the secret knowledge that Stormrage had entrusted to her, and her alone.

"Oh, you didn't miss much of anything," Ivy said, "but first, let's go home, and I'll tell you a bit about it along the way," she offered with a warm smile to stem the little girls insatiable curiosity. With a sigh of relief and her hand in hers, they made their way out into the bright morning sun that had begun to stream through the tall passageway of the ancient keep.

*   *   *

About the Author

Michel Savage has written & illustrated several short fictions in addition to his other novels, and has kept up his interest in writing through his careers as a commercial artist, an accomplished interior designer, various projects for major movie studios, and as an Art Director for numerous live productions. Sci-fi literature & fantasy artwork has always been a favorite subject, and suggests that when he's not busy dodging the bullets of international criminals and saving the world… you can usually find him either painting or curled up with a book and a healthy supply of chocolate.

…Always the dreamer.

www.Faerylands.com

Enter the Grey Forest

www.GreyForest.com

Portraits of the storyline Characters from the

Faerylands & ***Atlantis***
fantasy art series collection
by

Michel Savage